THE
RETURN
OF THE
PHARAOH

THE
RETURN
OF THE
PHARAOH

FROM THE REMINISCENCES OF
JOHN H. WATSON, M.D.

AS EDITED BY

NICHOLAS MEYER

MINOTAUR
BOOKS
NEW YORK

Published in the United States by Minotaur Books, an imprint of
St. Martin's Publishing Group

THE RETURN OF THE PHARAOH. Copyright © 2021 by Nicholas Meyer. All rights reserved. Printed in the United States of America. For information, address St. Martin's Publishing Group, 120 Broadway, New York, NY 10271.

www.minotaurbooks.com

Frontispiece maps and original illustrations by Rhys Davies

Image of the Rosetta Stone (page 55) reprinted by permission of
Heritage Images via Getty Images

Statue of Akhenaten (page 79) reprinted by permission of
powerofforever via iStock/Getty Images

Designed by Omar Chapa

The Library of Congress has cataloged the hardcover edition as follows:

Names: Meyer, Nicholas, 1945– author.
Title: The return of the pharaoh: from the reminiscences of John H.
   Watson, M.D. / as edited by Nicholas Meyer.
Description: First edition. | New York: Minotaur Books, 2021.
Identifiers: LCCN 2021021939 | ISBN 9781250788207 (hardcover) |
   ISBN 9781250788214 (ebook)
Subjects: LCSH: Holmes, Sherlock—Fiction. | Watson, John H.
   (Fictitious character) —Fiction. | GSAFD: Mystery fiction. |
   LCGFT: Detective and mystery fiction. | Novels.
Classification: LCC PS3563.E88 R48 2021 | DDC 813/.54—dc23
LC record available at https://lccn.loc.gov/2021021939

ISBN 978-1-250-85270-0 (trade paperback)

Our books may be purchased in bulk for promotional, educational, or business use. Please contact your local bookseller or the Macmillan Corporate and Premium Sales Department at 1-800-221-7945, extension 5442, or by email at MacmillanSpecialMarkets@macmillan.com.

First Minotaur Books Trade Paperback Edition: 2022

10 9 8 7 6 5 4 3 2 1

For Alan Gasmer

CONTENTS

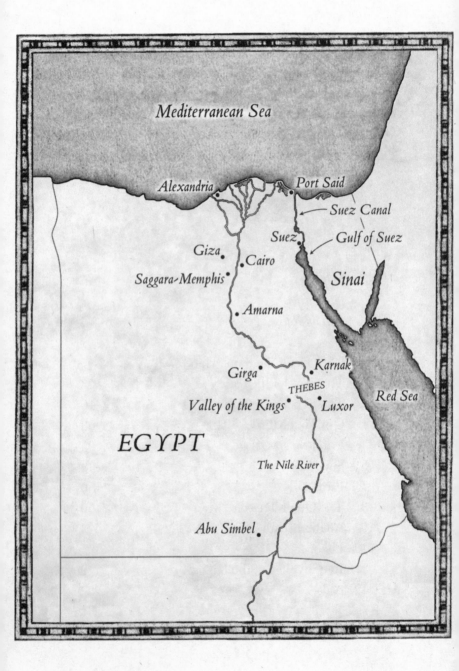

INTRODUCTION

Feb. 15, 2020

HIKARU MISHIMA
PRESIDENT & CEO, KUROSAWA HEAVY INDUSTRIES, LTD.

TOKYO, BRUSSELS, PANAMA & MACAO

Dear Mr. Nicholas Mayer:

As you know by now (the Internet allows no secret), I was the anonymous purchaser of the Watson journal at Sotheby's last year. Since my childish, I have loved Dr. Watson's accounts of the great detective. Please excuse my English. I attended Penn State many years ago, but I lack perfection. Also because I am with the flu at present, I have some confusion.

I was most pleased with the work you performed on the Protocols ms. but now confess I did not share the contents of the entire document with you at that time. Watson's dairy [sic] continues some years. Most of the entries are so-so. They mainly deal with W's medical practices and his marriage, also London Olympics of 1908, where he treated injured competitors. They could have been written by any doctor of the time.

But in 1910 Watson becomes again involved with Sherlock Holmes on a most bazaar [sic] case. If you are agreeable, I would entrust the pages to your labor as I am sure the world would (will? Please excuse) find them most bazaar [sic]. I am thinking he meant to publish one day as he gave those pages a title.

On this occasion I am prepared to offer a nominal fee for your services.

I send this to you via private correspondence and would appreciate your discretion until such time as we have made the agreement.

Let me know at your earliest, etc.

Very truly yours,
Hikaru Mishima
PRESIDENT & CEO

I was of course surprised by this communication, even more to learn there was more to Watson's journal than I had been led to believe when I edited the excerpt known as *The Adventure of the Peculiar Protocols.* Of course, I agreed to Mr. Mishima's proposal. As Watson says at one point in the ms., old habits die hard.

As Mr. Mishima rightly points out, this section of Watson's journal was evidently considered worthy of publication by the doctor, who gave it a good deal of attention, making my task considerably easier than my previous effort, where entire pages had been suppressed.

That said, some of Watson's Egyptian references have been shown to be inaccurate, due either to his own ignorance or the effect of subsequent discoveries that shed new and different light on his narrative. What follows must nonetheless speak for itself, with the remaining qualifications: there is some debate as to when Holmes actually began his years of retirement. Watson's journal herein may compound that confusion. When did Holmes formally begin bee-keeping on the Sussex Downs? Many scholars point to "The Adventure of the Lion's Mane" as evidence that Holmes was retired by 1909, when the case is ostensibly set. Other scholars—wouldn't you know—have theorized that "The Lion's Mane" itself is entirely bogus, not to be relied on for anything. So we must take what follows bearing these controversies in mind.

Another point: Watson was writing in 1910–1911 and evidently revising some time thereafter. Language, as we all know, is a living thing and vocabulary as well as prose changes with the times. What Watson wrote in 1886, for example, is not the way he wrote some twenty years later. His actual text—FedExed to me from Tokyo by Mr. Mishima— suggests a diary that was subsequently revised with a view to publication; thus tenses and perspectives sometimes shift. I have chosen to leave these inconsistencies alone as I think they convey the flavor of both the case as it unfolded and also Watson's later hindsights. Likewise, I've not corrected Watson's orthography or Mr. Mishima's English. I find Mr. Mishima's letter poignant as written and correcting his language, I feel, would dilute the emotion I believe I detect between lines written under duress. I've tried to keep footnotes to a minimum. You can always ignore them.

I have added illustrations and maps to Watson's text, which I hope will clarify places and things for the reader.

Finally, Mr. Mishima's letter, while self-explanatory, does contain a melancholy postscript. Shortly after I had agreed to his conditions, I received an email from his personal secretary, Mr. Watanabe, that the CEO of Kurosawa Heavy Industries had died. He was a vigorous eighty-four and had, as I understand, just returned from a Chinese business trip.

At the time, we in the United States were just becoming aware of the pandemic that would shortly change (or shorten) all our lives. By the time the legal aspects of the Watson journal entries were resolved, I was in lockdown in Los Angeles, stuck with only the ms. for company. I can only hope I have made good use of my time and Mr. Mishima's trust.

It should also be understood that I have no way at this point of knowing if this case is the last entry in the journal Mr. Mishima acquired with his Sotheby's purchase. As he originally chose not to inform me that the journals continued after the adventure of the Protocols, I have no way of knowing if the same journals continue beyond what Watson calls *The Return of the Pharaoh*. I have asked Mr. Watanabe this question but as of today's date have received no answer.

Nicholas Meyer, Los Angeles, September 2020

CURTAIN RAISER

As the Turkish police began to dig up the remains, Holmes and I gratefully sniffed the morning desert air. It was chilly at this hour but the heat would soon become insupportable.

"Remember Nietzsche's dictum," the detective remarked, lighting his pipe. *"Nothing not written in blood is worth reading."*

"Or writing, in this case," I rejoined.

He smiled in agreement. "Definitely one for the books. One of *your* books," he added with a twinkle.

Now that the ghastly business is well and truly over, I've been urged—by no less a personage than Sherlock Holmes himself—to set down the particulars. The detective, typically ambivalent about my efforts to chronicle his cases (his attitudes range from the sarcastic: "You have attempted to tinge it with romanticism," to the fulsome: "I am lost without my Boswell"), was uncharacteristically blunt on this occasion: "The whole thing is so fantastical, so utterly without precedent, it must be recorded, as we may be sure the official version will be a whitewash. Will there even be mention of the last three victims, let alone the identities of the first three?"

"Do you make it a total of six?" I asked. "Surely Bechstein was a fool and can we be certain Phillips—"

"Ah, but can we? The difficulties multiply with the cadavers," he interrupted. "And you are not counting the Swede, who, granted, took his own life. That would make seven. No, my boy, only you can tell the whole story, though," he added. "I very much doubt you'll be believed at all events. And mind, go easy on the scenery. There's plenty to go 'round."

Yes, the worst is now behind us. And yet, as I reflect on the whole improbable time, I cannot help but think what a close-run thing it was and how nearly Holmes and I—to say nothing of the poor duchess and Mr. Carter—came to grief. And so, bearing in mind his caveats, I shall now attempt to relate the entire wretched affair, consulting my journal when I kept notes, having recourse to my memory when I was too distracted to do so, and keeping scenery to a minimum.

To be completely accurate from the outset, there was in fact a seventh victim, though I am not certain he can properly be said to add to the body count, though his corpse was definitely among the rest. That would make a total all told of eight.

And that does not take into account the one who went mad.

In this, as in other matters, the reader must judge for himself.

1

I AM DEALT THE SAME HAND

Thursday, 3 November, 1910. Juliet's cough is back. She tries to conceal it from me but I hear it early in the morning when she wakes, and sometimes in the middle of the night when she imagines I'm sleeping. In addition, I can hardly miss the other signs—fatigue, occasional fever and night sweats. She appears to have scant appetite and her pallor is not her own.

Yesterday I finally persuaded her to visit Stark-Munro, who has taken over from Agar, and we went down together. Juliet insisted it was just a cold, but we both knew better. Understandably neither of us wishes to confront the likely reality. Unspoken between us was the thought that we have been so happy.

And also unspoken by me was the enraged thought that this couldn't be happening again.*

Stark-Munro was kindly and tactful but quite thorough. While Juliet waited docilely in his consulting room, pretend-

---

* Watson appears to be referring here to the death of Mary Morstan, his first wife.

ing to read a back number of *The Strand,* I stood beside the specialist as he peered through the microscope.

"There can be no mistake," Stark-Munro advised me, tugging off his gloves. "The bacillus is present." He stood aside, inviting me to see for myself.

As I stared through the microscope, my vision hopelessly blurred. I had attempted to prepare myself for this blow, but my colleague's diagnosis staggered me, made worse, if I'm not mistaken, by the very gentleness with which it was delivered.

Poor Juliet patiently endured the tedious and cumbersome X-ray procedure, which likewise revealed her compromised lungs.

"We still know so little of the disease," Stark-Munro remarked, now washing his hands with a thoroughness that put me in mind of Pilate. "You needn't worry," he added, mistaking my look as he turned off the tap and shook his wrists. "If you've not caught it by now, chances are unlikely you will."

"What about the girl?"

He shrugged. "She sleeps upstairs, doesn't she? Good. She would do well to keep her distance. Six feet, if possible, is a good rule of thumb. Otherwise, the usual precautions. Hot water and carbolic soap, etcetera. All that commonsense sort of thing. It's early days yet," he added, smiling. "And given the right circumstances your good lady may do very well."

"How would you define 'right circumstances'?"

His brow furrowed briefly. "Get her out of London, for a start. This is the worst winter I can recall, nothing but cold, snow, and endless rain. Everyone coming down with something. Take her somewhere where the air is dry and her lungs may well respond."

"The Alps?"

"Many consumptives go there. You could do worse."

"I must do better. The air may be dry, but the Jungfrau and Matterhorn will be cold and Juliet, slender as she is, abhors cold. What about the Riviera? That's warm, surely. Many folk choose to winter there."

"Too close to the sea. The object is to find someplace arid." Stark-Munro understood he was speaking to a desperate man. Seconds were ticking by, even if neither of us could hear them. "What about Egypt?"

"What about it?" I numbly repeated.

"Lots of people holiday there at Christmastime." I could tell by his tone that the idea pleased him. "The air is considerably warmer than Switzerland but equally dry. And there's no desert dust this time of year, certainly not in Cairo. I've sent patients there before with very promising results. There are now several sanitaria specialising in just this sort of thing"—he avoided the word "tuberculosis"—"and the temperature will rise steadily after January. Before it becomes intolerable, you will bring her home."

I grasped at his recommendation like a drowning man seizing a lifeline.

Later, in the taxi back to Pimlico, Juliet sat in silence, which I endeavoured to fill with a line of cheerful patter.

"It's no use, John," said she when I paused for breath.

"Don't say anything of the sort, dearest. Egypt! It is just the thing. What a time we'll have. You'll see the pyramids! I'm told they're just outside the city."

"Aren't the pyramids simply giant tombs? Will you build me one?"

"You mustn't talk such nonsense. I tell you this will be a wonderful adventure."

"What about your practice?"

"Hang my practice. Dearest, you mustn't take such a dim view."

She considered this, staring blindly out the window.

"How long would we be there?"

"As long as it takes!"

"That might cost a pretty penny."

Now I was on solid ground. "I can well afford it. Dearest, you know little of my finances, but allow me to enlighten you. Not only has my practice flourished over these last years, but I have a separate source of income that has been shrewdly invested in the City."

"A separate—oh, you mean your case accounts of Sherlock Holmes in the *The Strand Magazine*."

"I do. Truth be told, they've brought me far more remuneration than my doctoring. To be entirely candid," I went on, frowning at the thought, "I daresay the income from my case histories is larger per annum than Holmes's. I've frequently offered to share the profits with him," I rushed on, "but he always refuses. 'My fees are upon a fixed scale and I never vary them,' he tells me, 'save when I remit them altogether.'"

"Poppycock." Juliet had to smile. "Such grandiosity."

"Regardless, dearest, the fact is, we are flush."

The silence in the cab was now changed. I could feel Juliet's spirits mending as she doubtless contemplated the prospect of sunshine, warmth, and the undivided attention of a solicitous husband.

"Will we be back in time for the coronation?" she asked. "I should hate to miss the coronation."

Eagerly, I promised we would return in time for that milestone.*

---

* The coronation of George V was scheduled for June.

Mention of my finances put me in mind of my eccentric friend. Holmes and I had not been in touch of late, but this neither surprised nor distressed me. By this time the pattern of our relations was well established. We both led active but separate lives and over the years I had become accustomed to his silences and absences, equally unsurprised when a telegram or note would re-establish contact between us as though no time had elapsed. I knew from the papers he had recently been in Paris to attend to the affair of the stolen da Vinci.* He was not mentioned by name, but all the stories referred to the recovery of the picture and capture of the Italian thief with the aid of "a famed English detective," and so I knew my friend had added another triumph to his impressive list.

I remember thinking I should drop him a note of congratulations while at the same time informing him of our Egyptian sojourn and the reasons for it, letting him know I should likely be gone some months. On reflection, this struck me as premature. There were many arrangements to be made first and I fear that, in the press of events, writing the detective entirely slipped my mind.

The first order of business was settling on the best facility in Cairo for our purposes, which, to my annoyance, proved a time-consuming process. While speed was essential on Juliet's behalf, to do the thing properly involved days acquiring and poring through medical periodicals, correspondence, and innumerable telephone calls with still more specialists, and at least two consultations in Harley Street before the solution to my difficulty arrived from an improbable source.

---

* Confusion on Watson's part? "Stolen da Vinci" appears to refer to the theft of the *Mona Lisa* from the Louvre. That sensation occurred the following year, 1911.

It was on another Thursday when, true to form after my clinic, I went to the club to play billiards with Thurston. I cannot now recall but suspect it was his name that helped us settle on the day for our weekly game. He used to beat me handily enough in the beginning when we were just free of the army, but as the years have taken their inevitable toll, his eyesight and now coordination (he has developed a slight tremor) have tipped the scales in my favour. By this point, the game itself was little more than a pretext for an old soldiers' get-together.

"Cairo? The Paris of the East! Mother of the World! I knew it well after the war," Thurston remarked, struggling to line up his shot after I'd informed him of our intentions. I was not clear which war he was referring to, but his next sentence drove that consideration from my mind.

"There's a wonderful facility there, if I recall, which may be just the ticket." He scowled as his ball went wide.

"What sort of facility?" I demanded, setting aside my cue and wiping blue chalk from my thumb.

"The Khedivial Sporting Club. It's on the Jardin des Plantes, an island in the middle of the Nile, just off the western portion of the city. Three hundred acres, wonderfully green, you'd think you were in Epping. Splendid squash courts," he put in as an afterthought.

"I'm not sure a sporting club is what Juliet—"

"Oh, it's much more than that nowadays. The Al Wadi sanitarium is right on the premises, owned or at any rate managed by the army, and is reserved for the exclusive use of veterans and their dependents. Your missus will be in quarantine, of course. That's the usual procedure. The medicos are mainly Sikhs but top-hole."

"Really." I tried to keep the excitement out of my voice.

"I tell you the whole the thing is entirely up to date and as an ex–battlefield surgeon you'd easily qualify."

It all sounded too good to be true, but on the off chance that it wasn't, I let him win, determined later to ask Stark-Munro for a second opinion.

"You couldn't do better," was his answer. "The regimen is isolation, sunshine, fresh air, moderate exercise, mud baths, mineral soaks, and rest, while all the club's facilities would be at your disposal for the duration. You'd get to see her, from a distance, of course. I would've mentioned it straightaway, but I'd forgotten your military service, old man."

Many had. Once back from Afghanistan, years earlier, I'd been discharged with a mere nine months' veterans' benefits and my health in tatters. My wounded leg had a propensity to ache in inclement weather; therefore the notion of sunshine appealed to me as well. It now made eminent sense to apply for admission to the Khedivial Club and its Al Wadi sanitarium.

For once, matters military and medical were speedily reconciled, and a telegram from the Khedivial informed me that Juliet was eligible for treatment at Al Wadi and myself for adjacent club accommodations.

After that, things moved at an almost too-rapid pace. I booked passage aboard the P&O *Moldavia,* sailing for Alexandria from Tilbury on Monday, 12 December, mere weeks hence, sending Juliet and myself into a scrambling tizzy. There were trunks as well as Juliet's bulky and delicate glass X-rays to pack, travel documents and confirmations to obtain, my practice to sublet, and friends to bid farewell. Juliet, increasingly excited by the prospect of our trip, threw herself into preparations, seemingly forgetting its true purpose and choosing instead to view it as a genuine holiday, for which I could hardly blame her. I believe it was Sir Richard Burton who observed that action is the enemy of thought.*

Poor sailor that I am, I confess I was apprehensive about the prospect of a sea voyage, but the agent at Thomas Cook assured me the *Moldavia,* at ten thousand tonnes, was the last word in stability, equipped in deluxe fashion with all the latest appurtenances and remedies for *mal de mer.* Sparing no expense on my wife's behalf, our tickets were stamped: *POSH.*

None of which did either of us much good once we entered the Channel. A fierce gale roared down from the North Sea and the air was colder and wetter than ever. As Juliet was potentially contagious, we were obliged to keep to our stateroom, where we were both exceedingly ill. As a consequence, Juliet's coughing redoubled and my heart tightened within my chest every time I heard it.

But as we headed south and passed Gibraltar steaming into the Mediterranean, matters improved. The sun shone brightly, if not warmly, and the seas calmed, turning from angry grey to seductive azure. Alone and bundled on a deck chair in fresh air, Juliet posed no threat to others. Our stomachs settled and our appetites asserted themselves, a good thing, for the cuisine and company—always at a cautionary distance—were both excellent.

In a mere eight days we docked in the port of Alexandria, where the Egyptian weather was, as advertised, delightful. According to the glass, it was only fifty-four degrees,† but after frigid London it could have passed for the tropics.

---

* It was Joseph Conrad, not Richard Burton, explorer and translator of the Arabian Nights.

† It was not until 1961 that the UK began using the Celsius scale to record temperatures.

"You were here before," Juliet reminded me. "Did you spend any time in the city? Is it worth seeing if we can visit on the way home?"

I was obliged to disappoint her. "Our troopship put in at Port Said, more or less a hundred miles east, dearest, and thence we entered the canal, direct to Suez and the Red Sea. There was no sightseeing worthy of the name until we reached India."

But now the sights, and, it must be said, the scents of Egypt assailed us even as we set foot on the gangplank. "Mind the handrail, *effendi*!"

Alexandria proved no sleepy Arab backwater. A bustling seaport, situated at the mouth of the mighty Nile, the harbour was crammed with dhows and feluccas, Egyptian vessels whose shape and purpose had not altered in millennia. Laden with their cargoes, bulging lateen sails adroitly managed by Lascars, they plied the waters around and beneath our huge vessel, never somehow colliding with it or one another, while the dry desert air wafting from shore was perfumed with unfamiliar aromas, whose sum total proclaimed us strangers in a strange land.

We had scant time to admire, much less absorb, the cornucopia of alien stimuli. Ourselves and baggage were soon hefted by obliging, silent fellaheen, Egypt's ubiquitous peasantry, and whisked into the vast arrivals hall on the newly constructed quay. There we were inspected by customs and immigration officials. These in turn were supervised by British civil servants, looking, I thought, superciliously over the shoulders of their Egyptian counterparts.

"As-salamu alaykum, effendi! This way, *effendi."*

Everyone we encountered, native or European, was dressed in white or grey Egyptian cotton, punctuated here and there with red or yellow cummerbunds.

Our passports and travel documents briskly stamped and returned to us, our entry into the land of the pharaohs was officially noted. We were next ushered onto the adjacent platform where uniformed porters saw us swiftly ensconced on the waiting train. Our bags, which I half-expected never to see again, miraculously rejoined us, some in our compartment and the rest dispatched with the luggage. Almost immediately we were settled, a shrill whistle sounded, and we were headed south, staring at each other in happy wonder as a sun-baked landscape flew past our window.

"For almost five thousand years, Egypt has depended entirely on the Nile," Juliet, wearing her glasses, now read from her Baedeker. *"Outside its reach is uninhabitable Sahara; within it, the land is green and fertile and has been for over twenty centuries. The river itself is the longest in the world, its only competitor being the Amazon.* Think of that, John."

The trip to Cairo from Alexandria lasted some four hours, during which time Juliet alternately stared out the window, consulted the Baedeker, and finally slept. I attempted to follow her example, but my brain teemed with anxious thoughts. The entire trip, I knew, had taxed her resources to their uttermost, and thus preoccupied with the effect this might have on her fragile constitution, I have little recollection of the journey. It was well after nightfall when the train squealed into Cairo's Ramses Station, by which time the poor woman could barely stand.

It was almost eleven when we fetched up on the Jardin des Plantes* and were welcomed by the staff at the Al Wadi and the physician in charge, Dr. Amrit Singh, who towered over us. The white-bearded doctor—a Sikh Father Christmas—

---

* Today known as Gezira Island.

must have been well over six feet, and this not taking into account his lofty turban.

There were additional papers to fill and more questions to answer, but they could wait until morning. The bustle that had preceded our travel, the journey itself, and now the abrupt surcease of all motion combined to render us limp. Juliet offered no resistance when she was led to her room in the sanitarium and I to mine at the nearby Khedivial Sporting Club. We had been forewarned of these arrangements, but it still felt odd to be so close and yet separated. As flies were omnipresent, even at this time of year, every bed was draped in netting and we each were given fly whisks.

By daylight, Juliet's regimen had begun and, finally awaking from an almost narcoleptic sleep, I had the leisure to inspect the Khedivial and its facilities. These included tennis and the aforementioned squash courts, swimming pools, gymnasia, sculls for rowing on the Nile, and even a golf course. The well-named Jardin des Plantes included among its innumerable specimens blooming acacias, blood-red roses, and a variety of flora unknown to me. A stranger, waking to find himself here, would never dream he was surrounded by desert. Nearby were to be found elegant private homes on broad residential streets lined with superb flame trees.

But having completed my tour of inspection, I presently found myself at a loss. There was nothing to do but wait and see if the doctor and the desert would work their magic. I had stuffed books into my trunk, to be sure, and the Khedivial library boasted more, but I found myself unable to concentrate. I exercised, briefly took up golf, explored the byways of Zamalek in the island's northern extremity (there was a polo field where matches were almost daily in progress), but mostly

I remained in a state of bored anxiety, if that combination does not strike one as oxymoronic.

In those initial days, unwilling to leave Juliet, I confined my wanderings to the island, but as it was a mere two and a half miles in length, still less in width, such diversions soon began to pall. While Juliet had the benefit of scheduled activities, my day was shapeless. I saw her mainly at mealtimes—always seated at a distance and for a limited time. Like a lovesick schoolboy, I waited for those few opportunities to glimpse her, but it also occurred to me that my anxious countenance must not be doing her any particular good.

On Wednesday afternoons, to be sure, there were visiting lecturers giving talks on arcane subjects that held little interest for me. I recall one on philately (I couldn't trouble to learn what that was), and another on Lepidoptera, during which I fell asleep.

Juliet and other patients who wished to attend these talks were obliged to wear masks and white gloves, sitting apart from the rest on the farther side of the small auditorium. Thus veiled and separated, they bore an odd resemblance to Muslim women I was to encounter in the weeks to come.

Sunday, 1 January, 1911. The better part of a month has passed in this dreary fashion, enlivened only briefly by Christmas and some half-hearted singing of Carols. Eventually we realised how few topics remained unexplored by either of us and Juliet, nothing if not observant, perceived my ennui. "Dearest, you must not worry about me. Get off the island and explore the city."

"Nonsense. I'm perfectly content here."

But after another week, I could endure it no longer. I was starting to feel like Napoleon on Elba and dominated by the

same impulse to break free. Shepheard's Hotel, the one destination in Cairo known by reputation to many who had never
set foot in North Africa, was within walking distance. Armed
with a map, I traversed the narrow iron causeway that served
to connect the island to the western portion of the city, and
wandered into Ismailia Square,* treating myself to an urban
ramble before quenching my thirst.

Cairo proved to be a city of unrelated neighbourhoods, a
random juxtaposition of grand boulevards that might have
been created by Haussmann in Paris, exclusively populated by
Europeans and other Westerners. In Suleiman Pasha Street†
were many examples of the city's former French occupiers,
whose architecture, language, and signage still predominated,
but round a corner and a hundred paces farther you found
yourself in a Muslim or Jewish quarter amid narrow alleyways, seemingly unchanged for centuries.

The pyramids, as I'd been informed by Thurston, were
indeed not far off, but I decided to postpone that visit in the
hope that one day Juliet might accompany me.

Instead, referring occasionally to my map, I wandered
through the vast metropolis, glimpsing such sights as the recently opened Hotel Semiramis with its innovative rooftop
restaurant and the Egyptian Museum, housed in attractive
pink stucco and dominating the enormous Ismailia Square,
before briefly getting lost in the Khan el-Khalili *souq*. Con-
trasted with the expanse of the square, the *souq* proved a war-
ren of tiny, squalid, misaligned passageways dating from the
Middle Ages, swarming with flies and reeking with a pungent

---

* Today Tahrir Square. In 1926, the iron causeway connecting Gezira to
  the east bank of the Nile was replaced by the beautiful Qasr-El-Nil bridge.
† Today Talaat Harb Street.

mixture of cooking fires, orange peel, incense, and offal. I examined bolts of dyed cotton, hammered copper and brass platters, trays and kettle-ware, offered by sharp-tongued, dark-eyed bargainers, haggling through missing teeth. *"Salaam, effendi, baksheesh!"* In wooden cages dangling above us, parrots of green, red, and yellow plumage chattered like belowstairs gossips. Egyptian men, Muslim and those I took to be Coptics* were everywhere in evidence, as were Europeans and women (with their parasols), leisurely enjoying the Paris of the East.

Well-born Egyptian women, on the other hand, were typically veiled, while female peasantry wore overcoats, head scarfs, and Turkish-style face coverings called *yashmaks*. Only their eyelids, suggestively rimmed with kohl, glimpsed through varied masks, and the occasional jangling of jewellery, as I chanced near enough to hear it, hinted at other, more colourful, aspects of their lives.

Later my peregrinations found me at the beginning of Burjouan Alley of the famed Avenue Muizz where I gaped at the enormous Mosque-Sabil of Sulayman Agha al-Silahdar, established during the era of Muhammad Ali Pasha.

Time flew by without my realising it, but a gathering dryness in my throat put me again in mind of my original project, downing a brandy and soda at Shepheard's celebrated watering hole, the so-called "American" or "Long Bar," and there I made my way.

Given the events that were to unfold, I have wondered since at my decision. Would the outcome have been changed for any

---

* As opposed to Eastern Orthodox, Coptic Christians belong to one of the self-named Oriental Orthodox Christian sects, largely based in the Middle East.

of the principals had I simply returned to the Khedivial? Self-evidently not. The thing was already set down in the book of Fate. Some cosmic wheel or other was already spinning and I was a mere cog within it. No action I took or failed to take that day would have altered matters.

Wandering beneath Shepheard's vast porte-cochere and entering the sprawling edifice, I could not have been more surprised had I stepped into the basilica of the Vatican. Massive pink granite pillars, sprouting amid gigantic palm fronds, were evidently meant to evoke Egyptian or ancient Babylonian temples. (At the time I could not have told the difference.) With its lofty ceilings, gilt filigree, Berber rugs, polished teak, stained glass, gigantic mirrors, and terraced gardens, the hotel's opulence beggared many a palace. The famous "Long Bar" I soon discovered was so-named not because of its exceptional length but rather because of the wait before you were acknowledged by one of the overtaxed barmen.* The venue proved almost exclusively patronised by military personnel of various nationalities and ranks, all waving arms and stamping their feet for service. Many of the junior officers, I was bewildered to see, were milling about in uniform. In peacetime I could never recollect such a thing, but here were British, French, and American lieutenants, subalterns and the like, some even wearing what paltry decorations they boasted, clinking glasses and boisterously clamouring together, not unlike the chirping parrots of the *souq*.

Waving my hands for service like an agitated orchestra leader, I found myself standing beside a tall, rail-thin colonel

---

* Rebuilt since in pallid approximation near the site; the original Shepheard's burned to the ground in the 1950s.

in mufti. He sported a monocle, steel-grey hair, and a beaked nose I had seen before.

"Haven't we met?" I hazarded with a queasy sensation that we had.

"Arbuthnot," he introduced himself in an aristocratic drawl, not deigning to so much as glance in my direction.

But what really surprised me was his regimental green tie and pin, proclaiming him an officer of the Northumberland Fusiliers, my old regiment. No, that is not precise. What truly captured my attention—and indignation—as I studied his reflection in the mirror behind the forest of multihued bottles before it, was the large gravy stain on that selfsame green tie. To be still more precise, it was not the gravy stain itself but its shape that infuriated me. As I had so often noted before, that shape was reminiscent of Madagascar. I knew enough to lower my voice.

"You have *not* been in Afghanistan, I perceive. Holmes, why are you in Egypt wearing my regimental tie?"

2

THE FACTS OF THE CASE

"Maiwand, I should say!" the colonel bellowed in answer.[*]
"Ghastly business! Lucky to get out in one piece! I say," he
continued at an even higher pitch directed at the bar, "what's
about a libation for my friend here? Brandy and soda is yours,
isn't it, old man? Ice? Shouldn't if I were you. Never know
where it's been before they froze it. Good evening, Watson,"
he added in a lower tone, finally acknowledging my reflection
in the mirror.

"My tie," I repeated. "I wondered where it had got to."

"You abandoned it when you so imprudently deserted me to
remarry," the detective coolly replied. "Conceiving you had no
further need of it, I added it to my portmanteau of disguises, an
unpardonable liberty, I grant you, but as yours was an identity
I knew well, it greatly simplified my impersonation."

I was annoyed to find myself looking furtively over my
shoulder. A mere thirty seconds in the detective's company and

---

[*] "Arbuthnot" is here citing the slaughter at Maiwand during the Second
Afghan War in which Watson received his terrible leg wound.

already I was on the qui vive. One of the barmen set down my drink and I swallowed a large draught without ceremony.

"But what on earth brings to you Cairo?"

Holmes, or rather Colonel Arbuthnot, set down his drink in turn, removed his monocle, breathed heavily upon it, and commenced assiduously polishing the lens with his handkerchief, his head bent over his hands as he performed the task.

"I might ask you the same question," said he without looking up.

"But I asked you first." I heard myself sounding like a child.

He sighed and clapped the monocle back before his right eye.

"That is rather a curious story. Can you meet me at eight tomorrow in the *souq* for a spot of breakfast? The El Fishawy café? As always, your assistance might prove invaluable."

He walked off with a regal drunkard's lurch after slapping some Egyptian pounds on the bar.

"John, dearest, where on earth have you been? We looked for you at tea. Did you get lost? I couldn't sleep for worry."

Thus I imagined Juliet's remonstrance when I hastened back to Al Wadi, arriving only just in time for pudding.

None of which occurred. Dinner and coffee had long since been cleared by my return and Juliet retired for the night. More ominous, to my way of thinking, she had left no word for me, leaving me to my own guilty reflections. I ordered another brandy and soda and sat nursing it—and my guilty conscience—in the high-ceilinged common room with its fan softly whirring above me, a mocking, rotating halo.

What had just happened? And what had I got myself into as a consequence? Ought I to make a clean breast of it and tell Juliet Sherlock Holmes was in Egypt? I ruled out this ex-

pedient as soon as it occurred to me. In the wake of my previous encounter with the detective and what had come of it, I
had undergone something very like a collapse.* Were I now to
tell her Holmes was in Egypt and seeking my help, she might
panic and insist on returning to England posthaste.

I felt myself tugged in two directions, on the one hand
taking care of Juliet and seeing in every way I could to her
welfare; on the other, like an old warhorse summoning up
the blood upon hearing the bugle and collecting myself for the
charge.

It was an involuntary reflex but no less potent for that. And
as I continued to drink and take inventory of my emotions and
choices, I presently became aware of something else. The bitter
resentment I tried so hard not to acknowledge, that fate had
once again forced me to play the role, not of husband, nor even
doctor, but of nurse. I knew without even having to consider
the matter that Juliet had no desire to be ill. It was certainly the
furthest thing from her wishes. And yet, regardless of wishes,
here I was, once more assigned by kismet to repeat the same
disagreeable part I had played once before—unsuccessfully.

These feelings, I was all too aware, did me little credit.

Later, lying beneath my mosquito netting, I tossed restlessly in my bedding, unable to sleep.

What was I to do?

"You made sure you weren't followed?"

"Of course."

"And found the place alright?"

"Evidently."

---

* For details of this startling case, the reader is urged to consult Watson's
account, *The Adventure of the Peculiar Protocols.*

"I am truly sorry to learn of your wife's illness, Watson. I hope she enjoys a speedy and uneventful recovery."

I stared at the man in wonderment.

"How can you know anything of Juliet's health?"

The detective shrugged. "Rudimentary, my dear man. I espy you alone in far-off Egypt, furiously shouting for service at Shepheard's and, when it finally arrives, quaffing your drink at a gulp. Your skin is deeply tanned, informing me that you have been in these parts quite some time, which in turn suggests you've thrown over your practice in London at the busiest season of the year. What could it be that prompts such a migration? I see that your own health is indestructible as ever, but your haggard features and testy impatience over the matter of an old tie proclaim a set of circumstances that have robbed you of your customary equanimity. What can it be that brings you to Cairo in winter? Given the foregoing, it is not too great a leap to speculate as to Mrs. Watson's well-being. I can imagine your present situation prompts painful memories," he concluded with a sympathetic expression.

"Well," I huffed, irked but at the same time amazed to find myself once more on the losing end of a familiar exchange, "now you explain it, the thing becomes simplicity itself."

The detective sat back without comment and studied me, the tips of his fingers pressed together in his accustomed fashion. I determined to withstand his scrutiny, but was, I confess, touched by his unexpected solicitude. Those emotional aspects of his character were rare glimpses indeed and, as a rule, carefully hidden.

Thus we surveyed each other. That we had both aged

in the interval since our last meeting* was beyond question. Holmes had not troubled to colour his hair as part of his disguise; that silver was genuine and his brow had acquired additional creases, but his piercing grey eyes (one glittering behind his monocle) and imperious nose remained unchanged.

But under his penetrating inspection, I soon grew restive and took in my surroundings.

The El Fishawy café was located near the entrance to the odiferous Khan al-Khalili *souq*, the intricate vicinity I had visited the day before. Situated near a monumental stone gate that served as entrance to the maze, a brass plaque informed the curious in English and Arabic that the café was established in 1773. Reading the date, I was startled to realise that the numerals we take for granted are in fact Arabic in origin. Around us at nearby similar tables, sipping thick, black Turkish coffee and perusing Arabic newspapers, were local early risers. All wore the kaftan or *galabeya* as it is sometimes called, some cinched at the waist with colourful sashes or wide leather belts, others not, but all wore some manner of head covering, the tarboosh, red fez, or turban. A few were meditatively sucking on susurrating water pipes which the English refer to as hubble-bubbles.

"I expect you're wondering what I'm doing here, my dear fellow," my companion broke in on my thoughts.

"You will recall that is the very question I put to you last night," I responded somewhat tartly; his appropriation of my regimental tie I had still not forgiven, but my grievance ran

---

* The last record of their meeting was 1905, but since this excerpt of the journal has bypassed intervening years, the detective and doctor may well have met since then.

deeper. In truth I was annoyed to find Holmes in Cairo and more annoyed yet to find myself having agreed to meet him. His presence had given me a sleepless night and it was only that Juliet was already getting her mud bath that left me once again at loose ends, succumbing to my undisciplined curiosity.

"Very well, I shall attempt to enlighten you," said the detective, pulling out his briar and packing it with Balkan Sobranie from his battered pouch. He was eager, I sensed, to distract me from my difficulties, and perhaps his own. Like Scheherazade, he would beguile me with someone else's. "For it is a curious business, as I remarked last night." He paused, stretched his long legs, and held a flame to the tobacco, puffing contentedly while I waited. The familiar odor of his pipe had a soothing effect.

"Where to begin?" The question was evidently posed to himself. "Last night I confess I encountered you at a most inauspicious moment."

"Oh?"

"You know about the purloined *La Giaconda,* I imagine."

"The what?"

"The *Mona Lisa,* it is also called." He favored me with an impatient grimace. "A lot of fuss having to do with the lady's smile. Personally, I am not sure I discerned anything noteworthy about it, but that was no affair of mine. The picture had been stolen from its place in the Louvre, and the French police, not unlike our own, found themselves baffled and I was discreetly asked to step in. At first a Spaniard called Picasso was suspected, but I quickly ruled him out. In the end the matter proved a trifling one and the true perpetrator, an Italian, Peruggia by name, was apprehended. I had just returned from Paris and unpacked my bags when I was nettled to discover that as a result of my Paris sojourn I had missed the apprehension of Dr. Crippen, the wife murderer.* In its way this was the final straw. As you know, I have spoken lately of retirement. In fact, I have my eye on a property in Sussex which I've a mind to acquire and where I shall rusticate. Mrs. Hudson isn't getting any younger and those stairs do take a toll on her.

"I'd spoken of my intention and asked if she would be interested in keeping house for me on the Downs. You can imagine my relief when I learned she was amenable to the idea. As by this time we are both rather settled in our habits, I think neither of us relished the prospect of starting—"

"Holmes, what are you doing in Egypt?"

He smiled, shook his head, and blew smoke. "I grow garrulous," he conceded. "Well, well, all these arrangements were in process when Mrs. Hudson knocked on my door to hand me a visiting card which proclaimed my caller in the entryway below to be none other than the Duchess of Uxbridge."

"The Duchess of—"

"Uxbridge. The name is familiar to you?"

"The only Uxbridge I ever heard of lost a leg at Waterloo. Unless one counts Uxbridge Elixir. One cannot escape their advertisements."

"Just so. The grandson was in trade. I daresay their miraculous tonic water is ladled no farther than the Isle of Dogs, still it seems harmless enough. As it happens, the woman who swept into 221B ten days ago, swathed in black furs, before shedding them like a molting snake to expose a cloud of grey chiffon, is a Brazilian, Lizabetta del Maurepas, Duchess of Uxbridge, whose husband claims descent from the selfsame

---

* According to this, Holmes was still in residence in Baker Street. Whenever and wherever he did retire, it wasn't for long. As for Dr. Crippen, look it up.

elixir and battle. It appears His Grace, Duke Michael, the eleventh of that name, has gone missing."

"Ah."

"An excitable type, I should say."

"The duke?"

"Possibly, but I was referring to the gentleman's wife. Not precisely what you, with your vast experience of the fair sex, Watson, would term a classic beauty, but striking, in possession of a good figure, and definitely *a la mode*. Tempestuous, but perhaps with reason. The duke, it seems, is fond of wintering in Egypt, but presently no one seems able—or willing—to locate him."

"Stop a bit. Now I seem to recall. Wasn't this Uxbridge involved in a motorcar accident some years ago?"

"Excellent, Watson. Your memory is ironclad as ever. Yes, a car accident involving drink, as I am given to understand, in the wake of which His Grace came here to recuperate. And while here, he fell prey to the local mania."

"What mania?"

"Egyptology."

"What's that?"

The detective glanced around briefly before leaning forward and speaking in a confidential undertone.

"Grave robbing." My expression must have startled him. "Of a sort," he amended. "Your coffee's getting cold, old man." I swallowed a bit of the muddy concoction but now confess Scheherazade had my complete and complicit attention.

Satisfied that he had obtained it, the detective resumed. "Ever since Schliemann uncovered Troy, Flinders Petrie and Arthur Evans* the ruins of Crete, scientists, but also men of

_____

* These gentlemen may lay claim to being the fathers of modern archaeology.

means—sometimes they are one and the same—have descended on this part of the world in search of ancient plunder and modern notoriety. You know of the Rosetta Stone?"

"What has she to do with this?"

My question brought forth a hearty laugh. "Ah, Watson, you remain the one fixed point in our changing universe. Let us meet that Rosetta when we come to her, which we doubtless shall. Egyptology is a branch of archeology, the search for artifacts from its vanished civilisation, pottery shards, faïence, and the like—and, if one is lucky, a mummy or two."

"Mummy? You mean those ghastly—"

"The preserved remains of their dead. By first extracting the body's entrails for separate burial in canopic jars, the brains first dragged out through the nostrils, apparently those ingenious Egyptians of yore had mastered the art of embalming or mummification to such a degree that the corpses of their kings and such have survived several millennia. Surely you've seen examples in the British Museum?"

"Hang that place. All roads seem to lead there. I really must tour beyond the Reading Room sometime."

He shrugged. "The secrets of such corporeal preservations have been lost to us, but the collecting urge lives on as it does to some degree, I suspect, in most of humanity. The likes of the American, Theodore Davis, Lord Carnarvon, and the Frenchman, Verneuil, come here every year when the sun is not roasting, to dig for pharaonic treasure, unearthing most often mere fragments of dynastic Egypt, but every now and then"—he hesitated—"an item of purest gold."

"Gold!" The word roused an instinctive echo on my part. Scheherazade was now in full flow.

"The Egyptians boasted an awesome supply, and still more obtained through neighbouring conquests such as Nubia. It is said the pharaohs were buried with their hoards for use in the afterlife, though that may prove a mere farrago, as there is nothing to substantiate the notion."

"If true, it sounds a most pleasant arrangement."

"My dear fellow, much of this is common knowledge. Do you not recall our evening some years ago at Covent Garden, when we heard the great de Reszke as Radamès in a memorable performance of *Aïda*? Tenor and soprano buried alive, but in love at the finish?"

The pained look on his face as he perceived my own put paid to that question. The detective looked about him. "Shall we walk? I should acquaint myself with my surroundings."

"By all means," I said with some relief. "I've only just begun exploring." I confessed my tendency to stay close to the sanitarium but was pleased to accompany him through the convoluted *souq*. Once accustomed to its pungency, the place was not without its charm, and presently my attention was drawn to a hammered copper chafing dish I felt sure would become Juliet's kitchen.

"*Salaam, effendi,* look! Bargain! *Baksheesh!*"*

"It's as well to walk," Holmes murmured. "A moving target is best."

That reeled me back in. I had no idea what he was getting at but, looking about me, fell into step. "Go on about the gold."

I thought I saw him smile but could only make out his monocled profile by my side. The market stalls, as they enveloped us, swarmed with flies. Holmes squinted at the insects in disgust, waggling his slender fingers in a vain attempt to drive them off.

"As you may imagine," he continued, "the search for those

---

* *Baksheesh* at that time would seem to be something between a tip and a bribe.

tombs is a most addictive though possibly lucrative hobby, albeit there are two drawbacks."

The detective, I knew, was no stranger to addiction.

"Oh?"

"The first is that no pharaoh's unopened tomb has ever been found."

"I'm not sure I understand."

"For the simple reason that a hundred and fifty generations of tomb robbers have beaten these modern pirates to the punch. All that typically remains are immovable stone sarcophagi and the occasional mummified corpse inside, wrapped in shredded linen in their remarkable states of preservation."

"But surely there must be some tombs as yet unearthed?"

"That is the holy grail of all 'Egyptologists,' but it is an expensive one. Diggers as well as scholars must be paid. And while those who can afford it hire the local peasantry to sweat in the sun, gouging holes like gophers, it's all the government can do to impose some order on their efforts and attempt to restrict the booty these gentlemen are shipping back to European museums or private collections."

"You said there were two drawbacks."

"Did I?" Holmes retained his taste for the dramatic. I knew it would be necessary to prime the pump.

"I take it you number the duke among these Egyptian enthusiasts?"

The flies now mercifully dispersed in search of fresh blood.

"So it seems, though very much a neophyte." He looked about, alert to every detail as we prowled the winding alleyways, leaving behind my copper chafing dish which I feared I would never manage to locate again. He now paused to

examine some parti-coloured linen scarfs, ignoring the owner's torrent of encouragement, before he returned to his narrative. "But as I say, he is currently not to be found."

"And the duchess?"

"I was certainly startled by my visitor, a singular combination of English aristocrat and flamboyant South American, a
sort of Latin Viscountess Astor, if that helps.* Her English was
perfect but intermittently speckled with Portuguese, which is
Greek to me. As she paced my rooms, stepping carelessly on
her discarded fox—which I made haste to retrieve and sling
over the nearest antimacassar—the duchess explained that for
the past three years she had visited her husband during the
'digging season,' always staying in Cairo. Luxor she'd heard
was not amusing and she declined to join him there.

"'I pay no particular heed to the bric-a-brac of my husband's Egyptian mania,' she informed me. 'They do not interest me, but Cairo for a few weeks in winter can be diverting.'

"'A pleasant alternative to Uxbridge Manor in December,
no doubt,' I suggested.

"'*Sim.* Just so,' she agreed.

"'And when was the last time you heard from His Grace?' I
asked, gesturing to your old chair and hoping she would avail
herself of it.

"'Not for almost three months,' was the answer.

"She remained standing and shortly recommenced pacing with mincing steps occasioned by the snug contours of

---

* Nancy Langhorne, Virginia-born socialite, married Lord Astor and in
  1919 became the first female Member of Parliament to take her seat.
  Brooklyn-born Lady Randolph Churchill, (mother of the future prime
  minister), is another example of an American who married into the
  English aristocracy.

her ensemble. Truly, Watson, I cannot understand the ways of fashion. What women nowadays put themselves through."

"Holmes!"

He shrugged apologetically and resumed. "'My letters addressed to His Grace at Shepheard's have never been answered,' said she.

"'Nor returned?'

"'Nor returned, Senhor Holmes.' Here she finally subsided with a swish of satin onto the settee, betraying at last a modicum of vulnerability beneath the hauteur. 'I have been to the Metropolitan Police and spoken with a certain Chief Detective Inspector Lestradinho, who I learned is shortly to retire. He was of no help whatsoever, suggesting I file a missing persons report or some such nonsense when I know perfectly well my husband is here in Egypt. He then suggested I talk to Scotland Yard, but they informed me Egypt was out of their jurisdiction and recommended I speak with the Foreign Office and so I called at Whitehall with equally abysmal results, except that a Senhor Le Carré, showing me the door, suggested I consult you, which I am doing.'

"I found myself jotting down bits and pieces of her narrative in my pocket book. Her story, as she told it, made little sense. That a British nobleman of some ancestral distinction should go entirely missing with no official acknowledgement, let alone explanation, was bewildering to me.

"'Can you recollect nothing your husband might have said about his Egyptian hobby that might prove useful?' I asked.

"Her handsome features contracted in thought as she struggled to remember something about a topic which held no interest for her, but after some moments her countenance brightened.

"'He spoke several times about something called . . . what was it?' A polished fingernail raised briefly to her mouth to assist her memory did the trick. 'Tuthmosis.'

"'Tuthmosis,' I echoed. The term meant nothing to me, but I wrote it down phonetically as I heard it.

"My methodical action appeared to try her patience, for it was followed by a torrent of Portuguese invective, which I judged both agitated and anguished. I thought it justified, for it certainly appeared the woman had been given the runaround."

"I should say!"

"As you know, Watson, it is the outré that commands my attention. Thoughts of retirement on the Downs receded. Like a gambler who cannot walk away from the table, I found the woman's dilemma an intriguing one, and agreed to make some enquiries. Ascertaining she was stopping at Claridges, I betook myself to White's, where His Grace was a member, in search of data. One cannot fashion bricks without clay. At White's I was discreetly informed the duke had been black-balled. Rather a bad hat, it seems. Debts at whist."

"Astronomical," I suggested, "to be cashiered from an establishment as louche as White's. Not covered by Uxbridge Elixir, I take it?"

"The family no longer owns the enterprise. But there was more," he went on, before I could pursue this. "It seems the duke got into an altercation there with a Swede by the name of Ohlsson. They were to visit Egypt together, something to do with a piece of paper or chart in the Swede's possession—the steward insists he didn't actually get to see what it was. At all events, they came to blows in the smoking room."

"Blows?" I echoed, then shrugged as I considered. "I expect that sort of thing happens at White's now and again. Isn't that why so many are eager to subscribe?"

"Possibly, but I daresay the sequel is less common. In the fisticuffs that followed, the duke seized the paper held by the other and made off with it, fleeing the premises, at which point this Ohlsson repaired to the upstairs billiard room and blew his brains out."

"You can't be serious."

"Entirely. Of course the thing was hushed up. White's has probably done worse on occasion. Swift referred to the place as the bane of half the aristocracy. Ohlsson was probably neither the first nor last distraught member to do away with himself in those precincts. So I had a vanished nobleman, a mysterious paper, and nothing further to show for it. Ohlsson was an affiliate with guest privileges only and nothing much seems known about him other than the fact that he was a member of minor Swedish nobility with more money at his disposal than brains."

"Fewer brains following his suicide," I was forced to concede. "What about Mycroft?"

"To be sure. It was but a short walk from White's to Pall Mall. The Diogenes has gone most dreadfully to the dogs, by the way. The furniture in the Strangers' Room is quite threadbare and so, I might add, is old Harcourt in his fraying livery."

"Did you see your brother?"

The detective sighed. "Poor Mycroft. He has lost some weight, which must be counted good news, but now has gone quite deaf and carries with him everywhere a cumbersome electric contraption that is supposed to improve his hearing. I'm afraid its utility is questionable."

"What did he have to say?"

"Effendi!"

Holmes was briefly diverted by a heated argument between a rug merchant and a Turkish Begum, both gesticulating like whirling windmills and shouting in separate languages while nearby tradesmen looked on, some helpfully joining the dispute with comments in what I took to be dialects of their own.

"Holmes?"

The detective recollected himself. "I told Mycroft of my client, though without identifying her by name. I had to repeat myself a good deal and talk in a louder voice than was customary at the Diogenes so as to make myself heard.

"At length he nodded, poor man, indicating he'd finally made me out. I then enquired about conditions in Egypt. I knew in advance he would twit me with your nettlesome observation that my knowledge of politics was 'feeble,' but this I endured, as it seemed to amuse him.

"'The thing is deuced complicated.' As he said this, he was fumbling with a cigar and clipper while endeavouring to balance the hearing device resting precariously on his lap without dislodging the wires leading to his ears. 'The present state of Anglo-Turkish relations is a most delicate one.'

"'Why does that fail to astonish me?' I could not resist replying.

"'*What?*' Cupping a hand to one ear.

"'Never mind! Pray continue!'

"'The Ottoman Empire is crumbling,' Mycroft informed me, 'and Egypt is presently balancing as uncertainly between Turkey and England as this wretched machine perched on my lap. While nominally ruled by Abbas the Second, the Turkish viceroy or Khedive on behalf of Sultan Mehmed the Fifth, the crown of the Ages and Pride of all countries, the Greatest of Caliphs, Successor of the Apostle of the Universe, the Victorious Conqueror, the Shadow of God on Earth'—Mycroft rattled off the titles without difficulty or comment—'in prosaic reality, Egypt is presently a Crown Colony in all but name.'

"'That does not seem a durable status quo,' said I, reaching to help steady the hearing device.

"'The furthest thing from it,' my brother agreed after I'd

repeated myself. 'The place is a vipers' nest of competing agents and agendas, with Brits, Turks, and Egyptians vying for hegemony and, of course, control of the Suez Canal, which must remain in our hands. The Khedive insists he is pro-British, but we have reason to suspect he's playing a double game. If you insist on going there, which I take it is the reason for your visit today, my only advice to you is, Don't rock the pyramid.'

"He smiled as he said this, evidently pleased with himself, then tore a page from his engagement diary, as is his custom, scribbled something on it, and handed it to me. 'Just in case, this is the best I can do,' were his final words, 'because once in Egypt you will be on your own. I can help you craft a new persona, but besides this'—the scrap of paper—'His Majesty's government will not interfere.'"

"Where have we heard that before?" said I ruefully.

Holmes nodded in agreement, taking another swallow of cold coffee. "I placed the torn page with his writing in my pocket book, after which we said our goodbyes. He looked frail as I left him, which startled and saddened me. It seems mere moments ago we were boys together," he added with a startling wistfulness.

"But why are you incognito?" I asked, hoping to dispel his melancholy. "Why are you 'Colonel Arbuthnot'?"

We were now on the farther side of the *souq*, facing yet another enormous mosque just in time to hear the muezzin in the turret above us summoning the faithful to prayer.

"I don't think it would help my search to advertise my participation," the detective explained as those near us genuflected Muslim fashion, prostrate and facing east. "Nor do I wish to alert London's criminal element to my repeated absences, for they would seize the advantage. I managed to keep my name out of the French papers for just that reason. As Colonel Arbuthnot, a fledgling Egyptologist, I am here to rendezvous with Duke Michael, to search for Egyptian gold, but alas, upon arrival, I find my friend has disappeared. Don't turn around, my dear fellow, but I find already I am being shadowed."

I had to resist the impulse to do exactly that.

"By whom?"

He shrugged. "A stout fellah* in a fez, fingering the bolt of red-dyed cotton behind me. I shall keep in him view for the present. You will recall I said there were two drawbacks to this profession or hobby, if you prefer. Finding an unopened tomb is one difficulty, but it seems Egyptology itself can become a rather dangerous business. Have you read about Professor Jourdan?"

"Ah, yes, some months ago. Don't remind me." I held up a forestalling hand. "A Frenchman who . . ."

"Had his throat cut at a place called Karnak."

"By bandits?"

Holmes shrugged doubtfully. "Left, mark you, to rot in the sun."

I nodded. A dangerous business indeed, I reflected, when gold is at stake. The duke's disappearance now began to assume a more jaundiced complexion.

"You've made enquiries regarding His Grace?"

"It's early days yet. I had just completed my initial attempt when you appeared beside me at the bar last night. Neither of us was in the best humour."

"I take it you have met with no success thus far?"

He regarded me with an unfamiliar expression. "It's more peculiar than you can imagine, Doctor. Upon my arrival yes-

---

* Fellah: the singular of "fellaheen."

terday at Shepheard's I asked for Uxbridge. The duchess informed me he usually occupied suite seven-eighteen and her letters to him were invariably addressed there. But when I enquired, I was informed that not only had the duke not arrived this season, but there is in fact no room seven-eighteen in the hotel."

"What?"

I turned casually, but the stout individual in the fez Holmes had described was nowhere to be seen. I turned back to the detective. "No room seven—"

"Eighteen. As you may imagine, I kicked up a rumpus. 'See for yourself, *mon colonel.*' Monsieur Charpentier, managing director of the hotel, helpfully escorted me in the lift to the seventh floor, where we walked the endless corridor, its entirety covered with exquisite Persian carpeting. In truth, the even-numbered rooms, those with the view of the Nile, end at seven-sixteen. There *is* no seven-eighteen."

"How queer."

"The yellow wallpaper on the seventh floor is atrocious, by the way," the detective added, heaving a sigh. "Monsieur Charpentier showed me His Grace's mail, a smallish packet tied with string. It contained business correspondence from England and of course a half-dozen unopened letters from the duchess. According to Charpentier, His Grace always stayed in suite seven-sixteen and he apologetically intimated the duchess's memory was in error. In any event, suite seven-sixteen is currently occupied by a Mr. and Mrs. Irvington from Delaware, leaving on the fifteenth. As the duke was annually expected at this time of year, they had marked his mail: 'Hold for Arrival.'"

"But if His Grace never arrived, how can you know His Grace is even in Egypt? Perhaps at the last minute, he altered his destination without informing—"

"Precisely what I endeavoured to ascertain, but I was initially confronted by a brick wall. Egyptian Customs and Immigration, under the watchful eye of His Majesty's government, does not give out such information. Nonetheless, with discreet *baksheesh*, I learned His Grace entered Egypt two and a half months ago, precisely according to his yearly schedule."

"And there is no record of his leaving?"

"That information was beyond my powers of persuasion. But do you not perceive the anomaly that excites my curiosity?"

"How do you mean?"

"Think, my dear doctor. According to my unofficial source, the duke has been here since mid-November. Even without tonic water, a man such as His Grace, with vast holdings in England and abroad, in property and business, with those who manage his estates, his investments in South African mining shares, to say nothing of his ruinous debts, must have a sizable correspondence, if only from innumerable creditors, dunning him with invoices. By now they surely must know where His Grace is typically to be found at this time of year."

"I should imagine so, assuming his seasonal migration is consistent."

"Well, where is it then, if all Shepheard's can produce is a small packet of such correspondence? I should estimate no more than a week or two. Naturally, the management of Shepheard's has no thought of turning these letters over to one who represented himself as a mere friend of the duke, but regardless, where are the rest? Are they withholding it? If not, what has become of two months' worth? Was it being forwarded to His Grace elsewhere? Where might that elsewhere be?"

"I begin to see what you mean."

As the muezzin called out above us, I mentally reviewed all

Holmes had told me, trying to think like the detective, a fruitless endeavour, as I knew from a lifetime of similar attempts.

"Did you form an impression of the duke and duchess's marital relations?"

"An excellent, if delicate, question, Watson, and therefore difficult to answer. Short of obtaining the duke's post and reading the duchess's unopened letters without her permission, I should surmise those relations were . . . cool. Talking to her, I infer their interests and lives are essentially separate, though for form's sake they adhere to society's expectations. They have no children, which might or might not be suggestive. In London, the duke had the amusements open to a gentleman of means. Or had, as I understand those means have shrunk considerably. I expect theirs could be termed a marriage of convenience. Such has long been the subject of three-decker novels by Mr. James, in which impoverished aristocrats with colourful escutcheons are set afloat once more by American heiresses in search of titles, such as Lady Astor. The only difference in this instance is that the heiress in question is South rather than North American. Brazilian copper, if you please."

"Did you ever question the duchess about the Swede, Ohlsson, and the affair at White's?"

"The name meant nothing to her and she knew of no piece of paper or chart, though it's always possible she is a convincing liar. Women have been known to specialise in that sort of thing."

"No more so than men," I found myself retorting. I had not realised until that moment how much of Juliet had rubbed off on me.

The detective thrust forth a lower lip in dubious concession. "Be that as it may, as of today, I find myself in a cul-de-sac."

"Will you report your lack of progress to your South American client?"

He chose not to look at me, but direct his gaze upwards instead at the distant figure of the chanting muezzin. "I've no need. The duchess is here."

"What? In Cairo?"

"With her brother-in-law, the duke's younger brother. I attempted to dissuade her," he added hastily, "a woman alone in a strange society where members of her sex are treated . . . differently, and so forth, but I hadn't reckoned on that Latin temperament of hers. 'How would it look,' said she, stamping her foot, 'if I failed to take an interest in the fate of my husband? Besides, I shan't be alone. Lord Darlington will escort me.' Her arguments I found difficult to counter. Hoping to attract less notice, they are stopping at Osiris House, just off the Ismailia Square."

I took this new information on board, stealing a glance at my watch. It would be Juliet's luncheon by the time I made my way back to the Al Wadi, but I, too, found it difficult to walk away from the roulette wheel. "And the brother-in-law, this Darlington?"

"Lionel, a schoolmaster near Staines, if one can imagine such a thing. Naturally, as a younger brother he has little or nothing to speak of in the way of income, but he's a prepossessing devil, I'll be bound—a youthful forty, slender, blond, blue-eyed, clean-shaven, and . . ." The detective groped for the right word. "Diffident?" he chose finally, on an upturned interrogative. "What the Americans term 'a smooth customer.'"

"But here presumably out of concern for his brother."

With a cocked ear, Holmes listened to the muezzin's call, running a meditative thumb across his lips. "Presumably," he allowed after some thought. "While awaiting my findings, he says he will occupy his time doing research at the university with a view to writing a monograph on Napoleon's Egyptian campaign."

Holmes shrugged again. His recital had depressed him.

"And 'Colonel Arbuthnot' is an expert Egyptologist, I take it?"

He favoured me with a sheepish look.

"*Aïda* notwithstanding, alas, no. I boned up as best I could in the Reading Room at your hated British Museum where you toiled with Constance Garnett those long years since[*]— Old Kingdom, New Kingdom, mummification, that sort of thing—but I hadn't much time as our ship was shortly due to sail. I read voraciously once on board, to be sure, but the journey as you know is not a lengthy one and there are a great many names and facts to digest over three thousand years. In addition, I was diverted by the death of a second Egyptologist that I read of in the ship's newspaper, a German named Bechstein who apparently wandered from his dig into the desert, curiously omitting to bring his compass. The Sahara apparently swallowed him whole, for only his remains picked clean for carrion were found." He sighed. "I am therefore still very much a novice in all directions and have arranged for a tutor. If you are free later, you shall meet him."

"Perhaps he'll be able to explain Tuthmosis," I attempted to raise his spirits.

"Perhaps he will."

---

[*] As recounted in *The Adventure of the Peculiar Protocols*.

3

THE EXPERT

Even partially concealed behind his large desk, Dr. Amrit Singh cut an imposing figure. Turbaned as always, and imperturbable in his white coat, he thumbed through his notes of Juliet's case while she and I sat silent, awaiting his prognosis. I don't know that either of us was holding our breath, but it felt like it.

"You have been here some five weeks," the doctor remarked, quietly turning another page. I stole a look at my wife, her expression hard to make out in the dimly lit room, but she appeared tranquil and only mildly interested as the solemn physician held her London and Egyptian X-rays side by side up to a sunlit window. Unfortunately, one of the former had been dashed to pieces in transit, but the other had miraculously survived the voyage.

"It doesn't do to expose a patient too often to this procedure," Dr. Singh murmured, scanning the images with a magnifying glass, "but we do learn so much from it."

Again, we waited. What an odd position for a doctor to be in, it occurred to me. I was so accustomed to being the white-coated figure behind the desk.

"Has she made progress?" I finally could not refrain from

asking. The films looked very similar to me as I stepped to the window to examine them.

"Progress," he echoed in his mellifluous voice. "Progress is being made."

Juliet and I both exhaled simultaneously, though her exhalation trailed away in a slight cough.

Perhaps we had after all been holding our breath.

"Your lungs show signs of improvement." Using a pointer, he directed our attention to the second X-ray. "Especially the right. But more time is required for conclusive results."

"We expected as much," my wife surprised me by saying.

The Sikh responded with a faint smile as he set down the delicate glass plates. "I hope you are enjoying Egypt," he said, "because it seems Egypt is enjoying you."

After profuse thanks which the doctor acknowledged with an inclination of his massive head, both of us, more sanguine about Juliet's situation than I suspect either had been in some time, enjoyed a light repast. For this festive occasion I was admitted to the Al Wadi refectory, where several other patients dined, though we were placed at a separate table. Juliet was very like her old self, animated and eating with enthusiasm. Her appetite more than anything I had heard reassured me. While she was in such good spirits, I judged the moment propitious to tell her what else was going on. My news came as a definite surprise.

"Sherlock Holmes is in Egypt?" A warning fleck of red appeared on her cheek. In the sunlit refectory, it was impossible to miss.

"On a case, dearest. I encountered him by merest chance."

"And now he wishes you to help him?"

As always, your assistance might prove invaluable, Holmes's words rang in my ear.

"Not in so many words," I fumbled, alarmed by the knitting of her brows.

"I'm quite sure he didn't have to use any," Juliet retorted with some heat. "Really, John, you must decide to which of us you are married."

"That is most uncalled for. I did not seek him out. It was you, remember, who suggested I tour the city. If I hadn't obeyed your instructions, the meeting would not have occurred."

Juliet said nothing but set down her fork.

"My dear, you mustn't take on so. Just when you've begun to mend. Consider, I beg you. I am not in darkest Russia. I am not separated from you by thousands of miles.* I am here at your beck and call."

She sniffed, conceding I had scored a point.

"I only worry," said she at length. "The last time you two went adventuring you had nightmares for months afterwards. John, on that occasion I sometimes feared for your sanity."

I remembered those nightmares all too well. On occasion—though I strove to conceal the fact—they have recurred. But my pressing need at the moment was to reassure Juliet and overcome whatever misgivings she might entertain regarding any enterprise that involved the detective and myself.

"Dearest, this is merely a missing persons dilemma. Nothing cataclysmic, and if it distresses you, I will remain here on the Jardin des Plantes 'til the crack of doom. You've only to say the word."

She smiled at this and, after a moment's further reflection, took up her fork. I immediately did likewise.

In the end Juliet came 'round and a compromise was

---

* They were separated on a case which took Holmes and Watson to Russia in 1905.

reached. "I can't have you endlessly moping about this island while I have my treatments," she acknowledged, clever girl that she was. "Only promise me you two won't get up to anything foolish."

"That's an easy promise," I answered at once. There seemed no point in alarming her with other details. Bechstein had simply forgotten his compass and I told myself the Frenchman, Jourdan, murdered months ago, was an entirely unrelated affair, likely the handiwork of bandits. I blush to say I did not associate the suicide at White's with anything in Egypt. (The Swede, after all, was not even a full member.)

"Aside from pharaohs who've been dead for centuries, we've not a thing to worry about."

Whatever prompted me to say that?

While I was placating Juliet, Holmes spent the morning at Osiris House, fending off the duchess and her brother-in-law. Learning of his intention to visit the Egyptian Antiquities Service to speak with someone acquainted with the duke, they were intent on accompanying the detective with questions of their own. Holmes was obliged to be tactful.

"It's a devilish business conducting a proper investigation with one's clients breathing down one's neck, hanging on to one's coattails, getting underfoot, and generally second-guessing one's every move," he complained as we made our way among innumerable desks. The vaulted place was crammed with files teetering uncertainly on sagging shelves. Around us, huddled figures bent over what I took to be parchment fragments,* made entries in huge black ledgers, or scurried clutch-

---

* More likely papyrus, Egyptian "paper" made from the plant, which preceded parchment.

ing papers and notebooks through the narrow aisles, generally presenting the aspect of a beehive run amok. Not a single typewriter was to be heard. The department was the over-burdened nerve centre charged with cataloguing discoveries, but also with dispensing digging permits to the hordes of Western adventurers bent on excavating and expropriating Egypt's past. While the department might have wished to deny many of these "concessions," as the licences were termed, there was simply too much money on offer for importunate requests to be refused. The unwieldy Ottoman Empire was chronically impoverished and few who toiled here proved qualified or incorruptible. Most were mere civil servants trying to justify paltry sinecures. Their hands, as I would learn, were out and open. *Baksheesh* was the order of the day.

"I finally succeeded in persuading Her Grace I was more likely to obtain information as a blundering friend of the duke's than by confronting those likely to possess such information as part of a posse," Holmes explained in a low tone as he led me through the chaotic space. He would continue his pose as an archeological dilettante but gave the duchess an assignment of sorts. She was to go to Shepheard's and demand the return of her husband's letters. "For the moment, she acquiesced, but it is clear that in the long run both must be reckoned with."

"Lord Darlington?"

"Curious chap. Blank expression. Speaks in a monotone. 'I'll only prove an encumbrance in either locale,' was his comment. He was off to the university to conduct his 're-searches.' Watson, allow me to introduce you to Mr. Howard Carter, Chief Inspector of the Egyptian Antiquities Service."

As he spoke we approached a long table covered with papers, whose sole occupant rose to greet us.

Howard Carter removed his glasses and took my hand in

his, shaking it once emphatically like a chore to be done with as soon as possible. His hand was calloused with manual labour but surprisingly small for a man his size. I judged him not yet forty, with a build similar to my own and the florid complexion of one who has spent much time in the sun. Like me he wore a moustache, but forgoing the ubiquitous Egyptian cotton, dressed in attire that would not have been out of place on the Marylebone Road in February.

"Mr. Ar—"

"Colonel," Holmes interposed, adjusting his monocle. "Northumberland Fusiliers, retired. My chum Watson and I were posted in Afghanistan once upon a very long time ago, and now by happy chance find ourselves reunited."

The detective's impression of fatuous English gentry was condescending perfection. Holmes was still a most accomplished actor.

Carter regarded me with a myopic gaze. "Northumberland Fusiliers," he repeated in a jarring accent at odds with his clothes. "And officers, I've no doubt. I boast no such credentials," he went on, though in truth it seemed very like a boast. "No public schools, no university, that sort of thing. No string of letters after my name. Still, it turns out I know my business."

"You certainly do, Chief Inspector," Holmes assured him in a confident tone, conveying a touch of noblesse oblige. "At the risk of repeating yourself, would you very much mind bringing my friend here into the picture? The Chief Inspector was kindly explaining to me where Egyptology began, were you not, sir? Something to do with Napoleon, was it?"

"It's everything to do with Napoleon," Carter agreed, donning his glasses, resuming his chair at the table, and gesturing us to do the same. Spread before us in profusion were

innumerable documents, maps, and illustrations. "Napoleon invaded Egypt in 1798, ostensibly to take on the Mamelukes*
and interdict British overland trade with India, there being no
Suez Canal at the time."

"Seems rather out of his way," I said, attempting to emulate the detective's idiotic aspect. From the corner of my eye I
thought I saw Holmes wince.

"Just so," Carter allowed, curtly impatient, "but the general was a highly intelligent man."

"Doubtless."

"Napoleon understood that Egypt was the gateway to human history. Determined to exploit that fact amid his military purposes, the general brought with him on the campaign
historians, botanists, archeologists, and painters—over a
hundred French experts from every one of the sciences and
professions—in order to discover and record everything this
ancient repository had to offer. It was only because of this
extensive fact-gathering expedition, undertaken, mind you,
during the very Battle of the Pyramids, that the Rosetta Stone
chanced to be discovered."

"Rosetta—"

The detective shot me a warning look.

Carter, on his favourite subject, was now full of unchecked
enthusiasm. "Do you see what is here?" he asked, unfurling a
large, thick document. I looked and saw some vaguely familiar
ink drawings I recognised as "Egyptian," possibly because I
suddenly recollected elements of scenic design from that long-ago performance of *Aïda*. Or perhaps they were from a visit to

---

* Descendants of slaves, the Mamelukes evolved as a ruling military caste
  in Ottoman Egypt until massacred by the viceroy Muhammad Ali in
  1811.

Madame Tussauds. The figures reminded me vaguely of those cryptic stick figure images whose meaning Holmes had deciphered in "The Adventure of the Dancing Men."

"Egyptian writing?" I hazarded.

"Bravo, Watson." Holmes pulled out his pipe, settling in for the duration.

"Kindly do not smoke," the fastidious scholar instructed. "This place is a firetrap and all these items are perishable. While most are mere copies and tracings made from unearthed originals, replacing them would prove time-consuming and expensive, to say nothing of all the digging permits housed here. And I suffer from asthma," he concluded as if that decided the matter.

"Of course. Forgive me. Do go on. Egyptian writing." Suppressing a yawn, Holmes tapped his mouth with the back of his hand.

Poorly concealing his annoyance, the expert doggedly resumed his lecture. "To be more precise, these images are called 'hieroglyphs,' and though men have peered at them for centuries on the walls of temples and looted burial sites, it was only thanks to Napoleon that we are able to uncover their meaning."

"Napoleon must have been a very clever chap."

"Not him personally," the Chief Inspector corrected me

with a moue of exasperation, "but the expedition's discovery of the key, the Rosetta Stone, that unique stele that fortunately for history repeats the same text in three languages, hieroglyphic, Demotic,* and ancient Greek. A Frenchman named Champollion eventually decoded the Rosetta text and the gateway to Egypt's past was opened. Do you see these ovals drawn at intervals around various clusters of drawings, birds and so forth?"

"Yes."

"That is where Champollion began," Carter explained. "He realised these ovals, which he termed *cartouche,* were seals enclosing proper names within them, oftentimes, but not always, belonging to pharaohs. These other repeated icons outside the *cartouches* prove often to be the names of their numerable gods, Isis, Osiris, Ra, Horus, Set, Anubis, and so forth. The next question Champollion had to address was

---

* Demotic: common or everyday speech. In this case, a late phase of the ancient Egyptian language.

whether or not each of these symbols represented individual words or whether they are merely syllables or what we would call letters. A very complex problem, you'll agree."

"Most complex!" cried the detective, dropping his languid pose and poring over the intricate drawings with undisguised interest. "Are these symbols to be read horizontally or vertically? Where does one begin?"

"Direction varies," came the answer. "There's a bird glyph usually to be found where the passage starts and depending on which way its beak faces indicates the direction to be read."

"The Rosetta Stone is today in the British Museum," Holmes noted quietly for my benefit. "I told you we would come to Mamselle Rosetta, Watson."

Touché.

THE ROSETTA STONE

"How did the British manage to obtain the stone from the French?" I asked, hoping finally to pose an intelligent question of my own.

"How did they obtain the frieze work from the Parthenon?" Carter demanded as if the answer was obvious. "Lord Elgin carried the marbles off to England for safekeeping. The Greeks of our time place no more value on their patrimony than the Egyptians do on theirs."*

"Doubtless why we obtained the Suez Canal," Holmes murmured. "We do seem to be a collecting sort of race. Tell me, Chief Inspector"—Holmes had evidently concluded the repeated use of his title served to curry favor with the prickly archeologist—"my friend Uxbridge, who was to meet me here and go exploring and who has evidently been detained, spoke to me of pharaohs who were buried with their treasures for use in the afterlife. Is there any truth to this?"

"Your friend Uxbridge"—Carter failed to keep the contempt out of his voice—"is a rank amateur. How did you manage to fall in with a chap like that?"

"We met at White's last year. Playing whist, as I recall, with a chap named Ohlsson. He started blathering on about Egyptian treasure and I was intrigued."

At the mention of White's, Carter struggled unsuccessfully to contain a sneer. "You are not close?"

---

* The "Elgin Marbles," taken from the Parthenon in Athens, reside to this day in the British Museum, the subject of an endless legal and cultural tug-of-war. The Greek government maintains the priceless artifacts were stolen and must be repatriated; the British, that they were saved from heedless destruction and would remain preserved in England.

"By no means. But I rather admired his dash and for a lark we agreed to join forces and put in together."

"I shouldn't if I were you," Carter advised. "The man's a poor excuse for an Egyptologist. Mind you, I've been doing this since I was eighteen years of age. In my line of work, precision is everything. Each find and every site must be photographed and mapped on a grid. This is the sort of thing I'm talking about," and he unfurled a regional chart, covered with notations I assumed were in his own hand. It didn't require much in the way of expertise to understand it was work demanding patience and enormous powers of concentration.

"Everything must be recorded," he continued. "The smallest camelhair brushes must be employed to scrape away earth and sand." This was followed by a querulous sniff. "But your pal hasn't the patience for any of this sort of thing. Like the rest of 'em, he craves instant results. Specifically, Egyptian gold. He applied here for a digging concession but refused to stipulate where he proposed to dig, expecting us to offer him *carte blanche*, which of course is out of the question, even for ready money. There was an Ohlsson out here once," he now recalled, frowning as he strained to remember. "A Dane, as I recollect. Only stayed for one season. Don't suppose it's the same chap."

Holmes chose not to follow this trail but returned instead to Uxbridge.

"Was he doing a great deal of Tuthmosis?"

Carter's face took on a bewildered expression in response to this casual enquiry.

"Tuthmosis?"

"Am I mispronouncing it?"

"Was he *'doing'* it?"

"Perhaps I've misunderstood," the detective temporised. "What precisely *is* Tuthmosis?"

From behind his glasses, Carter regarded Holmes, seemingly torn between irritation and suspicion.

"Not 'what.' 'Who.'"

"I beg your pardon." Holmes did his best to express chagrin. "It appears Uxbridge really is out of his depth."

Carter scowled and sat back.

"Not to that degree. Uxbridge is an amateur but not an ignoramus. He knew perfectly well Tuthmosis was the name of a pharaoh. Of several, in fact. Eighteenth Dynasty. But nowadays those of us in the profession no longer use their Grecian names, preferring modern, Anglicised forms; in this instance, Tuthmose."

"I see." The detective appeared preoccupied studying Carter's charts, but we both sensed suspicion had now trumped the latter's irritation. Seeking to divert him, I was on the point of wondering if the name Tuthmose bore any relation to Moses of the Old Testament, when Holmes decided a frontal attack was called for and dropped his blueblood persona.

"Where is the gold of the pharaohs?" he asked.

Carter allowed himself a thin smile. "Your man Uxbridge asked the same question when he first came to Egypt. He was determined to get his hands on some. I can show you what I showed him, but I tell you now it won't answer. Do either of you gentlemen ride camels?"

It is a mere four miles from Ismailia Square to the pyramids, but four miles precariously atop a dromedary with my wounded leg torturously locked around an unwieldy leathern horn (not unlike the pommel on a sidesaddle) rendered the short journey excruciating and interminable. My camel's undulating gait was nauseating. Thank heaven we did no more than walk the entire way. A trot or lope would have finished me.

It was only the stupefying sight of those gigantic white stone mounds when they finally hove into view that dispelled my agony. I fell more than slid from my saddle, landing in a heap, but struggled immediately to my feet, gaping in astonishment as our drover caught the creature's reins. Juliet must see this. A brief memory of her twitting me about building such a final resting place for her flitted through my brain.

No photograph could ever do justice to these immutable heaps. I had never given much thought to that hackneyed phrase "the Seven Wonders of the World," but with a start I now realised I was face to face with at least three and couldn't for the life of me imagine others that might give them a run for their money. The massive objects I confronted had withstood the ravages of man and nature, of wind and rain, of war and pestilence, of every human folly since before the beginning of time. Civilisations had come and gone, yet these blunt things endured. And presiding over all at the centre, older still, was the colossal Sphinx, its leonine body fronted by the carved features of a human face, the latter shredded by the elements but no less mysterious for their ravages. Arguably more so. These stone leviathans had been here so long it was impossible to imagine the place without them. Their reality defies explanation. It was as if Nature and not Man had caused them to be.

Even Holmes by my side appeared struck dumb with wonder. I half-expected him to reiterate one of his favorite maxims, on the difficulty of making bricks without clay. "But see what a mess they've made of it," was his only comment.

His words were true enough. On closer inspection we could see the blocks of both pyramids and Sphinx scored with innumerable ad hoc gougings and lewd inscriptions, dating back to the French occupation and some even before. *Pierre et Yasmine.*

Who knows what impulse prompts such desecrations?

But that was not all. Instead of the solemn silence these mysterious monuments deserved, our ears were assailed by a throng of yelling busybodies. Before and below these ancient triumphs, stirring like the human ants they were, shrieking guides followed by parasol-wielding tourists threaded their way through souvenir salesmen hawking their trinkets, all hounded by famished urchins like so many locusts, skeletal outstretched fingers beseeching alms. *"As-salamu alaykum! Effendi! Effendi! Baksheesh!"*

And if that were not enough, an endless procession of horse-drawn carriages, smoking tour omnibuses, and the occasional honking motorcar were making their pilgrimage to the place, disgorging still more gawkers.

Among these was a handsome couple, the woman swathed in lavender twill, her escort in grey linen. She wore a stylish pith helmet with a trailing white veil; he, a less fashionable straw sun hat.

"Oh dear," was the detective's comment. "We have been followed."

"The duchess?"

"And her chaperone."

Holmes introduced Lord Darlington and the duchess to Howard Carter and myself.

I saw very much the striking Brazilian Holmes had described.

If the Chief Inspector was awed by the lady, he gave no sign. In his time I imagined he had met and been obliged to entertain all sorts.

We were now standing in the shadow of the largest, or

"Great," pyramid, over five hundred feet in height, according to Carter, and variously attributed to Cheops or some other. Miraculously the oldest of the Giza pyramids, it was curiously the best preserved. Shielding her eyes from the sun with a gloved hand against the brim of her helmet, the duchess squinted upwards.

"I did not expect a ziggurat. These look like Aztec pyramids, their steps only larger to be sure."

As I followed her look, there were adventurous souls clambering up those giant steps, swarming over the man-made tor like so many insects or Lilliputians clambering up a monstrous blanched ant hill.

"Originally the steps were entirely surfaced with polished marble," the expert explained, "but earlier generations have stripped the exterior, using it for other purposes. These wonderful piles became no more than rock quarries. The stones beneath were left undisturbed. At twenty to one hundred tonnes, they remain too heavy to move, and the secret of their placement has been lost. You there! Don't be carving up my stones!" Carter made a feint at a clutch of chirruping urchins carrying crude implements with which to make their marks, shooing them back. "Savages," he mumbled, rejoining us. "They've not the least conception, and the guards are useless."

"And these giant tombs were built by Hebrew slaves?"

"By no means," her brother-in-law corrected, speaking for the first time. "That is a common myth. The pyramids were built by free-born Egyptians, isn't that so, Professor Carter?"

"Quite so," Carter answered, not troubling to deny the title Darlington bestowed upon him.

"And you brought my husband here?" the duchess demanded.

"Two years ago. This was our first stop. It usually is for visitors to Cairo. I took him inside the Great Pyramid and propose to conduct Colonel Arbuthnot and Mr. Watson there as well, if they are game. Will you and Lord Darlington be joining us? The only way in is an extremely tight fit, I must warn you. The robbers' entrance is the only one and your costume may make crawling upwards difficult and backing down even more so." He seemed to relish the idea of her discomfort.

Her Grace had apparently seen enough. "Thank you, I shall refrain. I have a terror of closed-in spaces," she admitted. "I shall remain outside and confer with the Sphinx. Perhaps I can solve his riddle."

As an official of the Antiquities Service, Howard Carter had the authority to lead Holmes and myself into the tiny hole on the southern base of the Great Pyramid where a toothless fellah stood guard. From a distance the aperture appeared no larger than a fox burrow; close to, it was not much bigger.

"Remove your jackets, gentlemen. You will do better in shirtsleeves. The boy will see to them."

Setting an example, Carter removed his own herringbone, folded it, and set it on a desiccated canvas camp stool at the impassive fellah's feet. The "boy" was sixty if he was a day.

"Once inside, it will be black as pitch and there is no turning around 'til we reach the treasure chamber and I light my torch," Carter warned.

These were sobering tidings, but as Holmes did not hesitate, I followed his example and removed my jacket. Carter showed his credentials to the guard, who nodded at the paper without troubling to examine it, and then, signing us to do as he did, Carter got on his stomach and crawled into the small aperture. I followed with Holmes bringing up the rear.

What followed was both unforgettable and indescribable.

I've said that Carter's build roughly matched my own, but in truth I was somewhat larger. The tomb robbers of yore must have been considerably smaller than either of us. Their chiselled passage bent upwards at roughly the same angle as the structure itself, an inclination Carter informed me was over fifty degrees. We were in effect crawling on our stomachs up a steep hill.

"You understand, it took several generations of thieves to tunnel through all of this," he called over his shoulder. "Decades and then some. These men weren't robbing for themselves, but for their descendants."

I was obliged to relay everything he said to Holmes behind me. There was barely room for me to inch upwards and my fingers soon grew raw from clawing at the robbers' chiselled handiwork. The detective, thinner than either of us, seemingly experienced less difficulty. As we squeezed up that steep gradient, the temptation to lose one's nerve and scramble backward was difficult to resist. Only the knowledge that any such undertaking would prove futile steadied me. I could neither turn around nor, with the detective below my heels, simply back my way down. By this time I was soaked through with sweat and totally blind.

"What determination these robbers displayed," I called ahead, grasping at conversation as my best defence against terror.

"The very grandeur of these tombs proved their undoing," Carter called back. "The pyramids were monumental advertisements, literally pointing to buried gold. What thieves could resist such a challenge?" His voice grew muffled as the distance between us increased.

"Didn't they post guards, the pharaohs?" I was panting by now.

Ahead, I thought I heard Carter chuckle as the odd stone fragment loosened by the pillagers centuries ago was dislodged by his boots and trickled past my face.

"How long could a dead pharaoh expect whatever guards he posted at the time of his internment to remain outside his tomb and do their duty?" The expert's prompt answer suggested he'd been asked—or had asked himself—this question long since. "One year? One day? One hour?"

It was Holmes who chuckled when I repeated this. *"Quis custodiet ipsos custodes?"* He laughed.

"What?"

"Who will guard the guards?" he translated. "And we may be sure, if the ancient Romans found themselves posing that question in Latin, the ancient Egyptians surely found themselves posing it before them. The problem persists to this day. What bank boasts a safe that hasn't been cracked? Watson, you surely recall John Clay?"

"How could I forget him?"*

"It seems Egyptology is not for the faint of heart," I gasped.

"The fatality rate is surprising," Carter agreed after I'd yelled my remark a second time. "Why, only three months ago Professor Phillips, as he liked to call himself, for he was no more a professor than I am, but a gold hunter like the rest, fell to his death at Abu Simbel."

"What?"

"Abu Simbel! Why the nincompoop was standing atop the head of Ramses the Second I'll never know, but from that height he smashed to bits when he struck the ground."

---

* The notorious Clay's ingenious attempt at bank robbery was foiled by Holmes and Watson in "The Adventure of the Red-Headed League."

I did not need to communicate with the detective, for I knew he was thinking the same thing: if we were keeping score, that made three dead Egyptologists.

Finally and improbably we emerged, heaving and sopping, into a large chamber.

Howard Carter struck a match to the torch he had strapped to his body before climbing and by its startling light was revealed nothing more than an empty, cavernous, stone-walled room, at once unremarkable yet simultaneously unlike anything else on earth. I was so disoriented by this point that I was hard put to estimate the place's dimensions.

The centre of a pyramid is inevitably unique. There was not a scrap of ornamentation, much less Egyptian "writing" or decoration on its rugged walls. How high the man-made cave reached was impossible to say, as the blaze of the torch and its inky smoke travelled out of sight to dim recesses above.

"As you can see," Carter said, "like every other pharaonic tomb thus far discovered, its owner is long gone and his treasure with him. This room was once filled with it and the rest of the pyramid built to protect it and its sole, lordly occupant."

As was his custom, the detective, on his knees, was minutely examining every inch and fissure of the chamber, but I could see his frustration; the place would yield no clues. Had any remained, hundreds before us had picked them clean.

"How did the thieves manage to locate this place?" Holmes demanded. "If as you say, the pyramid stands five hundred feet high, I make it half the height of the Eiffel Tower, yet their tunnel leads directly here."

Carter shrugged. "One of many secrets I doubt we will

ever uncover. For all we know there may be other chambers, likely never to be found."*

"How did they contrive to extract the sarcophagus and the treasure?" I wondered, seating myself on the floor and resting my back on those cold stone walls. Sweating before, now I found it was all I could do not to shiver as my dampened shirt and singlet turned clammy.

"The very question posed by your man Uxbridge, sitting where you are now, Doctor."

"Chopped it into a thousand pieces and slid them down piecemeal, I've no doubt," Holmes supplied, seating himself in turn and stretching out his legs.

"Very good, Colonel. The thieves and their progeny had no interest in the pharaoh, only in whatever gold had shrouded his royal person or was numbered among his possessions. A sarcophagus of imperial jade, for example, might strike them as being of value. And keep in mind, coffins were nestled inside one another, rather in the manner of those Russian dolls. The outermost made of stone, to be sure, and then others, successively smaller as one approaches the mummy itself, made of intricately assembled and painted cedar."

We sat in silence contemplating this.

"All very instructive," the detective remarked, "but none of which brings me any closer to learning what has become of my friend. What was his reaction when you showed him this?"

"He was hardly surprised, as I had warned him—as I did

---

* In the twenty-first century two other chambers, also empty, have been discovered thanks to imaginative use of modern particle physics to "X-ray" the pyramids with the help of something called muons. You need more letters after your name than I have to understand how it works, but that's how they found the other rooms.

you—there was no gold to be found here. But he was philo-sophical. Remember, this was two years ago and he was just beginning to learn the ropes."

"Did those ropes include Tuthmose?" Holmes was now at pains to give the name its correct pronounciation.

Carter smiled. "This torch will soon go out, I think. As you may have surmised, this space does not receive much air."

"You've not answered my question," said Holmes with a touch of asperity.

"You're two thousand years too soon, Colonel." It was clear the expert had had enough for one day. He looked about him. "Shall we descend?"

In truth, I was relieved to go. As we sat there, I found my-self periodically overcome with dread that somehow, notwith-standing the robbers' tunnel had been present for millennia, the place would abruptly cave in and bury us alive.

4

OUR FIRST MURDER

Juliet has made a friend. Emilia Cunningham, a fellow patient, introduced to me at supper, is the widow of General Sir
Roger Cunningham, K.C.B. Like Juliet, she is wintering in
Egypt in an attempt to inhibit the deterioration of her lungs,
though her condition, in my estimation, is far in advance of
Juliet's. We are all obliged to sit with the usual spaces between
our chairs, notwithstanding which Lady Cunningham, between bouts of coughing, kept up a merry line of chatter, re-
galing us with anecdotes culled from the years she and her late
husband spent in the Transvaal. I did my best, distracted as I
was, to pay attention to her tales of safaris and stray lion cubs,
but Juliet could see my mind was elsewhere. In addition to my
recent unnerving experience, I found myself unable to stop
thinking about the death of a third Egyptologist, as related
by Chief Inspector Carter within the Great Pyramid. If I'd
heard correctly, the man named Phillips had fallen from atop
the statue of Ramses the Second at a place called Abu Simbel.
I knew the detective well enough by this time to be sure this
intelligence had no more escaped his notice than it had mine.

And having one's throat cut as the Frenchman had at Karnak, while possibly the work of brigands, could not possibly be dismissed as an accident.

"John, what have you done to your hands?" Juliet exclaimed after Lady Cunningham had bid us good evening. Wearing white gloves herself, but flouting regulations, she took my hands in her own and was now perusing my raw palms like a Romany fortuneteller.

"Chafed them against those wretched camel reins," I lied, making no mention of my expedition within the Great Pyramid. "I hadn't the strength for the ride back," I added with a dose of truth, "but Howard Carter chose to return the way we'd come. An old camel rider, evidently."

Gently I withdrew my hands as I saw an orderly approaching with a disapproving expression.

"And Mr. Holmes?"

"He rode with us in the calash. It was not, I suspect, his first choice, but I think he judged it prudent to allow the duchess and Lord Darlington an opportunity to question the progress of his investigation, albeit it has only just begun."

"And I take it they did?"

"Most assuredly. It was a snug carriage ride," I recalled with some distaste. I paused to slowly extend my bad leg beneath the table. It had been a long time since I had so pressed my luck with it.

"And?" Juliet remained in good spirits as she typically was following her mineral bath. Finally left to ourselves, she was glad of my company and eager for details. I found myself adopting Holmes's perspective.

"What most people fail to understand, dearest—and my accounts of Holmes's cases may be partly to blame for this—is the dreary reality that much of a detective's job involves leg work." Here my limb, as if in silent agreement, favored me with another twinge.

"Are you alright?"

"Perfectly. Clients want instant results and lose sight of the fact that eliciting data from either those reluctant to provide it, or those who don't even understand they might possess it, requires patience and occasional subterfuge." Even as I said this, it struck me that a detective's work was not that different from an archeologist's, both toiling to uncover the truth of past events, but rather than letting my mind pursue this intriguing parallel, I resumed my tale. "Holmes's idea, remember, is to appear in Egypt as a friend of Uxbridge, not a detective at all. He must be circumspect in his enquiries so as not to put the wrong parties on guard."

"What wrong parties?"

I had blundered and was now treading on dangerous ground. I had promised Juliet not to get up to anything foolish. Did burrowing with Holmes inside the bowels of the Great Pyramid of Giza come under the heading of foolishness? I had no intention of finding out.

"Those parties who may know what has become of the duke," I soothed. "Easier to go 'round collecting information as an interloping 'Egyptologist' than one who suspects foul play."

Her eyes narrowed at this. Had my leg been more flexible I should have employed it to kick myself. I saw no point in adding to my difficulties by mentioning that in addition to two Egyptologists dead under suspicious circumstances I had neglected to mention, I had just now learned of a third. Instead, I hastily resumed my account.

"The duchess was not happy with Holmes's progress and

made no secret of her displeasure. She is certainly immune to his charm."

"Unlike some." Juliet laughed. I chose to ignore this pawky dig.

"She did not approve of Holmes's foray inside the Great Pyramid, which she deemed a pointless waste of time. She complained about the money being spent on his accommodations at Shepheard's and so forth. Like many people of means I've encountered in my practice and elsewhere, she runs hot and cold where expenses are concerned. She does not scruple to pay top price for whims she deems essential but on other occasions will cavil over the ninth particle of a hair."

"And how were her objections received?"

"With what I thought a remarkable display of forbearance. Holmes responded calmly and logically that he had entered the pyramid because Uxbridge had done so; that he chose Shepheard's because the duke always stayed and received his mail there, and he was searching for suite seven-eighteen, but that he was happy to move elsewhere, or, for that matter, give up the case entirely if she wished, and decamp to London. He reminded her in turn that she had agreed to turn over the packet of letters Shepheard's had held for His Grace. She was now reluctant to do this, but Holmes was politely resolute. It was a spirited discussion, but in the end I think Lord Darlington managed to pour oil on troubled waters and she backed down."

"And how did this Darlington person manage to soothe her ruffled feathers?"

I thought about this. "He's a hard one to make out. Splendid looking but taciturn. The sort who never speaks unless spoken to. All he volunteered was how keen he was to get on with his 'researches,' saying there was much significant Napoleonic material at the university. Strange," I now remembered.

"In what way?"

"They never looked at or spoke to one another."

"The duchess and her brother-in-law?"

"Yes. After we dropped them at Osiris House, Holmes and I walked for a bit. My leg wanted stretching. I believe his comment was, 'Methinks the lady doth protest too little.'"

She frowned. "You suspect an intrigue?"

I suspected Holmes might, but did not say so. The detective had always maintained it is a capital error to theorise in advance of facts. It was time to bid each other good night.

"What is on the programme for tomorrow?"

"It's Wednesday. My mud bath, even better than the mineral salts. Such a voluptuous sensation."

"Juliet!"

"I've grown to quite love them. So good for my circulation. And you?"

"A visit to the Egyptian Museum and its director. Apparently he knows Uxbridge fairly well. And in the afternoon I shall return in time to hear Miss Vautrin's talk about China."

"I plan to attend as well," said Juliet. "We can glimpse each other like Pyramus and Thisbe." I wasn't sure what she meant by this, but as she appeared amused by her own remark, I smiled as if I understood. And with this, we parted.

I did not trouble to mention that during our walk the previous evening Holmes had pointed out we were still being followed. Having failed to share this information on the previous occasion when the detective first brought it to my attention, I saw little point in going into it now.

That night, I lay awake, staring through my mosquito netting at the darkened ceiling, and tried to make sense of the eleventh Duke of Uxbridge. A ne'er-do-well, who drank to excess (the motorcar accident), with staggering debts (persona non grata at White's), kept afloat for the moment by his fabulously wealthy wife, he surely must have understood that the sands (he was in Egypt, after all), were running out. He now seemed to believe that what had begun as a hobby following his car accident might prove his salvation. He hoped, by some alchemical process comprehended solely by himself, to turn Brazilian copper into Egyptian gold. He was certainly not the first of his buccaneering breed to search for the precious metal, whether in the goldfields of California, the mines of South Africa, or, as he now found himself, a place where untold riches were in theory merely waiting to be uncovered beneath a few inches of desert sand. From these musings I drifted off and found myself dreaming of that long-ago Covent Garden performance of *Aïda* I couldn't recall attending with Holmes; only somehow it became my trip inside the bowels of the Great Pyramid and I woke gasping and bathed in sweat.

"You will pardon my saying so, Watson, but you rather coddle your readers."

"I beg your pardon."

We were once more seated amid the regulars outside the *souq* over another coal tar coffee the following morning at the El Fishawy. I could think of better ways to start my day than indulging the detective's carping dissection of my literary efforts.

"You spare them the drudgery of detective work, presenting them with my lightning conclusions but omitting the sometimes tedious and, yes, occasionally degrading chores associated with reaching them."

I was tempted to tell him that only the day before I had

made that very observation to my wife. Instead, I resisted a different impulse, namely to suggest that omitting the drudgery arguably accounted for my success and his reputation. I knew he was leading up to something but couldn't yet make out what it was.

"Such as?"

"Such as reading other people's mail," the detective sat back, pleased to have arrived circuitously at his chosen topic. "Even with their consent," he added. "The correspondence from Shepheard's was a disappointment, predictable perhaps, but frustrating nonetheless. I sat up in bed last night for the better part of an hour—for it took no longer—ploughing through it. Of course I've no way of knowing if Her Grace turned over all the letters she had written to her husband in Cairo. For all I know several contain passionate expressions of devotion."

I said I was sorry though, like the detective, not astonished, to learn this news.

"There was the smattering of creditors, to be sure. Some fuss about flagstones for a terrace. His Grace appears accustomed to spending a great deal on trifles conceived on what appears to be a whim. Studs from Berkeleys, a diamond tie pin from Bond Street, a Moroccan leather travel case from Asprey's with his initials embossed, and so forth. In that respect, he is not entirely dissimilar to his wife," he noted with a wry expression.

"And her letters to him?"

Holmes wrinkled his nose in an expression of disapproval. "'Faith, as cold as can be.' Matters of business, the management of the estate, and complaints regarding a long-time upstairs maid who ought to lose her place. Even Her Grace's eventual expressions of concern when her letters were not answered are couched in Arctic language such as the Esquimaux might employ." From his breast pocket he pulled out a letter written on thick stationery with the Uxbridge crest and read aloud: "*I am mystified by your silence, as you know we have matters of grave importance to resolve and Lloyds cannot be put off any longer. Please contact me regarding these matters at your earliest—* etcetera."

"Hardly the stuff of marital bliss," I commented.

"It does sound more like business than love, does it not? Although, as I said, she may have suppressed more intimate material." He pocketed the letter. "But I doubt it. Shall we head for the museum?"

"Ah, yes, gentlemen," Professor Hassan Tewfik said, smiling, "I can certainly tell you about Tuthmose—about all five of them, if you like, though it was number four who fascinates your friend and mine."

"I take it you've not heard from His Grace of late?" Holmes began.

"Alas."

Professor Tewfik, sleek, urbane, and well-spoken in his taupe linen suit, was very much the opposite of yesterday's Howard Carter, whom I was now inclined to regard as a self-important fussbudget, knowledgeable to be sure, but tiresomely querulous. His speech, which would not have seemed out of place in the mouth of a Covent Garden dustman, I found incongruous juxtaposed with his erudition, a prejudice to which I guiltily plead guilty.

Tewfik, by contrast, presently leading the detective and myself through echoing marble halls and atria, occasionally passing a chamois he carried for the purpose over dusty vitrines, the better to expose exhibits within, (one of which was, improbably, a mummified cat), was courtly, welcoming, and altogether agreeable. Clean-shaven, deeply tanned, and slightly vulpine, he was perhaps fifty years of age, though boasting the trim figure of a man ten years younger. His distinguishing physical characteristic was an intermittent protrusion of his eyes. Cerulean, they seemed to bulge reflexively to punctuate a sentence or emphasise a point.

The Egyptian Museum, imposing enough on the outside with its impressive Latin inscription and pinkish stucco, was something of a disappointment within. I suspected its reputation preceded it, as the place was not crowded.

As if reading our minds, the director held out his slender, manicured hands and addressed us in thinly sliced Etonian.

"When the museum was originally conceived, some forty years ago, it was anticipated that Egypt's treasures would soon fill it to capacity. We Egyptians had not reckoned on the likes of Theodore Davis and Lord Carnarvon, whose successes in the Valley of the Kings now furnish museums in England, Europe and America. Now we must content ourselves with the likes of this."

From a nearby shelf, Tewfik produced an exquisite aquamarine faïence hippopotamus which he held in the palm of his hand. "Isn't she a beauty?"

"Stunning," I agreed. The colour of the glaze quite took my breath away. I could not recall ever seeing another like it.

"More's the pity."

He dropped the thing to the parqueted floor, where it splintered into a hundred shards.

"What the devil!"

"Fake."

Holmes appeared as nonplussed as myself.

"A forgery. Less than thirty years old. Entirely worthless, I assure you. Don't trouble. It will be seen to. And we have hundreds more like it. My countrymen are impoverished but ingenious. Learning many years ago—probably as far back as Napoleon's time—the value foreigners placed on such baubles, they have become masters at re-creating them. But even then they are the losers. What they must sell for a pittance is resold in the West for hundreds, if not thousands. And this does not take into account phony treasure maps, some very convincing, to lead the gullible astray."

It was a sobering demonstration, but I could see mention of fraudulent treasure maps had caught the detective's attention as much as the shattered hippo.

"What is the Valley of the Kings?" Holmes enquired.

By way of answer, Tewfik led us to a mosaic map of Egypt, large enough to fill an entire wall.

"As Chief Inspector Carter has doubtless explained, the age of pyramids lasted little more than a century. Those magnificent wonders were catnip to tomb robbers, their unmissable presence challenging all comers." He paused and interlaced his fingers, his eyes bulging briefly as if to capture our full attention. "Imagine now that two thousand years have elapsed. Nothing has changed! Can you conceive? We are still in the same Egyptian empire, yet ruled by pharaohs, fed as ever by the Nile and governed by her floods and seasons. Time passes so slowly in Egypt that all history since would fit into its span."

Holmes and I struggled to visualise this. Eyeing us, Tewfik resumed, using a pointer to trace a line south along the Nile.

"And now a different pharaoh in a different age gets a different idea."

"What sort of idea?"

"It was Tuthmose the First—not *your* Tuthmose, but an ancestor—who cleverly thought that instead of building monuments to one's death and wealth, it might prove wiser to conceal both."

"Conceal, you mean—?"

"Just so. Hide them. Four hundred and fifty miles south of Cairo and farther south of Thebes, the old Egyptian capital, here"—the pointer tapped the map's ceramic tiles—"on the river's western bank was where the first Tuthmose found what suited his purposes. It has come to be called the Valley of the Kings. The pharaoh caused limestone, of which the valley is composed, to be cut and shaped into several chambers and in the inmost he was buried. The entrance was subsequently walled up and sealed with mud, then filled in with sand to conceal its existence. Following his example, hundreds chose the same expedient for the next five hundred years, rulers and nobles of the New Kingdom with their treasure, imitating the pharaoh's ruse, creating their ossuaries in this remote and desolate place." He shrugged. "Of course the Davises, Carnarvons, and Bechsteins have since dug them all up and packed whatever the previous robbers scorned off to the British Museum, the Metropolitan in New York, or the Neues Museum in Berlin."

He sighed as much as to say, "It is the way of the world," then resumed our tour, leading us past statues and fragments, pausing to explain and detail their origins. There could be no question some of these objects with their queer shapes and exotic picture writing served to spur one's imagination. Human figures topped with birds' heads, boats of the very sort that still plied the Nile, beautiful women in gold pleated robes, chariots drawn by horses while archers drew their bows, aiming arrows at rampant lions. There were endless snakes and vases dripping liquids. Viewing these mysterious things made old Egypt seem close by, which, in a sense, it was. Whose hand had grasped that spoon? What mouth had drained that cup?

One enormous statue in particular attracted our notice. Larger than anything else on view, it was a male figure of red granite, clutching the crossed scepter and shepherd's crook of command in disproportionately long fingers. He was seated on a regal-looking chair, and his concave face supported a high-backed crown within which nestled what looked like a smaller one.

"And who might this be?" Holmes enquired, struggling to pronounce the name on the dust-covered silver plaque near the base.

"Our most precious possession," Tewfik was gratified to inform us, "and the most controversial ruler in three thousand years of Egyptian history. Dating from the mid-Eighteenth Dynasty, which is to say roughly 1650 B.C., he is in fact the younger brother of that Tuthmose who so interests our friend the duke."

"Dear God. All these names."

"Yes, I know."

But with his reference to Tuthmose, Tewfik garnered our fullest attention. We stared up at the statue's bizarre countenance. The toes in his sandals I now perceived, like his face and fingers, were repulsively elongated.

"This pharaoh's name was Akhenaten. Or rather, he

changed it to Akhenaten from Amenhotep and in doing so plunged Egypt into a bloody civil war."

"Is there any other kind?" the detective murmured.

"How did he manage that?" I asked.

Tewfik's eyes performed their odd trick. "Thereby, as you may say, hangs a tale. Akhenaten, as he chose to call himself, broke faith with the pantheon of gods Egyptians had worshipped unquestioningly for two thousand years. Two millennia of faceless pharaohs, and finally one who differed. Instead of Amun and his brethren—Isis, Osiris, Horus, Anubis, and the rest—Akhenaten chose to adore but one. Convinced it was the origin of all life, he worshipped the disc of the sun, which he termed the Aten. Hence his new name."

"One could argue he had a point, the sun being the source of life," I remarked.

Tewfik made no answer to this but proceeded with his talk, which I inferred he had often given before.

"Akhenaten, as he was now known, withdrew his court from Thebes and built his own capital on the banks of the Nile two hundred or so miles north. The place is now called Tel-Amarna. The Egyptian art found there is radically different from all that came before—the rays of the Aten shine over everything and everyone. Notice how the rays culminate in benevolent hands."

"What happened to his nose?" I asked. The pharaoh's face transfixed me, his peculiar concave cheeks, drawn physiognomy, and stretched fingers reminding me irritatingly of something—or someone—but I was at present so out of my element I couldn't place it.

"The nose was hacked off, though as you can see, clumsy attempts were made to restore it. In fact, most of Akhenaten's images were destroyed after the insurrection that ended with his death, which is why we have so few of him. The old gods and their priests returned triumphant. Akhenaten's alternate capital of Amarna was demolished, buried beneath the sands, and Egypt went on as if he had never lived."

"Stop a bit," said the detective. "I must be confused. Did you not tell us this—"

"Akhenaten—"

"Yes, was the *younger* brother of Tuthmose—the one my friend Uxbridge talks about with such interest? Did I understand you correctly?"

"Indeed." Tewfik's blue eyes bulged briefly as he smiled in the direction of his brightest pupil. "Then why," he exclaimed, anticipating Holmes, "as the elder brother was Tuthmose the Fifth, as he would have been, not proclaimed pharaoh himself and this dreadful convulsion possibly averted?"

"My very thought. Does not the firstborn inherit here as elsewhere?"

"To be sure. But, as it happened"—here the eyes protruded again—"Tuthmose died young. And so younger brother," gesturing to the statue—"became pharaoh in his stead and wears the double crown of Upper and Lower Egypt. And what's more, he married his brother's attractive widow, Queen Nefertiti, to whom he was devoted and with whom he sired six daughters and a son.* See here is their group portrait, an affectionate family, all blessed by the rays of the Aten."

---

* Possibly Tutankhamen.

The portrait, even by my ignorant lights, was astonishingly different from other art I had been shown. It was touchingly intimate. We stared at the unmistakable image of a loving family three thousand years ago.

"Married with deceased brother's widow, that's an old story, isn't?" Holmes mused.

"Older than Hamlet, evidently," agreed the museum director.

The detective's expression changed. "You are not implying—" he began, but Tewfik cut him off with a laugh.

"Murder for a kingdom and a beautiful queen? Truly a familiar story, but without knowing where he is buried and examining his remains, who can say how Tuthmose died? Disease? A fall? A mischance while hunting? People live longer today. In the past they succumbed to a host of ailments and accidents, many of which are easily remedied now, though I ought to add that Egyptology itself is a profession not without risk. The desert is treacherous and allows for few miscalculations."

"So we've been told," murmured the detective, returning his gaze to the statue. I knew we were both thinking about the rash of recently deceased Egyptologists.

"There is a tendency," Tewfik went on, following his look, "to romanticise the old boy, the first monotheist and so on."

"Surely he must have been," said I, staring at the misshapen face, unable to place where else I had beheld it, certainly not in old Egypt. How could such a beauty love such a man?

"Technically a monotheist, perhaps. But not in the Judeo-Christian sense. He tolerated other gods at first but later became a fanatic, persecuting the priests of Amun and the old believers, attempting to extirpate the pantheon, thus prompting the rebellion that ultimately undid him."

"You said the American, Davis, and the others had discovered all the tombs in the Valley of the Kings." Holmes placed his fingertips together.

Tewfik offered an apologetic shrug. "All that we know of so far. Some threescore sites have been identified—all looted, needless to say."

"But not that of Tuthmose, who would have been the fifth of that name, the rightful heir-apparent whose early demise enabled *his* reign." The detective gestured to the odd-looking figure with the missing nose.

Tewfik positively beamed. "Precisely. It is Tuthmose the Fifth—as he would have been—that our friend is seeking. And in my opinion, he may be on to something."

"Did he confide in you?"

"Not specifically, no, but he was quite convinced there were parts down in the valley that had not received sufficient attention. That and his excitement at the prospect of an un-discovered tomb with its treasures intact, though I believe his application for a digging concession was unsuccessful. I do hope nothing untoward has befallen him. Dear me." The director consulted his watch. "I'm afraid I must leave you. I've a meeting with my staff. Please"—he gestured—"feel free to wander about and enjoy such exhibits as we can offer."

"Let me see if I understand the facts of the case," Juliet mused, over lunch.

"By all means. Juliet Watson, Consulting Detective," I encouraged.

She paused for a sip of water as she gathered her thoughts. "Michael, Duke of Uxbridge, winters in Cairo, seeking buried Egyptian treasure to solve his own financial difficulties."

"Correct."

"At White's, he somehow obtains some sort of map from a Swede that purports to locate the treasure of—"

"Tuthmose the Fifth. More or less."

"The map seemingly concentrates on this Tuthmose, the prematurely deceased elder brother of he who became pharaoh—" Here she broke off, laughing. "I can't pronounce his name—"

"Akhenaten," I supplied.

"Yes. The first monotheist monarch."

"Right again."

"Taking his cues from this map, the duke professes some notion as to where the missing tomb of brother Tuthmose is to be found, though he does not share its location."

"According to Professor Tewfik, yes."

"At which point the duke himself vanishes, along with the map and any evidence he ever stayed at Shepheard's, as was his annual custom."

"Bravo. You have summed up the known facts of the case

as succinctly as Holmes could have done," I told her, though omitting more troubling data.

She smiled, pleased by my praise. In truth, during our weeks of separation I had forgotten how perceptive and intelligent my wife was. I now realised she had been paying close attention to all I had confided. In fact, as I would learn, she had been paying a great deal more attention than I realised at the time.

"The question is, where do you and Mr. Holmes—"

"Colonel Arbuthnot."

"Forgive me, yes. Where do you and Colonel Arbuthnot go from here?"

"My dear, you have posed the question of the hour."

That afternoon at the Al Wadi, I found it difficult to concentrate on Miss Vautrin's talk about China. I remember it had to do with missionaries—she being one herself, from the American Midwest—but my mind was stranded in ancient Egypt, not present-day Peking. What was it that tickled the back of my memory about Akhenaten's malformed face? I looked over to see Juliet's delicate features, but hers were obscured by the white mask that covered her nose and mouth. The Al Wadi patients were obliged to wear these to public events, making them resemble so many nurses and surgeons. Her eyes, however, shone brightly in the direction of the speaker, and told me she was raptly attentive. Sitting beside her, Lady Cunningham appeared to be asleep. I suspected that when not the centre of attention she was easily bored.

So that we could see each other, I sat through the talk and smiled at my wife every time our eyes chanced to meet. When Miss Vautrin concluded her remarks and chairs were scraping back, I passed Juliet a note that I was going out and would see her at breakfast. The noise of the chairs served to rouse her, and Lady Cunningham woke with a startled expression, looking about in confusion before recollecting where she was. She adjusted her white mask and endeavoured to suppress a coughing spasm.

Receiving my note, I saw Juliet nod and wave her fingers in my direction. It was strange and melancholy to think what comparative strangers we had become in such a short time. It occurred to me that when our enforced separation eventually ended, as I told myself it must, we would in effect be obliged to know each other all over again.

My errand was in fact supper at Shepheard's with Professor Tewfik, Holmes, and his clients, the purpose of which—at their instigation—was to review our findings. For the occasion the duchess was attired in a clinging gown of white muslin; Lord Darlington, as was his custom—and befitting his purse, I assumed—appeared in his usual wrinkled charcoal linen.

We had not yet begun to discuss our museum tour and findings (slender as they were) when an incident occurred that was to throw all into confusion. Our heavyset waiter, a turbaned Sudanese, like all who toiled in the hotel's vast pseudo-Moorish dining salon, managed to spill his carafe of water onto Holmes, who leapt up in an instant.

"Clumsy fool!" Holmes shouted to the astonished man, drawing surprised glances from nearby tables. "Show me to the W.C. and help me clean up this mess!"

"*Effendi,* I did noth—"

"None of your lickspittle! Watson, lend a hand! Enjoy your soup," he urged the others in a very different tone. "We'll return directly."

Not pausing for further conversation or expostulation, he more or less tugged the hapless man in the direction of the washroom. As I made haste to follow, it occurred to me Holmes knew its location perfectly well, for we had just washed our hands before sitting down. As the salon was presently a hubbub of activity, our awkward exit occasioned little notice. "Chap's had too much bubbly," was the only comment I made out, but it wasn't clear to which of us he was referring.

At the washroom, Holmes fairly thrust the waiter inside. As most guests were already dining, it chanced there were only two gentlemen in dinner dress present along with the attendant, who was in the act of handing over a fresh towel.

"Police! Clear out, everyone!" Holmes barked in a tone that brooked no argument.

Having no desire for confrontation with an officer of the law, they hastened to obey.

"Watson, the door!" I knew from long experience what to do and held it fast after the place had cleared.

"Now then, this is the gentleman who has been following us of late. Don't bother to deny it; I've been watching you do it. What is your name?"

The man shook himself free and made some attempt to adjust his picturesque uniform and straighten his turban, knocked askew by the detective.

"I am Mustafa. I spilled nothing, *effendi*."

"*I* spilled it," the detective snapped, backing the man against one among the row of white porcelain sinks. "I did it so we might talk undisturbed. Why were you following us? What do you know regarding the Duke of Uxbridge?"

There was a tentative knocking on the door behind me which I ignored, pressing my bulk against it to keep it shut.

"That is why I was following you," the man who called himself Mustafa said plaintively, "but I could find no opportunity to speak to you alone and unobserved."

"We are alone now." The man hesitated. "*Baksheesh?* How much?"

Mustafa's features assumed a sly expression, but the knocking was now increasing in fervor and pressure being brought to bear against the door.

"Colonel—"

"Not here!" Mustafa exclaimed. "English pounds! Not Egyptian! Tonight, *Inch'Allah,* in the alley behind the Great Mosque of Muhammad Ali Pasha—after Isha!"

"'Isha'? What is—"

Pounding on the door decided the detective, who stood calmly aside and, looking in the mirror above the sink, adjusted his monocle, straightened his tie, and tossed a lordly hand towel to Mustafa as if he were the attendant, upon which I allowed the door to open and in burst several mystified gentlemen.

"I say, what's the idea?"

"And let that be a lesson to you, Fortunato," said Holmes to me as we made our way. "All yours, gentlemen."

Mustafa immediately made himself scarce as we returned to our table.

"No harm done," Holmes assured the company. "It was only Uxbridge water and will soon dry."

"What became of—"

"I sent the man about his business. He'll not trouble us again. Is that Nile perch? How considerate of you to have ordered for us."

And so the detective managed to steer our conversation into benign channels, extolling the knowledge and kindness of the museum director and getting him to explain at length which Tuthmose in fact was of such interest to Duke Michael.

"I expect my brother was rather hoping to find his burial site unopened." Lord Darlington surprised us all by dipping in his oar.

"Had he ever spoken to you of this?" Holmes enquired, setting down his fish knife.

"Never," was the laconic answer. "I merely inferred as much from your talk."

Silence greeted this exchange. Holmes resumed his meal, addressing himself to the fish getting cold on his plate. "What is Isha?" he asked Professor Tewfik, spearing a forkful of the delicacy.

The professor blinked, startled by the change of subject. "Isha? May I ask what prompts your question?"

"Curiosity merely. A comment I overheard in the washroom." Holmes was now slicing his haricots verts with surgical precision.

Tewfik patted his lips with his napkin. "Observant Muslims are called to prayer five times daily," he explained. "At dawn, the Salat Ul Fajr; at midday, the Salat Ul Zuhr; midafternoon, the Salat Ul Asr; at sunset, the Salut Ul Magrib; and finally nightfall, the Salat Ul Isha."

"The summons to prayer called Isha begins at nightfall?"

"It is not precisely timed," Tewfik allowed, making a gesture with one hand. "Ostensibly it begins after sunset and lasts until the rise of the 'white light,' the *fajr sadiq* in the east."

"That seems rather a long time," the detective observed with a smile.

Tewfik responded with one of his own. "The traditional time for Isha is typically closer to midnight."

"In effect halfway between sunset and sunrise."

"In effect," the other conceded.

"I've heard much of the Great Mosque of Muhammad Ali Pasha. Is it far from here?"

"Not far at all." Tewfik smiled.

"I hope you will not find my question impertinent, but would you describe yourself as observant?"

The man appeared in no way put out. "I do my best," he said, "but four years at Cambridge has rather eroded some of my habits. As you see, I wear no beard."

"Ah, yes." Holmes nodded. "Might I trouble you for the courgettes?" he asked Lord Darlington.

"By all means." The obliging schoolmaster passed the silver dish to the detective.

Throughout much of this the duchess sat ominously silent. "I have a headache," she now proclaimed, rising. Instantly Darlington got to his feet and held her chair as the rest of us stood.

"Mr. Holmes," she spoke, making no attempt to acknowledge the detective's incognito, "I am displeased by your lack of progress."

"If one is in the midst of a forest," Holmes responded, facing her calmly across the table between them, "it is impossible to tell how far one is from the road. It might be thirty trees or thirty thousand. We are not best placed at the moment to know." He did not, I notice, choose to divulge the potential lead proposed moments ago by our fugitive waiter.

"I give you forty-eight hours to find that road," his client responded, oblivious to the clatter of nearby cutlery and suppertime talk. "After that, your services will no longer be required."

"As you wish, Your Grace." Holmes inclined his head.

"Lionel." Instantly, the younger man proffered his arm.

Taking it, Her Grace swept from the noisy room with the serene assurance of a Nile steamer, waiters and diners parting
before her progress.

"Gracious," Tewfik murmured as we subsided into our
chairs. "Is she always like that?"

"I shouldn't be surprised," the detective rejoined, helping
himself to the courgettes and appearing in no way discom-
fited. "The duchess is accustomed to getting her way. Watson,
what time do you make it?"

"Eight-thirty-five."

"Excellent. Should we order coffee?" My friend gave no
appearance of haste.

"So late?" the professor exclaimed. "If you gentlemen will
excuse me." He now rose again. "It has been a long day."

"By all means. It certainly has. And many thanks for all
your patient explanations," Holmes added, rising as well.

"He made no mention of the duchess addressing you by
your right name," I said when the man was out of earshot.

"Possibly in the moment it escaped his notice. Do you know
which is the Great Mosque and where it is located? We have
not much time."

We did not stay for coffee. In the semi-darkened streets
and without the benefit of my map, it took longer than I would
have liked, but I eventually succeeded in leading Holmes to
the Great Mosque of Muhammad Ali Pasha. I had no thought
of returning to the Jardin des Plantes at present; like Holmes
I was on fire to learn what Mustafa knew.

The mosque was within the kasbah or old citadel, largely
deserted by the time we reached its precincts save for a pack
of mongrel dogs foraging for scraps.

"The moon will rise presently," was the detective's only

remark as we took our station at the cul-de-sac behind the vast and crumbling alabaster edifice.*

Waiting is the most wearisome aspect of detective work, as I had reason to know. Aside from the occasional dog bark, the place was ghostly quiet. I was on the point of lighting a cigarette when Holmes laid a restraining hand on my sleeve. We would do well to remain inconspicuous. How much time passed it became difficult to say before three things happened almost simultaneously.

The moon appeared as Holmes predicted, rising ivory and enormous above one of the minarets, making it bright as day, and by its light I made out the time. It was 11:35. Almost at once the muezzin called out the Isha, his cry resonating over the silence of this part of the city, far from the hubbub of colonial restaurants, night-clubs, and other establishments where Western visitors to the city spent their evenings.

"*I praise the perfection of Allah, the Forever existing,*" Holmes surprised me by whispering the translation. He evidently knew more than he had let on at supper and continued as the muezzin chanted above us, exhorting the faithful. "*The Perfection of Allah, the Desired, the Existing, the Single, the Supreme: the Perfection of Allah, the One, the Sole, the Perfection of Him who taketh unto Himself no male nor female partner nor any like unto Him, nor any that is disobedient, nor any deputy, equal or offspring! His Perfection be extolled.*"

The prayer was repeated several times in different registers, gathering force as we listened, before ceasing altogether and plunging all into stillness. Even the curs now slept.

The quiet was now absolute. Next to me, I sensed

---

* By 1911 the mosque was in danger of collapse. Years later it was renovated by King Farouk.

Holmes's tension, his every fibre taut like the strings on his old fiddle.

And then, without warning, came a bone-chilling shriek such as I hope never again to hear in my life.

"Watson!"

We dashed by moonlight down the uneven surface of that endless alley, glimpsing a dark figure at the entry racing away while I could dimly make out a second figure, half-crawling, half-stumbling, before finally collapsing twenty yards before us, and crying out as he fell.

"Quick, Watson!"

Holmes sped to the alley entrance as I crouched over the inert form. It was Mustafa. No longer dressed in his waiter's uniform, the man had tumbled forward on his stomach, one hand outstretched as if reaching for something, a finger twitching faintly before it stopped.

With some difficulty I heaved him over, for he was ursine in life and in death still more so. There was no pulse, but the man's eyes were wide with terror as if even now they beheld their fate. The reason was evident: his heart still held the knife that was buried within it, his other hand near the handle as if to pluck it forth.

Holmes rejoined me, panting. "Too many byways." He looked about, a bloodhound on the scent, and almost immediately gave an exclamation. "What have we here?"

Using his monocle as a magnifier, he slowly followed the corpse's outstretched arm to his hand, holding the glass finally over a patch of dust just beyond the plump forefinger that had ceased all movement. I struck one of my matches and by its light we could make out something scratched in the dirt by the dying man, the tip of the finger in question smudged with the granules he had improvised for ink.

"*VR 61*, it looks like," I said.

"Yes," the detective agreed somberly, "*VR 61.*" Using his handkerchief, with some difficulty he tugged the knife from the body by its handle and held up its ornate, scarlet-coated blade to the moonlight, an effusion of blood trickling from its source.

"Lapis lazuli by the look of it," he murmured, and indeed the thing appeared antique. "Here is no missing compass, no accidental fall, but murder beyond question."

"There's also Jourdan," I reminded him. "Whose throat was slit at Karnak."

Without addressing this point, the detective regarded Mustafa's inert form. "The man called out before he fell, did he not?"

"Yes. It sounded like—"

Suddenly we heard familiar police whistles of the sort we knew well in London.

"Hulloa! Stay where you are!" As luck would have it, an electric torch carried by two British Military constables flared in our direction and caught Holmes squarely in its beam, holding the murder weapon aloft, as if to strike. As the constables raced towards us Holmes managed to extend the toe of his shoe in time to erase the marks in the dust. In doing so he inadvertently crushed his monocle.

5

WINDOWS

"How long have we been here?"

"Hard to say," the detective rejoined quietly.

It was impossible to see my watch, which I now recalled had been confiscated along with the contents of my pockets at the time of our arrest. My furious protests and demands to see the British Consul were met with East End indifference.

"Consulate opens at nine, gentlemen. Cleaning crew comes at 'alf seven."

Indeed it was just as difficult to determine where we were as it was how long we had been here, for there was no light of any kind. I had anticipated some sort of cell, but the place in which we found ourselves was clearly spacious, high ceilinged and populated by slender columns of frieze work and flaking plaster against which—to my intense annoyance—I struck my head several times. In addition, the place contained a fantastic assortment of queerly configured furniture against which, as I restlessly sought to examine our surroundings, I was constantly barking my shins.

For all its sense of space, the odor of the big room was mildewed and airless. Using my hands, I felt fringed footstools, tasselled settees, curiously shaped chairs, and large, bolster-like cushions with goose down stuffing popping out from tears in the damask. Silken upholstery was frayed elsewhere beneath my fingers.

Colliding with these irregular objects, I was hard put to contain my temper.

"All this fuss over a piece of paper none of us has ever seen and which may very likely prove fraudulent," I fumed.

"I'm not sure I follow you, old man," Holmes offered mildly.

"I should think it obvious. This whole wretched business began when Duke Michael stole that map or whatever it was at White's and came gallivanting off to Egypt in search of buried treasure or some such nonsense. Professor Tewfik warned us Egypt is swarming with such items. You surely remember his blue hippopotamus. And here we find ourselves!"

"But how does all that connect with Mustafa and our present predicament? As for the map, I remind you the Swede Ohlsson certainly believed it genuine, so much so that when it was taken from him, he chose to do away with himself. It's possible, one must allow, the man was delusional and invested more faith in the document than was warranted, but—"

"Holmes, it is imperative I get back to the Jardin des Plantes before breakfast!"

"I understand your anxiety, my dear fellow."

"They are Military Police. Tell them who you are!"

I could sense his frown in the darkness. "Only as a last resort. Revealing my identity would lead back to Mycroft's part in the business of Colonel Arbuthnot's passport and on no account must I compromise him. Come, we are in a British gaol. Let us not surrender to panic."

His advice was impossible to follow. Were I not to appear at breakfast with Juliet and the reason for my absence inevitably become known, nothing would dissuade her from returning to London with me in tow.

By contrast with my own agitated state of mind, the detective appeared content to remain in thoughtful silence.

"Holmes, what can you be thinking?"

"About the unfortunate Mustafa, to be sure. And also about ancient Egyptian daggers with lapis lazuli handles. A singular choice of murder weapon, wouldn't you agree? What would you give to know what sort of knife was used at Karnak to cut the throat of Professor Jourdan, eh, my boy?"

His words meant nothing to me in my distracted frame of mind. In the gloom, I once again tried to make out where we were. If this was the British idea of a holding cell I was at a loss. Briefly tripping over Holmes's extended legs, I paced out the circular room. The detective was reclining on one of those oddly constructed items of furniture, a sort of divan seemingly designed to allow two people reclining side by side to face each other with back support in opposite directions. I could not imagine the reason for such an arrangement.

"Certainly suggestive," Holmes said, reading my thoughts. "Ordinarily, I might infer the foyer in a house of ill repute, but in this case, strange as it may be, I think we have been stashed in an erstwhile seraglio."

"A what?"

"Harem. Doubtless belonging to a previous owner, as the place is in a state of evident neglect. No self-respecting sultana would deign to set a perfumed foot here. Of course I could be mistaken," he added, but in truth his explanation accounted for some of the furniture's more unusual properties. In other circumstances I might have been intrigued; currently I remained distracted.

"What will we tell them?"

"The police? As much of the truth as possible is always best. You are here with your wife at the Al Wadi on the Jardin des Plantes for her health. At Shepheard's you chanced to encounter a former regimental comrade at the American Bar and attempted to help search for his missing friend. The waiter at supper offered to supply us with information as to that friend's whereabouts in exchange for the usual incentives. We somewhat naïvely agreed to meet with him where and when he stipulated, but the unfortunate man was attacked before he could speak and the rest, alas, is known."

"But he did say something," I now recalled. "Or tried to."

"Could you make out what it was?"

I shook my head, trying ineffectually to focus on the problem. "It sounded like—it was *T*-something. It began with *T*."

"Let us for the moment keep that information to ourselves. The less we give them to chew on, the better off we shall be."

His words, coolly uttered, calmed me for a time. But as more invisible minutes elapsed, I felt the floodtide of anxiety returning. How much time did I have to get back to the Khedivial Club with Juliet none the wiser?

"Holmes, really—"

I have no notion what my next words were to be, because at that instant, all unbidden in that curious way the mind works, I suddenly recollected what the features of Akhenaten had put into my head.

"Marfan Syndrome!" I cried.

"What's that you say?"

"Pharaoh what's-his-name's stretched-out face!" I was quite sure of myself as it all came to me in a rush. "Fifteen or twenty years ago a Dr. Marfan—French, if I recall rightly—

first described this condition in *The Lancet*.* The elongated
face, fingers and toes, a genetic disorder that runs in families.
Not very common, but the drawings and photographs in the
article I would swear matched those presented by the statue."

"Bravo, Watson. That is most—" But before the detective
could say more, a rattling of keys, footfalls, and voices interrupted us and drove all thoughts of Marfan Syndrome aside.
"Remember our narrative," Holmes cautioned as light flooded
the room.

Moments later, two privates in the khaki dress of British
Military Police escorted us up an enormous winding stair-
case of polished malachite and down another arched corridor
with bulky wrought-iron lamps, recently wired for electricity,
strung from massive chains overhead. This in turn led to yet
another set of stairs. As we walked, their metal-tipped boots
reverberated off tiled walls adorned with intricate, symmetri-
cal designs.

As we were shortly to learn, this sprawling building was
nothing less than the former palace of Suleiman Ali Pasha.
It served now as the British Consulate and British Admin-
istrative Headquarters in Cairo, adapted for both purposes
ad lib. Our belongings were returned to us at half past three
in the morning according to my watch, which I immediately
refastened on my wrist,† after which we were taken before a

---

* As a doctor, Watson was an avid consumer of medical literature,
which likely also explains his familiarity with the writings of Sigmund
Freud.

† Times change and Watson's timepiece with them. When he first met
Holmes, the doctor wore his late brother's watch on a fob. No longer,
apparently.

sleepy sergeant in his small office. A framed portrait of His late Majesty remained on the wall behind the sergeant's desk, and drooping from a short flagstaff nearby was a reassuring Union Jack.

"What's all this then?" The man spoke more to himself than us as he flipped through a set of pages. "Out for a midnight ramble and got into a scrap, 'ave you?"

"Nothing of the sort," Holmes assured him, and launched into our account of the evening's events.

The fellow heard us out, not troubling to suppress a yawn, his rattan chair rustling as he leaned back in it. The notion that a murder had taken place on his watch seemed not to interest him particularly, though I daresay his attitude would have been different had the victim been an Englishman.

"But you was seen a-pulling this 'ere weapon from the wog's body." He read from the arrest report and, rummaging carelessly for it, held up the distinctive bloodstained dagger.

"Pulling it out, not pushing it in," the detective emphasised. "See here," he went on. "You have my passport and travel documents. I am Colonel Arbuthnot, Northumberland Fusiliers, retired—in Egypt on holiday. My friend hasn't his papers with him, but you can easily obtain them as he's a registered guest of the Khedivial Sporting Club."

"Oh, registered at the Khedivial, is 'e?" This intelligence seemed finally to rouse the sergeant.

Nonetheless, the man insisted on taking us through the events of the previous evening several times more. The temptation to vary our answers simply on the basis of boredom was enormous, and in my case I had to suppress the wild impulse to implore the man to release me, babbling explanations about my wife and so forth, but following the detective's example, I adhered to what we had agreed as if it had been the Lord's Prayer.

During one of these catechisms the door was opened quietly and a bearded Turkish officer drifted into the room. The sergeant snapped instantly to his feet, stamping his boot, and performed a rigid salute.

"Sir!"

"As you were, Sergeant."

"'Evening, Major 'aki." The sergeant stood at ease, hands clasped behind him.

"Good morning," corrected the Turk. He extended a beige-gloved hand and the sergeant handed over the arrest documents. *"Shukran."*

Holmes signed to me to remain silent while the major lowered himself into a straight-backed chair and began to read. The sergeant reseated himself and fell to drawing circles on his desk blotter.

At length the man addressed as Major Haki looked up and regarded us with professional detachment.

The detective broke the silence. "Major, my friend's wife is taking the cure at the Al Wadi spa and she'll raise the roof if her husband here fails to join her for breakfast. All this is easily verified by Dr. Amrit Singh," he added. "In the meantime, if it's the man who held the knife who interests you, here I am."

The major studied us some more, fluffed his beard thoughtfully with the back of his gloved knuckles beneath his chin, but did not reply. It took me a moment to realise that what I'd presumed to be the man's knuckles was in fact something else. Haki's left hand had evidently suffered a catastrophic injury, his missing or deformed fingers now concealed by a leather shroud or cap that appeared to cover a perpetually clenched fist.

Oblivious to my scrutiny, the major used his good hand to uncover the dagger on the sergeant's desk where the man had tactfully concealed it beneath a large blue handkerchief. The major held it to the light and squinted at the darkened bloodstains with the same disinterested expression. To him it was merely evidence, a piece of the puzzle, nothing less or more. The sergeant, abruptly determined not to appear idle, now busied himself with paperwork, seemingly indifferent to what came next.

At length the major rose slowly to his feet, and mumbled something to the sergeant, before turning to me. "You may go," he said, handing me back my belongings. "Not you," he instructed the detective as Holmes made to rise.

"Colonel Arbuthnot—"

"Not to worry, old man. I'll send word."

I did not stay for him to change his mind.

"John, you've not shaved," said Juliet, studying me over her porridge.

"I know, dearest. I had rather a late night." In truth the night had run so late it was all I could do to arrive at breakfast moments before the appearance of my wife.

"You were with Colonel Arbuthnot?"

"Yes. The colonel and I dined at Shepheard's with Professor Tewfik, the duchess, and her brother-in-law. There was a bit of a fracas involving one of the boys."

I spoke in a low voice so Lady Cunningham and others breakfasting at the stipulated distance could not hear our talk. Taking Holmes's advice as my model, I told Juliet as much of the truth as possible, omitting merely the incidental fact of a murder and our arrest as suspects. Even as I censored my account, I had the dim conviction this was a mistake and that a reckoning would one day come due. I had in fact no idea what had become of Holmes following my release from the sultan's harem (Watson, can you hear yourself?) by that mysterious Turkish major (what was his name: Haki?) with his club hand and felt guilty to be sure—always guilty—about leaving my friend when and where I did.

Instead, I concentrated my summary of events on the duchess's displeasure and the time limit she had set on the detective's progress, conditions I could not ever recall being imposed on any of his investigations before. Forty-eight hours was not a long time and we had squandered at least four of them in British custody. For all I knew, Holmes was still under arrest, clapped by now in a real prison, and heaven knows what difficulties would be incurred trying to free him. But he had enjoined me in the most emphatic terms not to reveal his identity to the authorities.

Following his instructions, I therefore attempted nothing of the kind and happily spent the day in Juliet's company. With Dr. Singh's permission, following breakfast, we went for a slow ramble about the leafy precincts of Zamalek on the northern portion of the island. I suspect Juliet was pleased to escape Lady Cunningham's clutches. "She is most amusing," she conceded, her voice as always slightly muffled behind her face mask, "but sometimes a little of her goes a long way. We were running low on lion cubs," was her wry conclusion. I could not see whether or not she was smiling.

The weather was warming and our stroll so leisurely it placed no strain on my leg. I confess it was a relief to escape the horrible events of the previous evening, and while it was maddening to walk with space between us, forbidden to touch, I think we were both overjoyed to regain some of the intimacy we had been obliged to forfeit in the earlier days of her illness.

I took comfort as well in Stark-Munro's opinion that if I'd not contracted the disease by now, I was unlikely to do so, but felt it best not to antagonise the head of Al Wadi by flouting his instructions.

On the polo field there was a lively match in progress and we enjoyed several chukkas before I heard Juliet clear her throat. The sound was not large enough to be termed a cough and certainly nothing compared to those in London before Christmastime, but it was enough for me to conclude we had best return. Indeed she looked quite done in by the time we got back to Al Wadi.

"Time for a lie-down." She smiled, pressing the back of her wrist briefly against her forehead before blowing me a kiss.

I was making my way back to my residence at the sporting club when a white-clad orderly on a bicycle squealed to a stop before me, Dunlops crunching the gravel.

"Dr. Watson?"

"I am Dr. Watson."

He glanced at the envelope in his hand. "Dr. John Watson?"

"I am Dr. John Watson."

"That's alright then," said he, shrugging and handing me a telegram which I opened at once.

I AM THE BIGGEST FOOL IN EGYPT [it ran]. *MEET ME OUTSIDE SHEPHEARD'S AT SIX. WILL BE-COME CHILLY AFTER DARK.*

There was no signature. I reread the terse message several times.

"Any reply?" the lad enquired with a touch of impatience.

I shook my head. Wordlessly he remounted his bicycle and pedaled off.

I looked at my watch. It was close on five. I sent a note to Juliet explaining I was fatigued myself (which was true), and in for the night (which was not). I then hastened for a shower and thence to my room for a change of clothing and a sweater, arriving breathless outside Shepheard's at a few minutes past six. I found the detective pacing agitatedly before the enormous porte-cochère.

"The biggest fool in Egypt, Watson!" he repeated at the sight of me.

"Colonel, how did you manage to—"

"How many windows do you count?"

"What?"

"Up there!" He pointed. "The seventh floor! How many?"

Taking my time and using my finger, I counted up seven stories and then, going from left to right, ticked off the number. The setting sun, reflected in the windows, turned them into orange mirrors, easy to count. "One, two, three, four, five, six, seven, eight, nine, ten—"

"Ten windows!" he fairly shouted.

"But . . ."

"Now we must wait."

"For what?"

"Night."

"Only on condition that you explain yourself." I tugged his sleeve to turn him towards me. His grey eyes were glittering as when the game was afoot.

"How often have I twitted you that you *see but do not observe*? Well, now we may lay that charge at my own door. How many times since my arrival have I beheld those windows yet failed to notice their number—one for each suite with the Nile view on this side of the hotel? Mark you, Watson, as it grows dark, you will see the lights in all those rooms turn on. All but one!"

Sure enough, as we waited and smoked the sun made its slow descent beyond the farther side of river. As the light vanished, so did the orange mirrored windows. They turned dull black but, as Holmes predicted, began almost at once to light up within, one after another, including two on the seventh floor as occupants throughout the building began dressing for supper.

"Colonel . . ."

"Patience, Mr. Watson."

And so we stood there as it darkened and felt the desert chill. I was glad the detective had forewarned me to dress warmly. Still I had no idea what to make of all this.

"Colonel, how did you obtain your release from police custody?"

"What? Oh, that. You recall my telling you Mycroft slipped me a page of his engagement diary before I left the Diogenes?"

"Oh, yes, now you remind me, but—"

"I kept that ace up my sleeve and I played it. What Mycroft had written on it was sufficient to command Major Haki's attention. At my suggestion he summoned Professor Tewfik, who kindly came at once and instantly vouched for both Colonel Arbuthnot's identity and his character. I felt rather like the upstairs maid presenting her references, but it seemed to answer. With the major's permission, I showed the professor the murder weapon. Tewfik turned quite pale and then informed me it was Egyptian, Seventeenth Dynasty, and wondered when the legalities were concluded if he could add it to the museum's— Look!" he interrupted himself, seizing my sleeve and pointing upwards. "There's another! Hotel guests turning on their lights! What could be more natural? Soon they will all be lit, but I wager not the tenth at the end of the seventh floor. There! You see! Dark as Plato's cave."

I followed his finger once more to the now conspicuously black window at the end of the seventh floor.

"Perhaps they're already at supper."

"They are not, because the salon does not begin service before eight o'clock and *because the room does not exist.*"

"I'm not sure I follow—"

"The thing is simplicity itself. As you can see, this side of the hotel uniformly boasts ten windows on each floor, all facing the river. One set of windows and a balcony for each suite. The duchess says her letters were addressed to suite seven-eighteen, which would be the tenth even-numbered room on the end of the seventh floor. But Monsieur Charpentier of the management insists there *is* no suite seven-eighteen and allows me to walk down the corridor and confirm this fact for myself."

"So you told me."

"I began at the first even-numbered room, seven hundred. There should be a total of twenty rooms on the seventh-floor corridor. That is to say, ten rooms on either side. Ten which face the Nile and the odd-numbered, doubtless less expensive rooms with the less attractive views, facing the city to the east."

"Very well."

"But each side of the corridor has only nine room numbers! Why?" He did not wait for me to speculate before answering his own question. "The odd-numbered side is easily accounted for. It is typical that there would be no room seven-thirteen, as superstitious builders and occupants sometimes eschew that reputedly unlucky number. But how does one account for only nine *even*-numbered rooms overlooking the Nile, when I count *ten* windows from where we stand?"

At which point, with a jutting forefinger, he again emphasised this fact, and now fairly bursting with manic energy, he pulled forth his notebook and pencil, shoving both into his trouser pockets. Before I knew what he was about, he had peeled off and handed me his alpaca.

"Colonel—"

"Wait here, Watson, and hang on to this, if you please. There's a good fellow."

In another instant he had grabbed hold of one of the wrought-iron columns of the hotel's massive porte-cochere and began shinnying up, crawling across the glass awning and reaching for the cornerstone masonry. From there, as people noticed and gathered about me, the detective, imitating Poe's agile monkey,* commenced scrambling upwards.

"Holmes!" In my alarm, I forgot his alias. Clasping his coat to my chest, I watched, along with multiplying spectators in evening dress, as my friend, by no means a young man, scaled his way higher and yet higher, clutching the cornerstones until he gained the seventh floor, by which time he resembled nothing so much as a large spider. From there, as we gaped, he began a hazardous aerial journey, leaping from balcony to balcony, slowly but inevitably progressing to that lone, dark window.

Now cries could be heard, occasionally from rooms above where the detective's presence had understandably alarmed the occupants (I distinctly heard a woman's high-pitched scream),

---

* That climbing orangutan is featured in E. A. Poe's "The Murders in the Rue Morgue."

and several cries came from the throng gathered where I stood.

"What's the chappie doin'?"

"Some kind of wager," another was convinced.

"Look at him. The Great Houdini," a third sniggered.

Having finally lunged onto the last balcony—to gasps from below, some of them mine—Holmes turned his attention to the window behind him and peered briefly into its blackness before returning to the balcony ledge. By the light overflowing from the adjacent suite I could make out he was doing something with his hands on the railing.

"Looks like he's writing!" someone with sharper eyes than mine cried out.

Squinting, I could imagine this was likely the case, as he'd taken his pocket book and pencil with him. We watched in puzzled silence for some moments.

"A suicide note!" someone suggested helpfully.

More exclamations greeted this possibility.

"Here, you ladies best be off," a gruff voice to my right advised. The women, I suspect, were only waiting to be told, and with a swish of skirts many quitted the vicinity, retreating inside to the foyer.

After another few moments, during which time we'd all now congregated directly below the balcony in question, the detective finished whatever he was doing and waved his hands.

"*Señor* is going to jump!" a Spaniard shouted in alarm, but I knew better and stepped forward.

"Stand back!"

Obedient to my confident command, the crowd withdrew a few steps, and I pushed my way through, waving his alpaca above my head, knowing the lights down here would enable Holmes to see it and me.

In another instant, with an emphatic gesture of his right arm, the detective flung the notebook into the air, where it fluttered down some thirty feet from where I stood, landing on a topiary camel.

"Out of my way!" I cried. "That is intended for me!"

"Well, no one said it wasn't," a bystander mumbled as I pushed my way unceremoniously towards the hedge.

The small book lodged just out of reach in the cleft of the camel's hump, but by dint of shaking the entire shrub furiously, the thing obligingly tumbled to my feet.

Ignoring the bemused stares of those clustered about me, I took the small volume into the light and opened it to the last page, where Holmes had scrawled his message. Reading the words twice to make sure I understood them, I pocketed the book, tucked his coat under my arm, and waved up to him to acknowledge my possession of the book and its instructions. By way of reply, he clasped his upper arms, indicating he was cold.

Waving again, I entered the hotel and made for the front desk.

"I wish to see Monsieur Charpentier at once," I told the clerk who stood behind it. A polished brass nameplate before me identified him as *Mr. Dumfries.* The man surveyed me with a bureaucrat's condescension.

"I'm afraid you are not properly dressed—" he began.

"Read this." I held the book open before him that he alone might see what the detective had written. He scanned it with a bored expression, but the colour drained from his face as he comprehended, then stared at me with the surprised expression of one who has just been slapped.

"Please follow me."

It has been said that if you enjoy sausage you would do well to avoid seeing where and how one is made. I had experienced examples in hospitals, in the army, and on those infrequent occasions when I found myself backstage at the theatre where the chaotic arrangements and the troops of enablers bore little or no resemblance to the effortless airs and graces produced by the actors and the production's scenic effects in view of the enchanted audience. Yet none of these quite prepared me for the clattering mayhem that was just out of sight at a luxe hotel. While well-paying guests enjoyed spotless linen, crisp sheets, furniture redolent of beeswax, sparkling crystal and gleaming cutlery framing artfully presented food, the veritable army required to achieve this agreeable result toiled just out of view. Only a wall and occasional swinging door separated diners in formal dress from piles of laundry in trundling carts, dozens of chefs and *sauciers* in scalding kitchens, multitudinous maids scurrying to and fro, dozens more pressing on steaming irons, butlers and menservants forcing passage through narrow hallways and corridors crammed with houseboys on their errands. Simply maintaining an establishment as large and complex as Shepheard's required a company of carpenters and electricians. It was the opposite of what one imagines pondering the workings of a Swiss watch, where the innards are as pristine as what is seen on the clock-face.

Dumfries—I was not sure of his title—led me through this maze of activity with determination and assurance. If I anticipated our trek would culminate in an imposing command post wherein M. Charpentier presided at his ease over the Shepheard's kingdom, I was again disabused.

Monsieur Charpentier, a Frenchman in his forties, occupied an office that was smaller than his responsibilities might have suggested, but his large walnut desk was perfectly organised with what looked like topless tin dispatch boxes separating his multifarious tasks for easy disposal. Much of the scant wall space was devoted to photographs of M. Charpentier with some of his more celebrated guests. Richard Francis Burton had evidently stopped here on more than one occasion and a photograph of his unsmiling widow, Isabel Arundel, adorned the wall, as did a portrait of Charles George "Chinese" Gordon, though that had obviously been taken before the advent of the present hotelier.

As we entered, Charpentier himself looked up in surprise, then checked his watch. Clearly everything in his domain ran according to a prearranged timetable and the appearance of the clerk I took to be the concierge was not anticipated.

"Dumfries? What brings you here?" He was looking at me as he posed the question.

"Monsieur Charpentier, this gentleman"—indicating me— "has something to show you that would seem to warrant your immediate attention." The man nodded in my direction and I opened up the detective's notebook to the same page and held it before the hotel manager.

Charpentier adjusted his pince-nez and read what Holmes had written. I had seen men turn grey before, from illness or wounds incurred in combat, but never, I think, from merely reading three sentences of English:

You will immediately break open the concealed door to suite seven-eighteen or I will smash the window on the balcony where I am standing and unlock the door from within. Watson, please send for the duchess and Lord D at Osiris House. Kindly hurry, as I am cold. Sherlock Holmes.

6

SUITE 718

"Efficiency" was one of the many watchwords that might apply to Shepheard's. In almost less time than it takes to write, two of Charpentier's Berber workmen, manipulating accordion-like Chinese silk screens, had partitioned off a section of corridor at the end of the seventh floor. Behind these and out of the public's view as I watched, they deftly employed razors to slice through the yellow wallpaper Holmes had described, revealing the outline of the door whose existence the detective had inferred. The door's panelling and bevelled edges had been cunningly overlaid with plaster to produce a flat effect for the wallpaper and the doorknob itself removed along with any trace of a room number.

Monsieur Charpentier favored me with an unhappy expression as he withdrew a key from his pocket and, punching the wallpaper at intervals, after several attempts succeeded in locating the covered keyhole and unlocking the door.

"*Shukran,*" he addressed his carpenters. "Leave the screen." Tipping their fingers to their foreheads in salute, the fellaheen silently withdrew.

"Please hurry."

Nodding, Charpentier pulled open the door using the inserted key for a handle. I followed him into the darkened room and hastened to unbolt the double window, admitting the detective and handing him his coat.

"Good lord!" was his first exclamation. "Thank you, my dear fellow!" was his second.

He looked about, rubbing his upper arms to warm them. Spying the light switch, he turned it on, bathing the large, beautifully appointed, if dust-covered, room with amber illumination. Somewhere there lingered the faint aroma of perfume.

I closed the window panels, secured them once more, and drew the curtains, turning in time to see the detective face the hotelier.

"Now then, Monsieur Charpentier, it is time for us to speak candidly."

"And you, *monsieur*," the hotelier replied, attempting to recover his composure. "You are not Sherlock Holmes. In Dr. Watson's accounts he is much taller. You are Colonel Arbuthnot, whom I have previously met searching for this room!"

This was a surprising start to the conversation, but Holmes, I cannot resist saying, rose to the occasion and, taking full inventory of the man, addressed the Frenchman thus:

"You were born in Marseilles towards the end of May. Your father was a shipwright and your mother a seamstress. Your older brother is a doctor and your sister drowned when she was twelve in a boating accident. You were educated at L'Ecole du Saint Esprit in Grenoble and studied hostelry for a time in Zurich. You have been with Shepheard's for approximately fifteen years, starting as third bellman."

Before the open-mouthed hotelier had time to expostulate, Holmes went on, "This gentleman will confirm my identity," indicating me. "He is the selfsame Dr. John Watson who so

ably chronicles my"—he hesitated—"exploits in the pages of
The Strand."

"That is so," I answered promptly and with conviction,
inwardly delighted that the detective's approval of my work
was now part of the public record. "I am Dr. Watson and this
man is definitely Sherlock Holmes and he is exactly as tall as
I say he is."

"As I was saying," Holmes pursued before this case of identity stretched into reductio ad absurdum, "I believe you have
some explaining to do."

The man pinched the bridge of his nose, red from the em-
brace of his pince-nez and squared his shoulders. "And if I
refuse?"

"Monsieur Charpentier, a British subject has disappeared
and you have not only failed to report the fact; you have con-
nived to conceal its occurrence."

"I did report it!"

"Oh?" We were both startled by this response.

The Frenchman sank into the nearest chair.

"What do you wish to know?"

Holmes, who had been meticulously examining the room
with his habitual attention to detail, now gently tugged a long,
ebony hair from behind a cushion wedged on a small green
settee, holding the strand to the light, where it glistened.

"Shall we start at the beginning? The Duke of Uxbridge
was a guest in suite seven-eighteen every year," he prompted.
"This suite."

"Yes."

"He arrived this year, as usual?"

"Yes."

"The date being.?"

"November the first."

"But he was not alone." Holmes dangled the hair close to the man's face.

"Not this year, no." The man averted his eyes, refusing to look at it.

"Monsieur Charpentier, I am neither a dentist nor a barber. I am no more interested in pulling teeth than I am hairs. The duchess and her brother-in-law will be here shortly, so you must speak quickly. Who was this woman?"

The man tugged at his own locks, smoothing grey curls back behind his ears.

"A dancer." Holmes raised his eyebrows. "The wrong sort of dancer," the hotelier acknowledged. "She specialises in *Raqs sharqi.*"

"*Raqs sharqi?*"

Holmes's repetition of the words appeared to embarrass the Frenchman. "An Egyptian or Turkish dance in which the torso and pelvis take precedence over hands and feet. Their claim to Egyptian tradition is ridiculous despite the occasional resemblance to ancient wall paintings. Westerners and European tourists flock to her performances. Natives, too, it must be said—but men only. Such exhibitions are not deemed fit for polite company. The duke very likely encountered her at her place of employment. They resided here together."

"The date being?" Holmes was once more writing in his pocket book.

Charpentier tugged at his curls again. "Late November? We do not keep strict records of such—"

"Irregularities? For how long?"

"Over two months. We—the management—as I say, are accustomed to . . ." He hesitated, in search of the euphemism that best suited his present requirements—

"Turning a blind eye?"

"*Exactement,*" he whispered.

Holmes took a turn about the room. Charpentier seized the moment to blow his nose. Our movements had stirred the room's unattended dust and motes floated and danced in the light.

"And where are the duke and his inamorata now?"

"That's just it!" wailed the other. "We've no idea! On the third of January they left together. The porter remembered carrying a valise of Moroccan leather and a red carpet bag to the hotel omnibus which took them to Ramses station, but nobody knew where they were going and we deemed it—"

"Impolite?"

"Indiscreet, to make enquiries. We assumed from their luggage their trip was to be a short one." He shrugged. "Then, as time passed—"

"How much time?"

"Two weeks! By which time, when they failed to return, the situation . . ." He trailed off.

"Became a burden," Holmes supplied.

"To put it mildly, *monsieur*! What were we to say—and to whom? The woman in question—"

"The dancer of the 'wrong sort'—"

"Precisely. We knew she was of interest in certain quarters."

"British or Turkish quarters?"

"That is where I made my mistake!" he cried. "I went to the Turks. Egypt is officially under Ottoman control, as you are doubtless aware. I spoke with a Major Haki who, acting, he said, under directions from the office of the Khedive, told me under no circumstances to make mention of either the affair or the disappearance."

"Why on earth not?"

Charpentier blew his nose again. "He saw no reason to explain matters to me! I carry a French passport. Cairo is"—again, searching for the right words *juste*—"complicated. Porous. Wheels within wheels. Shepheard's ability to function is dependent on a variety of permits. Licences. Inspections. A clutch of regulations that can change at any time. *Baksheesh!*" he added peevishly, as the last straw. "Complying I deemed the lesser of two evils," he concluded, hanging his head. "How relieved I am Monsieur Shepheard did not live to see this!"*

As Holmes studied the hotelier, pondering the latter's rationale, I wondered what would have happened with Major Haki had the detective not managed to preserve his incognito.

"What is the dancer's name?"

"She is known throughout Cairo as Fatima. I am unaware of any other."

"And where does she dance? No evasions, please. Time is short."

"At the Cave of Ali Baba. In the French Quarter. Such entertainments are 'after hour' affairs. As such they generally do not commence before midnight. We have since made discreet contact, but no one at that establishment has either seen nor heard from her. The proprietor, a certain Majid, is most upset. A bit of a character," he added, without elaboration.

Holmes surveyed the room again, lost in thought. There were, I sensed, a great many directions in which matters might unfold and it was incumbent on my friend to choose the right ones.

---

* This has to be taken with a ton of salt. Shepheard, the hotel's original co-creator, was long dead before Charpentier was on the scene.

"And His Grace's bill?"

Charpentier eyed us with another injured expression. He seemed to possess an endless repertoire. "Remains outstanding. And astronomical."

Holmes and I exchanged looks. The same word had been used to describe His Grace's gaming debts at White's. Duke Michael appeared to be running true to form.

"What have you done with their possessions?"

"I disposed of them."

"It is a mistake to lie to me, Monsieur Charpentier. You did nothing of the kind because for all you knew, they might at any time return and reclaim them."

Charpentier jumped up, hands outstretched, imploring.

"But they haven't! What were we to do, I ask you! Defy the Turkish authorities, reveal a scandalous liaison, and face a host of enquiries from His Grace's . . . relatives or other . . . interested parties with questions we would be quite unable to answer! And so, we—I—thought it best to—"

"Pretend the man had never been here."

There was a leaden exhalation. "I panicked."

"And relied on the discretion of your staff."

"They are Sudanese and entirely reliable."

"Not entirely," I struck in. "Your man Mustafa was ready to talk."

His head jerked up at this.

"Mustafa? Many are called by that name."

"The heavyset waiter in the dining salon."

Charpentier blinked in recognition. "What did he say?"

"He said nothing. He was murdered before he could tell us what he knew."

The hotelier doubled over as if punched and tripped backward onto the settee.

"*Mon Dieu.*"

"*Monsieur,* you are being disingenuous at best," Holmes said quietly. "Cairo, where three competing national interests jockey for primacy, is inevitably honeycombed with spies, and Shepheard's, with its international clientele—many in uniform—wining and dining, must be the locus of endless intrigue. I'll wager half your staff is listening to the other half while many of your guests are doing the same. Waiters are ideally positioned to eavesdrop on all. It wouldn't take long before your man Mustafa learned there was an Englishman asking questions about the Duke of Uxbridge. Or that his suite had been concealed."

Charpentier said nothing.

"Where are the possessions of Fatima and His Grace?"

For a time no answer was forthcoming. The man's head drooped between his knees, and he breathed with difficulty. The detective allowed him several moments' grace before prompting him.

"Monsieur Charpentier."

"In the luggage room. In the basement. Six trunks."

Holmes considered for some moments, staring at the Persian carpet, then looked up with decision.

"Have this room cleaned and aired immediately and bring all their effects back as they were. When the suite is presentable have your Mr. Dumfries conduct Her Grace and Lord Darlington here. They are stopping at Osiris House."

Charpentier did not look up. "It shall be done as you say, Monsieur Holmes."

Once again, we were obliged to wait.

"I know this room." Almost two hours later, the Duchess of Uxbridge stood uncertainly on the ragged threshold, framed in the open doorway by torn strips of yellow wallpaper.

"Of course you do," the detective concurred. "It is suite seven-eighteen, where you stayed with His Grace when you visited Cairo in previous years."

"You said it didn't exist," the duchess accused the detective, literally as well as figuratively standing her ground.

"Is that your rationale for not entering?" Holmes enquired. "In truth, until ninety minutes ago this room had indeed ceased to exist. It had been carefully concealed. It was I who exposed it." Holmes was not without vanity and the duchess had offended him with her ultimatum.

As if to show she was unafraid, the woman now entered, sniffing suspiciously. The place had only just been cleaned and was still redolent of the efforts to rid the rooms of their musty odor.

"Will Lord Darlington be joining us?"

The schoolmaster, who had remained in the corridor, hearing his name, now wandered absently after his sister-in-law, looking about with his usual blank expression.

Holmes watched the duchess in silence as she inspected the room, evidently recalling time she had spent here.

"I smell *eau de Cologne*."

"Yes."

"Not mine."

"No. What I have to tell you may prove distressing," said he, eyeing Lord Darlington. "Would you prefer to hear it alone?"

She faced the detective. "Please explain yourself. Darlington can hear whatever it is you have to say."

"Very well." Holmes waited, untroubled by the silence between them.

"Is my husband alive?" she asked after a pause.

"I cannot say." Her shoulders sagged at this. "But I know a good deal more than when you allotted me forty-eight hours to progress in my investigation. Be kind enough to open the right-hand wardrobe door behind you."

This was not what she expected to hear.

"The right-hand wardrobe door," Holmes repeated in a firm tone.

Frowning, she obeyed and opened the door. Inside were an assortment of her husband's clothes, singlets, hose, morning coats and cutaways from Jermyn Street and Savile Row, shirts from Turnbull & Asser, his Winchester tie and several hand-stitched brogues and patent leathers, also a carbine in its long holster from Purdey & Sons. On the shelf below was a dish of cufflinks, studs, and stick-pins alongside an old, silver-backed hairbrush from Yardley's. I know for I had recently placed them there.

Holding it at arm's length, with evident distaste, the duchess now drew forth an aquamarine faïence hippopotamus, which she set down without comment, as much as to say, "Here is all my husband has to show for his Egyptian enthusiasms." Remembering her previously expressed scorn on the subject as well as Professor Tewfik's demonstration, Holmes and I thought it best to remain likewise silent and refrain from spec-ulation as to the object's value or provenance. Learning the thing was worthless would merely serve to stoke her anger when the detective would prefer her attention.

"Now open the left, if you please," he instructed.

I began to wish I were someplace else.

The duchess stared at the contents of the open left-hand door. Jumbled in silken profusion were the colourful garments that belonged to another woman. These included scarfs, shoes, dresses, blouses, gowns, stockings, and several items of a more intimate character. Their style, moreover, was less European than Asiatic. There was an open red leather box of service-able paste jewellery, shiny earrings, a garnet necklace, and the like. And emanating from the midst of the closet, more of the perfume the duchess had detected on her initial tour of inspection.

For a time, she faced the wardrobe, motionless, her rigid back to us. Blinking uncertainly, Darlington tactfully closed both doors and, taking his sister-in-law by the elbow, turned her to face the detective. Her face was a mask, the features fro-zen as if her countenance would fragment were she to adjust her expression.

"Please sit."

Like an automaton, she allowed Lord Darlington to lead her to the chair lately occupied by Charpentier. Born in Brazil, married in England, and now betrayed in Egypt. Were it not for her previous disrespectful treatment of my friend, I might almost have pitied her. As she sat, Holmes rose to his feet. He was, I knew, still attempting to marshal his thoughts, deliberat-ing such facts to lay before her as she could tolerate on the one hand, while retaining certain others he was not yet prepared to divulge.

"Almost three months ago here in Cairo your husband met and contracted an intimacy with . . . an exotic dancer. She took up residence with him here." With a sweeping gesture, he indicated the suite. "A little over a month ago they both departed for what the staff of this hotel assumed was a brief excursion, from which they never returned. Are they alive? Have they met with an accident or foul play?" The detective ticked off the possibilities on his fingertips. "At this juncture it is impossible to say. For reasons beyond my understanding at present, the hotel felt compelled to conceal this suite, rather than acknowledge either had ever occupied it. Last night at dinner our waiter attempted to sell me information on the subject, but he was murdered before he could speak."

Her mouth opened and closed soundlessly. I noticed Holmes made no mention of what Mustafa had scratched in the dirt as he died, nor did he allude to the man's last words—if indeed what I heard could be called words.

We sat in silence for several moments.

"Is it possible they were kidnapped?" Darlington wondered aloud.

"It is not."

"How can you be sure?"

"Over a month has passed and there has been no ransom demand."

The duchess cast her eyes upwards, seemingly unsure where to look.

"You and His Grace were not, I gather, on intimate terms of late?" Obliquely phrased, the detective's meaning was nonetheless unmistakable.

"We were not on intimate terms." Her voice was so low it was hard to hear.

"I am sorry for your difficulties, Your Grace."

"Do you—do you think they have run off?" the duchess asked, after an awkward pause.

"No." Both appeared surprised by his answer. "But they did decamp on short notice. I take it your husband was fond of his comforts?" Holmes gestured to the wardrobe. "We are creatures of habit, most of us. This Yardley's hairbrush, for example. The silver handle with his engraved escutcheon is scratched, suggesting long usage. Was it a gift from Your Grace?"

"It is one of a matching pair, one for each hand. He has

numbered them among his toiletries for as long as I have known him."

"The mate has not been found. Would I be correct in assuming it is hard to imagine the duke, long accustomed to such niceties, setting out to reinvent his life without at the very least his familiar brushes and their reassuring, if tarnished, ancestral crest, to say nothing of the rest of his private necessities? When a man has a cherished personal possession, a hairbrush or favorite article of clothing, he is unlikely to abandon it, whatever other claims may be made on his attention."

"You forget," Darlington pointed out in his usual monotone, "my brother had ample motive for wishing to disappear. Such a motive may have trumped a sentimental attachment to a hairbrush which he could, for a need, replace."

The detective regarded Lord Darlington as if seeing him in a new light. But he shrugged. "The motive, perhaps, but not the means. How would he replace them? What would he use for capital to mount his resurrection? His financial well-being is currently buried in the copper mines of Brazil, or am I mistaken?"

"Our finances are complicated." Like Charpentier, people seemed always to utter the word in a whisper. "I control the copper."

"To be sure, but the estate and title itself cannot be claimed without ascertaining the fate of His Grace. And there is this."

Holmes rose and opened a drawer on the left side of the wardrobe, taking out a dark blue velvet reticule, whose contents he emptied onto the low table between them next to the aquamarine hippopotamus.

We four stared at a necklace which comprised a dozen large, gleaming black pearls. Unlike the costume jewellery or the Egyptian faïence trinket beside them, the pearls were doubtless genuine.

"I don't imagine Miss Fatima received these from your husband. Not in his straitened circumstances. But however she obtained them, I cannot imagine any woman, no matter how amorously susceptible, setting out to restart her life and leaving these behind. Can you?"

The duchess stared at the pearls as if hypnotised, her silence an answer.

"And if escape and disappearance was your husband's intention, why not use these? They would take him far. No," the detective answered his own question, "His Grace had pinned his hopes and limited expertise on the gold of Tuthmose, possession of which he was convinced would dwarf all other solutions." Holmes paused, allowing his conclusions to sink in before adding, "No one witnessed any act of coercion, nor did your husband sense any need of protection. He did not trouble to bring this carbine. I therefore infer their journey was conceived as a short excursion, prompted perhaps by news or information of some sort. The pair didn't plan to travel long or far but were sufficiently eager for His Grace to forgo the mate of a favorite hairbrush, yet not so entirely heedless that he overlooked his toothbrush. After all, they had a train to catch. The hotel omnibus took them to the station with light luggage, principally a fine Moroccan travelling case. Sightseeing perhaps. An overnight trip or possibly merely a picnic. And then something happened."

He did not allude to the fates of any other Egyptologists.

"What is to be done?" the duchess demanded finally in the same whisper.

"What is to be done must be done without your interference or supervision," the detective explained in a firm but not unsympathetic voice. "When I have news to convey you may be assured I will convey it. Otherwise, I must be turned loose to pursue the case as I see fit. Are you prepared to accept these conditions? If not, I will reluctantly suggest you seek assistance elsewhere."

The duchess hesitated, looking briefly at Darlington, the first time I had ever seen them exchange glances.

"Will you at least tell me what direction you intend to pursue?"

Now it was the detective's turn to hesitate. Clearly the duchess had no intention of slipping the leash entirely. He placed his fingertips together in a gesture I well understood.

"I will not."

Another silence followed this. Her Grace was unaccustomed to confrontation, much less denial. After some moments, the woman extended her hand without looking, and as before, Lord Darlington was there to take it, gracefully helping her to her feet.

She cast a look at the detective but said nothing before the pair silently left the room.

Holmes appeared momentarily at a loss following this exchange. He fumbled for his tobacco, struck a match on the chrome ashtray strike-plate, and puffed on his briar. I do not believe it gave him any pleasure to enlighten the duchess regarding her husband's infidelity, though I sensed this was by no means a unique occurrence for her. I took the occasion to light a cigarette and we sat for a time in companionable silence. Cleaned and spruced once more, the room was decidedly agreeable.

"What do you make of her?"

"The duchess?"

"The dancer. One might easily make the case for such a woman, obliged by circumstances and her sex to live by her wits, throwing her cap in the way of a duke, but how long, one is forced to wonder, before his own situation became clear to her? After all, she has proved sufficiently clever to acquire these." He indicated the pearls on the table where he had placed them.

"And what then?"

"Precisely, my dear Watson. And what then?"

Unable to answer his question, I posed one of my own. "I observe that when you spoke with Her Grace and Lord Darlington just now you made no mention of VR 16, whatever that may be."

"Sixty-one," he corrected me, tapping out ash from his pipe on the ashtray. "Give that woman an inch and she will demand a league." He sat back. "I have been pondering those marks in the dirt and for the life of me I cannot associate the letters *VR* with anything other than the late queen, which would hardly seem pertinent. Likewise the numbers six and one suggest nothing at present."

"May I ask another question?"

"By all means."

I gathered my thoughts. "If I am keeping a correct count, three Egyptologists, a waiter, and a Swede in London some years back are now all dead. It is clear that there is some connection between these fatalities, but what can it be? Bechstein may have been merely foolhardy, neglecting to bring his compass, but why was he wandering away from his dig in the first place? And do you believe Phillips really fell to his death? Professor Jourdan was murdered; that is beyond question. Was it a mere robbery or something more? And as we know, that Mustafa person was on the point of giving us information regarding this subject when he was summarily dispatched. That makes five. Excepting Ohlsson, are we meant to imagine they were all somehow struck by the same hand? If gold is at the bottom of all this, the pattern is decidedly irregular."

"Decidedly, on first glance," my friend agreed. "But put aside for the moment the suicide in London. The other deaths all occurred here in Egypt. What have the victims in common? As you yourself said, Doctor, the pursuit of treasure. That would seem to be some sort of pattern."

"But while Jourdan and Phillips died violently," I objected, "Bechstein seems merely to have left his compass—"

"But did he leave it? Or was he relieved of it? If the latter, what then befell was not mischance but violence of perhaps a more subtle cast. That would make three dead treasure hunters in toto. Are you fatigued, my dear fellow?"

"Quite the contrary. Overstimulated."

"Good. Mustafa's clue must wait, for the curtain is about to go up and we must not miss the performance."

"Performance?"

"At the Cave of Ali Baba. Weren't we told the risqué event begins at midnight?" Holmes was replacing items back in the wardrobe and closing the double doors as he spoke. "It is time we learn about *Raqs sharqi.*"

"I beg your pardon?"

"Belly dancing."

7

FATIMA

The Cave of Ali Baba in the French Quarter was nothing of the sort, but rather a low-ceilinged room of modest dimensions, off the avenue Mansour. It contained perhaps two dozen small tables spaced in tiers about an aproned stage with a raised platform at the rear, presently occupied by four bored-looking musicians, cradling instruments that were unfamiliar to me. To the right, three false arches in the distinctive Mogul style made of what looked like pasteboard upheld diaphanous red curtains with gold trim. Electric sconces had been shaded with pink glass to contribute a presumably exotic effect.

It was almost midnight and the smoke-filled establishment was crowded but not overflowing with an odd assortment of clientele scattered among the tables. Some were Arab, puffing on burbling hookahs or sipping a date-alcohol mixture called Arak, permitted Muslims; others, clearly Western, in evening attire, had obviously dined beforehand and now, with wives and families safely tucked elsewhere, had come laughing and jabbering, waving cigarettes or cigars, for their late-night diversions. All were male. Waiters, also male, and startlingly young (bare-chested boys in gold-tasselled red vests and matching skull caps, who looked no more than twelve), threaded their way among the tables, supplying drink, nuts, yogurt, and beans of some sort in response to imperious finger snaps. The aroma of smoke and drink added to the ambience and was here inhaled as a kind of incense.

"*Salaam, effendi*. Welcome to the Cave of Ali Baba. I am Majid." Majid wore a strange assortment of Arab and Western dress, trousers of cavalry twill with Persian slippers that would have done justice to Ali Baba himself. "Have you booked a table?" I judged him roughly forty years of age, though it was apparent he dyed his hair, as clumps of untended white appeared here and there amid the boot polish black. His dark, glistening eyes and not-unpleasing features—the Levantine skin, the beaked Arab nose—were marred by an ivory gash across one cheek. It lent him a faintly piratical aspect and suggested other occupations at other times. I recalled Charpentier referring to him as "a bit of a character."

"Assuredly," Holmes answered, slipping Majid several Egyptian pound notes which the man deftly palmed, leading us to one of the empty tables and snapping his fingers at the nearest boy. "Arak!"

We had scarcely been seated and served the ghastly potion when there was a crash of cymbals from the stage that caused all talk to cease. The musicians, prompted by some invisible cue, commenced performing on their odd instruments, one plucking multiple strings, another blowing shrilly into a pipe that looked fit for a snake charmer, while the remaining two, moving their arms in rotating unison, struck a tattoo on slender drums that resembled tambourines, though larger than any I had ever seen in any Gypsy caravan.

The resultant sounds, barbaric, pulsating, and wild, served to introduce nine barefoot women who sprang from the three false arches. All were clad in a variant of the same gauze-like material as the curtains. All tapped miniature cymbals between their thumbs and forefingers as if they were casta-nets, though producing a metallic clang rather than the hol-low Spanish *clacking*. Small bells around their ankles jangled as they spun. Below their heavily kohled eyes, the lower por-tions of their faces, in Muslim fashion, were draped with veils, but in a kind of mockery of the modesty proclaimed by their faith, these veils were as transparent as the curtains and their pantaloons, revealing flesh and features as clearly as if there had been no covering at all. Most shocking, their navels and midriffs were bare for all to see.

And if the foregoing was not sufficiently sensational, the convolutions of their bodies in synchronicity with the insistent music displayed postures, movements, and supple gyrations one would not have dreamed possible of the human form. And all the while, the undulating waggle of their hips and backward bending of their torsos was accompanied by those finger cym-bals and ankle bells, the whole capped by an unearthly ulula-tion produced by their flicking tongues. Their ages, as best I could determine, ranged from little more than young girls to women bordering on matronly.

Why their tall, spangled headdresses failed to topple amid their contortions I could not fathom. To be sure, this was the sort of thing I had glimpsed on certain French postcards, but in motion and accompanied by the pulsing beat the effect was quite different. A photograph, after all, left something to the imagination.

Throughout this exhibition, the audience of men responded with hoots and rhythmic clapping, urging the dancers to ever more brazen choreography. Arak seemed the inevitable com-plement to the spectacle and I found myself throwing back the

fiery brew without hesitation, gritting my teeth at the spiky fla-
vour. There was, I noticed, no difference between the response
of Arab and European men; all were caught up in the same
frenzy of enthusiasm and manifested their approval in iden-
tical fashion. The dancers, not insensible of the encouragement, strove to satisfy the crowd. To the intoxicating formula
of smoke and drink, human sweat was now added.

I stole a look at Holmes and was mildly astonished to see
that the performance interested him not at all. A finger held
statically aloft, he was summoning one of the youthful waiters and handing him a note, torn (like Mycroft's communi-
qués) from his pocket book, as well as two crumpled Egyptian
pounds. Over or perhaps below the riotous cacophony, Holmes
whispered to the boy, who nodded vigorously and departed
with the items in his fist.

Surrounded by tables of onlookers, the dancers on the tiny
apron were performing virtually and deliberately under our
noses, vibrating as close as possible to the glazed eyes of the
spectators. I confess it required an act of will to tear my eyes
from the extravaganza and watch as the boy handed Holmes's
note and money to Majid, hovering near the entrance. Reading it, he frowned, bent low, and whispered something to the
little messenger, who in turn wheedled his way back to us,
whispering (or shouting? It was heard to tell) in the detective's
ear.

Nodding, Holmes rose, plucking me forcefully by the
sleeve. I followed him towards the disappearing figure of Majid, who was in the act of flinging aside a beaded curtain I
hadn't noticed before.

We followed him into the darkness, where he waited.

"What is this about?" He did not append the salutation
"effendi."

"We came here hoping to experience Fatima," Holmes said.

The man spat. "May Fatima rot in hell. She has bankrupted me."

"Fatima?"

"Why do you think half the tables are empty? When Fatima performs there is no room even to stand," the impresario snarled, lighting a cigarette with a match that briefly illumined his scar. "It takes nine of those cows"—with a head jerk he indicated the gyrating women—"to equal one of her. And she has a contract!" he added with bitter indignation.

"Where does Fatima live?" Holmes held up another pound note that disappeared like a fly in the mouth of a frog.

"Why do you want to know?"

Holmes set more pound notes among the tubes of cosmetics and greasepaint on the shelf between them. Majid swept the money into his pocket without taking his eyes off the detective.

"Where?" Holmes flourished another banknote.

"Sixty Suleiman Pasha Street near the avenue Muizz." Brows drawn together, he glowered at the detective as if to hold him responsible for his present difficulties.

Holmes handed over the money.

"But she's not there. I have a man watching the place and I will know if she returns."

"Ah."

"But she won't. Not anytime soon."

"Oh?" Another note.

Majid dropped his cigarette on the floor and snuffed it with the curled-up toe of his Persian slipper, reminding me in that moment of where Holmes kept his tobacco years ago in Baker Street.

"She's at Shepheard's with that damned Englishman."

"Englishman?"

"Some viscount or other. They won't let the likes of me in the place, but mark you this, and I don't care who hears me: if I ever lay hands on either, that vixen or her drunkard lover, I'll kill them, kill them both." Uttered in a conversational undertone, this threat seemed all the more chilling.

Holmes produced yet another banknote.

"When did she take up with the Englishman at Shepheard's?"

He scowled at us, remembering. "November sometime. Ruined," he added in a tired voice.

"You have been most helpful, Monsieur Majid. Good night."

Majid replied with a surly grunt by way of farewell. "If you see them, tell them what I said!" he called after us.

As we left, we squeezed past the bevy of panting dancers traipsing offstage following their exertions and onto the avenue Mansour, well-nigh deserted by this hour. With my head throbbing, I slumped against a kiosk plastered with successive layers of posters and notices it was too dark to read.

"I'm too old for this sort of thing," I protested to no one in particular.

"Can you recall what Mustafa cried out as he died?"

I shook my head. "One word—if it was a word. It sounded like . . . something that started with a *T*? 'Tourette's'? I know that can't be right. I'm sorry." I was unable to suppress a yawn.

"Watson, get thee to bed."

"I will." The detective started off. "And you?"

"I'll return to my digs at Shepheard's. It is quite a three-pipe problem."

"What of VR 61?"

"That is the three-pipe problem."

And thence we parted. There was no transportation to be had at this time and place. The Jardin des Plantes and my bed were not far off, but I was in truth at the very limit of my strength. I stumbled across the now interminable Nile causeway and made my way to the Khedivial Club, where I was obliged to knock up the sleeping porter to let me in. I swallowed an Aspirin, ignored my mosquito netting, and fell into my bed fully clothed, where I slept like a dead man.

"Dr. Watson, *effendi*! Dr. Watson?"

"What is it?" I squinted against the glare of the sunshine as the boy raised the blinds.

"It is nine o'clock," he responded, misunderstanding my confusion. My head felt like a split melon, which I judged were the effects of last night's intake of Arak. "Today you are taking your wife to the pyramids!"

I could swear he looked gleeful at my discomfort, whose origin he appeared to have no difficulty diagnosing, but in truth I could hardly open my eyes to make him out in the sudden access of sunlight.

"Have you forgotten? She is waiting."

I might have drawn the bedclothes over my head, but he had thoughtfully arrived with black coffee, which I would have inhaled had that been possible. How could I have forgotten that today was Juliet's big day, the long-promised trip to the pyramids? A calash, driver, and guide had been laid on.

I will omit the details of my painful ordeal. My powers were so much under a cloud that even Juliet, exhilarated like a child loosed from school for the holidays, noticed.

"John, are you ill?"

I explained I had merely awakened with a migraine which would doubtless pass.

"Poor you!" she moaned in sympathy. "Today of all days. Should we postpone our jaunt?"

"By no means," I insisted, knowing that was the last thing she wanted. "May I borrow your parasol?"

"Of course. Are you certain? Poor you."

The weather had begun to warm since our arrival in November, which was not to my advantage at present. I slept partway in the calash, only to be jostled awake when Juliet first caught sight of those stupendous mounds. The day, or certainly a good part of it, dragged on while I suffered her chirping exclamations of wonder. "Really, this is beyond anything!" Her inquisitive nature prompted an endless number of questions put to our guide, many of which he was unable to answer. "We do not know," or, "No man can say," was at least part of his threnody.

Pleading my ailment, I remained in the carriage while Juliet descended and, in what seems a visitor's ritual, stood for some time in contemplation before the Sphinx, after which, while the driver helpfully raised the roof of the calash for my benefit, she reclaimed her parasol and marched to the edge of the Great Pyramid. It was only with difficulty that I finally succeeded in persuading her not to exhaust herself and to return.

"You've no idea what you've missed, John!" she said, adhering to Dr. Singh's instructions and sitting across from me. Feebly I reminded her that I had in fact visited the place already, but her enthusiasm remained unchecked. The calash hood was folded down once more to ensure nothing interfered with the free circulation of air between us as we wound our way back to the city.

"I'll go again another time," was the best I could manage, heartsick at having disappointed her but simply unable to keep my eyes open or my head from throbbing.

"Poor John!" she suddenly wondered, a gloved hand to her mouth. "I pray you've not come down with—"

"Nonsense. I'm feeling better already."

In this fashion we trundled back to the Jardin des Plantes. I attempted to comfort myself with the reflection that at least I was not astride a camel. Referring to the excursion, Juliet kept repeating, "I'll never be the same," at regular intervals, finally blowing me a farewell kiss as she returned to isolation at Al Wadi, while I stumbled off to the Khedivial's common room for tea and sandwiches. I was awake now and hungry.

"Have I the honour of addressing Dr. Henry Jekyll?" Sherlock Holmes was brushing crumpet crumbs off his lap as he clambered awkwardly to his feet. "Or had I best salute you as Mr. Edward Hyde-and-Seek?"

I shrugged, too tired to either appreciate his humour or dispute his analogy. I had certainly been burning the candle at both ends, companion to a semi-invalid by day and turning into Count Dracula by night. Or something along those lines. I helped myself to the remaining crumpets and asked the steward for some cucumber sandwiches.

"You needn't tell me about your day"—the detective smiled sympathetically—"as I'll wager it was not half so rewarding as my own." He stretched awkwardly and groaned. "I believe I've thrown out my back."

"How did you manage that?"

"I spent the better part of the day burgling the premises at 60 Suleiman Pasha Street."

"You don't say." This news failed to surprise me. By now I

knew and to a certain extent could anticipate a great many of my singular friend's habits of action. There was no question entering Fatima's flat had been on his mind from the moment he learned its whereabouts.

"It was no great business gaining entry. The fellah Majid had posted on watch had long since concluded there was scant possibility of Miss Fatima's return. I had to wake him to offer *baksheesh*, which, as you may anticipate, he had no trouble accepting. He'd been told to watch for the woman, after all, nothing or no one more. The rest was entirely none of his bailiwick. The concierge was of the same opinion and similarly accommodating. The lady's rent was paid up and he did not seem particularly surprised to receive a visitor who pressed pound notes upon him."

"This investigation is proving expensive," I noted as my sandwiches arrived.

"Her Grace can well afford it," the detective replied. "And I keep strict accounts. In any event, someone had been to the dancer's flat before me."

"What?"

"The place had already been, as the Scotland Yarders would put it, 'tossed.' Small wonder the concierge appeared unfazed. I felt like the second man who'd invented the wheel."

I was now fully awake. "Tossed? By whom?"

"Amateurs. Or at any rate people who didn't expect to find anything. Their efforts appeared cursory."

"Sent by Majid?"

"In addition to his watchman? I doubt it. Whoever they were, they anticipated she would be too clever for them—as indeed she was. The place is well furnished but conspicuously ordinary, if such a thing is possible. A single woman's residence, tastefully but not richly appointed in the French fashion, as befits the vicinity. Some inferior nudes by Vernet on one wall, risqué cartoons by Daumier on another. The noteworthy exception being her extravagant wardrobe and varied collection of footwear, which those who came before me had flung in all directions. Fatima evidently does, or did, a fair amount of entertaining, even maintaining a cabinet of spirits, some of which had evidently been sampled direct from the bottles by my predecessors. There was a gramophone which they had smashed to bits, unaware, I suspect, of its agreeable purpose. Or perhaps regarding its function as blasphemous. They also slashed the goose down mattress on an enormous bed that would not have been out of place in our gaol of the other night. Who knows, perhaps they found something hidden there, but I suspect not. A woman in her line of country is unlikely to be indiscreet about her private life, what with various guests and visitors having access to the place. And certainly, when she moved her field of operations to Shepheard's she took her most valuable possession with her."

"The pearls."

He nodded.

"So you found nothing of interest?"

"Far from it. I did claim to have had a rewarding day. Those who came before me were lazy and had persuaded themselves theirs was a fruitless errand. I worked from no such assumption and arguably have more experience in these matters. For a start, here is her portrait."

Reaching into his breast pocket, he carefully withdrew a photograph of a remarkably beautiful dark-haired woman with blazing eyes, a cruel mouth, and an inscrutable expression. Obviously taken for professional purposes, the picture had the single name, Fatima, in gilt cursive, emblazoned on the grey nether border along with the name and address of a photographer's studio in Alexandria.

"It was by no means hidden," he added, observing me closely as I studied the image. "It lay among several on an escritoire, along with bills of no great import. Invoices from the florist. The drawers were empty, to be sure. Anything of value had already been seized, but I doubt she was so careless as to incriminate herself on exposed paperwork."

"If she dances as well as she looks," I remarked, setting down my sandwich, "one can readily imagine standing room only at Ali Baba's Cave every night. But what did you actually uncover?" I knew my friend so well by now that I anticipated his love of the dramatic flourish.

He smiled as much as to say he appreciated my understanding and again reaching into his breast pocket laid down on the table between us a French passport, a faded *tricoleur* stripe on its binding.

"Open it," he commanded.

I did so and found a very different photograph of the same woman. Here she was blond, Caucasian, perhaps a bit younger, grinning like a schoolgirl, and was identified as Ghislaine Marie Zelle, age 23, born in Aix-en-Provence.

"So she's French," I remarked.

Holmes said nothing, but set beside it a tawny-hued Dutch passport with embossed lettering on the front. Inside was yet another image of the same woman, this time identified as Margareta Gertrude Grumet, 25, born in Rotterdam.

"Well, well."

"And this."

Her Turkish passport, a simple yellow page covered in Arabic with fragmentary English underneath, in which the same woman was identified as Fatima Johar, 26, born in

Constantinople/Istanbul.* In this photograph she wore the *niqub,* appeared Levantine, and was virtually unrecognisable.

"And this."

In her blue American passport, placed beside the others, she was Mary Jane Owens, 25, with freckles, from Nashville, Tennessee.

I sat back, staring at the documents before me. "Where were they?"

"That large, immovable bed of hers made me curious. Its corners pinned down a multicoloured Persian carpet. Its bulk and weight may have discouraged the others, who may have missed it in any case, but by dint of much straining and shoving, I managed to free one corner, hence my back injury. Crawling under the bed among the goose feathers and rolling back the liberated portion of rug, I found the knot in the floorboards that triggered open the ingenious cache beneath."

Holmes looked pleased with himself and I was tempted to applaud.

"So the woman is some kind of spy."

"Exactly," the detective agreed. "But for which side? Or, to put it another way, in whose pay?"

"Good questions," I allowed. "But has she taken up with the duke on assignment or from purely private motives?"

Holmes gave a derisive sniff. "Let us assume, for the present, her motives were professional and mercenary. And let us not forget: for all we know the lady is carrying yet another passport on her person as we speak. I should think it highly likely."

This was a daunting thought, but Holmes was pursuing

---

* It was around this period that the Turks began to transition the city's name.

his first. "Who might wish to know what about the Duke of Uxbridge?"

"Mycroft and his crowd? I believe you said you'd never named your client when you met with him at the Diogenes."

"True," the detective mused, "but regardless what could Uxbridge know of value to Whitehall? He couldn't even manage to obtain a digging permit, his chief object. Nothing then, unless he was somehow in league with the Turks, but if that were the case, why would he be so desperate for money? Spies are expensive. The Ottomans may be impoverished but surely would pay well for whatever services they imagine he could render. But, as we know, his bill at Shepheard's remains 'astronomical'"

"So we are dismissing the notion that Miss Fatima was in British employ?"

"For the present."

"Could she be working for the Turks? She carries a Turkish passport." I tapped the yellow paper.

Another snort. "That hardly signifies, given her collection. But the idea is not implausible. According to Mycroft, the Turks are rabidly suspicious of British objectives and intentions in the Mid-East. He suggested the Khedive is playing a double game. The Turks would give much, I've no doubt, to learn His Britannic Majesty's long-range plans for the region, especially the canal. Perhaps the lady is on retainer, plying admirers of different ranks and nationalities with music and drink in her flat, hours after hours, if you follow me."

"I do."

"Then at some point in all this maneuvering, the Turks stumble upon Uxbridge, a down-at-heels nobleman in desperate straits and attach someone to learn if Egyptology is in fact his real motive for being here or does he in fact harbour ulterior objectives? They worry he's playing the fop while spying for His Britannic Majesty and they engage Miss Fatima to keep an eye on him."

We pondered this possibility before the detective added, "If the Turks *are* her masters that might well explain the Khedive's orders to Monsieur Charpentier via Major Haki not to report the couple's disappearance. They are—or were—confident she would keep them apprised of the duke's movements."

"Speaking of which, ought we not report that disappearance and Miss Fatima's activities to the authorities? The duke may be in danger."

"Aye, there's the rub, my boy," Holmes rejoined. "Which authorities? We don't wish to repeat Charpentier's mistake and approach the wrong party. Do the British in point of fact desire to let the Turks know they've unmasked La Belle Dame sans Merci? If we report the lovers' disappearance, we may be reasonably sure that will happen. Everyone here is playing a deep game. Is our Major Haki working for Constantinople or Whitehall? Does anyone besides us know about Ohlsson's map, authentic or not? No," he concluded after a moment's further reflection, "for the present let us play our cards close to your regimental necktie."

"None of this brings us any closer to their whereabouts."

"It does not." He attempted another stretch. "Does this place have a steam room and might an honourably discharged Northumberland Fusilier obtain the use of it?"

They did boast such a room and Holmes and I shortly found ourselves basking in the facility, along with several other towel-draped patrons. Still reeling from the effects of the previous twenty-four hours, I must have dozed off. When I awoke,

Holmes's slender form was still beside me, motionless, but his eyes remained open. I sometimes wonder if he ever closed them.

"Have you made any headway on VR 61?"

He scowled. "I've cudgelled my brains and even dreamed about that wretched code, for it must be something of the kind, all to no avail. I keep writing it down and staring at it. 'Vacuum,' 'Vale,' 'Variety,' 'Veal,' 'Vector,' 'Viceroy,' 'Victoria,' 'Voisin,' *'Volte-face,'* 'Road,' 'Route,' 'Royal,' 'Rue,' 'Roi,' and so on. I have tried every possible combination in English and French, but perhaps we're dealing with another tongue entirely, German or Italian or who knows in what language the wretch was scribbling as he died?"

"Or have we just imagined he was scratching out anything at all?"

"An even worse possibility, though I'm sure we were seeing something." Exasperated, he slammed a fist into a neighbouring palm. "Are we dealing with a proper name? Someone's initials? Violet Something or are we back to Victoria Regina? A little calculating confirms her reign lasted sixty-three, not sixty-one years. Regardless, I cannot for the life of me reconcile the late queen empress in any form with Mustafa's dying revelations." He shook his head. "The possibilities are infinite. I even stopped at the British Consul this morning before my house-breaking and put it to the *chargé d'affaires,* but no one could tell me anything. And the number sixty-one was likewise no inspiration to anyone within hearing. There *is* a Victoria Road, but the numbers stop at 49, a milliner's emporium." He sighed and stretched again, evidently a painful endeavour. "Absent any progress I must allow time for what Dr. Freud would call my 'unconscious' to grapple with the problem."

Shortly thereafter, we made use of the showers and Holmes, finally feeling more like himself, departed in time for me to join Juliet at supper. She was still full of the day's adventure—poor woman, so long accustomed to segregation and routine, it was a major achievement to have ventured forth, and to my relief and delight she seemed none the worse for it.

"John, you are looking quite your old self," she observed in turn.

"It took long enough," was my moody rejoinder, "but I'm so pleased that today was a success."

"Have I ever told you of the time I was nearly gored by a water buffalo in Durban?" Lady Cunningham called to us from her end of the table.

And so our meal concluded and after a brandy and soda in the Common Room back at the club, I retired for bed, anticipating a much-needed night's rest.

But sleep did not come. I had been overstimulated by sights, sounds, and mysteries. I did the usual tossing and turning and finally gave it up, switching on the light and trying to switch off my brain by reading the copy of *Martin Eden* I had brought from home, but even Jack London's magic, which I normally enjoyed, was unable to divert me.

Finally, I threw aside the netting, put on my robe, and sat at the small desk that was part of my room's Spartan furnishings. As ex-military men, I suppose we were intended to find such simplicity a nostalgic plus.

I pulled out a sheet of foolscap and, like Holmes, wrote down *VR 61* as traced in the dirt by the dying waiter.

Then I wrote it out again. And again. And . . .

Then I saw something—something that astonished me. It was not Holmes's unconscious but my own that had performed the miracle. I squeezed my eyes shut, then opened them again and sat staring at what was essentially my accidental handiwork, hardly daring to move for fear that, like a dream after waking, the whole thing would abruptly vanish forever.

But vanish it did not. Hardly daring to move my eyes from the page, I fumbled for my clothes and stole from the room.

The city was deathly still in the hours before morning prayers, broken only by a distant cock crow. And it was chilly. In my haste, I had neglected to throw on a jumper, but as I limped as quickly as possible across the causeway, I soon grew accustomed to the temperature. Or perhaps I was too excited to care.

Shepheard's was likewise somnolent when I entered. Charwomen were beating and airing the omnipresent carpets, while others polished the teak and mirrors. The American Bar was conspicuously empty save one fellah washing an infinite number of drinking glasses and rinsing out carafes. I spied serried bottles of Uxbridge Elixir on a shelf behind him.

At the front desk, I asked for Colonel Arbuthnot's room. There was some difficulty about this at first as the clerk enquired who I was and gave me the usual folderol about not being allowed to give out such information.

"Mr. Dumfries, do you not recognise me? Must we pay another call on Monsieur Charpentier?"

That brought it all back to him.

"Colonel Arbuthnot is in room two-seventeen in the annex," he explained, and pointed me down another of the hotel's innumerable carpeted corridors, towards the end of which I located the lift operated by a sleepy boy, who shaking himself awake and mumbling apologies, took me up.

I knocked on the door of 217. I hated the idea of waking

the detective, especially as he was suffering the effects of back strain, but my discovery could not wait.

"My dear fellow." Holmes stood in the doorway, clad in a pale blue dressing gown.

"Were you asleep?"

"By no means. Come in."

I would not have conceived Shepheard's letting such a small space to any of its guests. It was clear Holmes had, from the first, attempted to economise on the duchess's behalf.

In the centre of the room he had assembled a nest of pillows and cushions, whose indentations informed me he had—as was his custom when meditating—been squatting there. The small place (perhaps originally intended for someone's maid) was choking on stale tobacco. It had proved more than a three-pipe problem.

"What is it, my dear fellow? You seem quite worked up."

"I am. Holmes . . ." Here I hesitated. What if I were mistaken?

"Would you like some water?"

I shook my head. "May I show you something?"

"By all means."

I looked about. "Have you some paper?"

"There's always my notebook. Will that do?"

"Of course."

He switched on a small lamp on a nightstand beside his monk-like bed, little more than a pallet, and flipped to a blank page. I couldn't help noticing that the page opposite was filled with repetitions of *VR 61*. The combination had been tried frontwards, backward, and in many random permutations.

"Holmes," I began again, "what if we didn't correctly make out what Mustafa scratched in the dirt?"

He blinked. "How do you mean?"

"Well," said I, trying to keep my voice steady, "we thought he wrote 'VR 61.'"

"That is what we both agreed we saw."

"But the man was dying; his hand was unsteady. Suppose what he actually wrote was this?"

And I showed him.

8

THE OTHER TREASURE MAP

It would be no exaggeration to say the detective's eyes bulged as he read what I had written.

"Watson!"

"I may be wrong—"

"You are not wrong!" He staggered about the room, a hand clapped to his brow, then returned in a rush to stare at the page. "There are moments in my work when intuition strikes like lightning and the truth is illumined in a single, stunning flash. You, my dear friend, my luminous light conductor, like Oedipus!—no, like Prometheus!—you have solved the riddle of the Sphinx!"

"Holmes, you are mixing metaphors. Contain yourself."

But he was unable to do this. "Don't you see, dear chap, what a vista this opens? What now lies before us?"

I was privately overwhelmed. The detective had, on occasion, sometimes grudgingly and at others with frank admiration, praised my efforts, but never in such a fashion as now.

This is what I had written: *VK 61.* In my room at the Khedivial I had not intended to write it; I was merely and numbly repeating the original lettering as Holmes had done, trying without method to force some meaning out of that senseless combination of letters and numbers. But with repetition and fatigue my hand had produced a different result. A *K* could be mistaken for an *R* if written by a trembling hand that inadvertently slurred the top of the *K*'s vertical column with the angled projection to the right.

The detective, circling the room and its pile of cushions ("excuse my little Ottoman empire," he said, gesturing to the pillows), muttering to himself as he envisioned the hapless man's predicament. "Mustafa, dying, cries out something. It could be an exclamation of agony, but that would more likely be a vowel than the consonant you maintain you heard. The latter suggests he was trying to articulate something specific. On the ground, impaled by the knife, he can barely move his forefinger to delineate his message. *V* he can manage, as he is not obliged to raise his fingertip from the ground. But *K*? *K* is well-nigh impossible. He achieves the downstroke but in extremis cannot lift his finger to form the rest, and what emerges instead is a messy *R*." He looked at me. "But he meant *K*. VK: Valley of the Kings."

"Yes, I thought 'VK' might somehow refer to the Valley of the—"

"More, my dear chap! Much more. Do you not recall Professor Tewfik's words when we asked how many tombs had been unearthed there? He said . . . 'some threescore,' which would indicate sixty sites, but he was generalising, wasn't he? Hence his use of the qualifier 'some.' As Dr. Freud has remarked, 'we must listen as well as observe.'"

"So '61' refers to—?"

"You will doubtless also recall Howard Carter explaining to us that every tomb site and its location in the valley has been numbered, photographed, and mapped on a grid."

"Oh, yes. Now I—"

"If I'm correct, sixty-one—assuming we've correctly read what was scratched in the dirt—must pertain to the supposed location of Tuthmose's theoretically unopened grave. This forms the basis of Duke Michael's conviction and his quest."

"I was thinking something along those lines."

He went on as though I had not spoken. "You know where we must go this morning, do you not?"

"I think I do."

"Without doubt, old man. Without a doubt in the world." The detective was throwing on clothing as we talked, hastily improvising an ensemble, using the small basin in the place to splash water on his face and clean his teeth. Normally meticulous as a cat in such matters, he was wasting no time.

"It must have happened something like this." With the toothbrush in his mouth he was hard to understand. "The duke and Miss Fatima were in the dining salon at supper. Mustafa, he of the long ears, serving at their table or nearby, likely overheard them talking excitedly of the place where His Grace was convinced the tomb of Tuthmose and its golden hoard were to be found. Is he, like everyone in this confounded place, on another payroll besides the hotel's?"

"Major Haki's?"

He rinsed his mouth. "We cannot be sure, but he now has information of conceivable worth. Does he report that information to those who pay for such extraneous gossip or does he choose to keep it to himself for the time being? Let us suppose, for the moment, Mustafa decides on the latter course of action—or rather of inaction. But then another Englishman appears, a retired army colonel, sporting a monocle and asking questions about the missing nobleman. This he does in fact report, after which he is instructed to keep me in sight."

He paused to lace his shoes.

"But then he came to us—"

"Not quite, Watson. He merely improvised when I recognised him as my shadow and we cornered him in the washroom. He claimed he was simply trying to speak with me alone, but in that moment I surmise he saw the chance of earning twice the coin for the same information. Sell us what he was already peddling to his paymasters, whoever they are. Cupidity got the better of his judgement. He thought to be rewarded from multiple sources for the same data. He wouldn't be the first to play that game," he added, holding out his hand.

I handed him his tie—my own tie, as it happened.

"You don't imagine they are still in Luxor, the duke and his lady friend? Over a month with only a carpet bag and travel case between them?"

"It appears unlikely, I grant you," the detective rejoined, knotting the tie, indifferent to its ownership. "What time does the Antiquities Service open, do you recall?"

"Ten, I think I remember seeing on the door when we were first there."

"Then we have time to breakfast. Good, as I suspect this will prove a longish day."

How right he was.

The huge dining salon had just begun serving by the time I entered and there couldn't have been a half-dozen guests in the whole of that palatial space. Knowing his preferences, I ordered for the detective, as he was occupied at the front desk sending a telegram. Notwithstanding the country's religious prohibitions, Shepheard's served its clientele rashers of bacon and all manner of ham. (Where they raised or harvested pigs for this purpose was something I never thought to ask.) In addition, I ordered eggs, porridge, and biscuits, though the latter, when they arrived, did not rival for lightness those prepared by the inimitable Mrs. Hudson.

Holmes returned from his errand and tucked into the food without comment, eating like a man who had not been fed in days. I fancied I could see the wheels churning inside his head as he gulped his tea.

It was my turn to do a bit of mind reading. "Do you really imagine Uxbridge and Miss Fatima have located the first entirely sealed tomb in modern times?"

"We have yet to ascertain for a fact the Valley of the Kings is where they actually went," was his only remark, "though I daresay we shall learn soon enough." He refused, however, to be drawn on the subject and kept taking out his watch. "And Mrs. Watson?"

"Today is Wednesday—mud bath day."

"What a voluptuous prospect that sounds."

The door to the Egyptian Antiquities Service had no sooner been unlocked by the commissionaire than we barged through it.

"Where is Chief Inspector Carter to be found?" Holmes demanded. His question occasioned some consternation. Wondering perhaps if the man spoke no English, the detective looked over his head in search of someone who did.

"Not here," the commissionaire informed him. "Carter gone."

"Gone? I beg your pardon!" he shouted to one of the clerks removing his hat, having evidently arrived from a different entrance. "I am Colonel Arbuthnot. You will perhaps remember I was here some time ago with my friend?," he said, gesturing to me. "We were talking to Chief Inspector Carter?"

The same look of consternation appeared on the clerk's face as he came over to us. "I am Abdul," he introduced himself. "I remember. Will you please to follow me?"

As he spoke, the establishment began to refill with those busy bees I had witnessed during our previous visit to this singular hive. The shuffling of papers had begun.

Puzzled and impatient, we followed Abdul, who led us to Carter's old workspace, which we found disconcertingly barren. On the long table where documents and charts abounded on our previous visit, there was now only wood scored with innumerable scratches and idly inscribed initials. The instinct to vandalise was not limited to the pyramids. Abdul indicated two chairs.

"Please to sit."

"What has happened?" Holmes demanded, still on his feet. "Where is Chief Inspector—"

"Mr. Howard Carter is no longer Chief Inspector in the Antiquities Service. He has resigned."

Of all the news we might have anticipated, this was the most shocking.

"Resigned?" The detective began to sink into one of the chairs, then evidently thought better of it and remained standing.

Abdul sighed. "It has been a long time coming. Years in fact."

Holmes shook his head like a pugilist who had absorbed a blow to it.

"Please explain more fully. It is most urgent that I confer with him."

Abdul sighed yet again, aware that others were now gathering about us. "Five years ago in Saqqara, the Chief Inspector got into a fracas with a crowd of French tourists he felt were defiling the excavation and flouting restrictions designed to keep the dig pristine. As I think you know, he is passionate on the subject."

I remembered Carter shooing off Arab children proposing to scar the pyramids with their handiwork.

"As he should be," Holmes commented.

"In the aftermath there followed an enormous to-do and brouhaha. One of the tourists in question proved to be a Frenchman of some consequence and relations between France and Egypt (that is to say, Constantinople) have been strained. A diplomatic rupture was threatened, a lawsuit was filed in Paris, and so on." Abdul sighed again. "The whole thing has dragged on interminably with the upshot that two days ago the Chief In—Mr. Carter, that is, gave his notice."

We sat in silence for a time. And then, assembling his faculties, Holmes asked, "Where are his maps?"

"Maps?"

"The Chief Inspector explained that all the sites and discoveries are mapped on a grid and—"

"Ah. *Those* maps. He has taken them."

"What?"

"Those maps are the personal property of Mr. Carter. He compiled them during the time of his employment with the Lord Carnarvon."

"All?" Holmes's look was incredulous.

"Most. Mr. Carter has in fact gone back to work for the Lord Carnarvon."

"In Cairo?"

Abdul gave a rueful smile.

"I believe he is currently back once more at Saqqara."

"Where is—?"

"Saqqara is near Memphis, for a time the capital and most

important city in ancient Egypt. There's a dig in progress there. There are regular trains," he added, anticipating the detective's next question. "It's only fifteen miles from where we stand, on the western bank of the river, just south of here."

Holmes stood for some moments, irresolute, before recollecting himself.

"You have been most helpful, Abdul. *Shukran*." Wearily he pressed pound notes into the man's hand.

Abdul gravely bowed his head, closing his hand around them. *"As-salamu alaykum."*

Outside the building, accustoming our eyes to the glare of the morning sun, which I now remembered Professor Tewfik explaining the infamous pharaoh Akhenaten referred to as the Aten, we were found by the telegraph messenger Holmes had instructed to seek us here.

Holmes tore off the envelope and handed the yellow page to me without comment.

3 4 5 JANUARY ONLY WINTER PALACE LUXOR NO LEFT LUGAGGE BILL OUTSTANDING H

"No reply," he told the boy, giving him some coins.

"Shukran." The messenger touched his cap, remounted his bicycle, and disappeared into plentiful mid-morning traffic.

Holmes looked about him. "So they came and went. Three days only."

"Went where? We seem to be back where we started."

His glum silence implied agreement. At length, he turned to face me.

"I must have a look at Carter's maps, Watson. It appears I must visit Saqqara."

"I will accompany you."

"That won't be necessary; I should be back by nightfall."

"That enables me to come along," I pointed out.

If Holmes was pleased by my offer, he gave no sign, but flagged a calash to take us to Ramses Station, where I dispatched a telegram of my own:

DEAREST WE ARE SIGHTSEEING BACK BY NIGHT-FALL YOUR DEVOTED J

As the place lay less than twenty miles from the Jardin des Plantes, I felt confident I should be back for supper, with no need for luggage of any kind.

On the dilapidated local, whose windows contained no glass, we travelled at a snail's pace, accumulating heat and dust from the Sahara, both of which soon flooded the carriage.

Holmes, a handkerchief tied over his mouth and nose, sat with eyes closed, his body oscillating gently with the motion of the train. Thus attired, he gave the appearance of a somnolent Wild West desperado.

Briefly out of sight of the Nile, there was nothing to behold but an ocean of sand. Soon my eyes fell closed as well, and thus without entirely realising it I began speaking aloud.

"So His Grace and Miss Fatima left The Winter Palace, which we are to surmise is a hotel of sorts, in Luxor on 5 January. Where did they go next? No one we know has reported sight of them in over a month and we've established His Grace did not have much money. In Luxor he failed to pay The Winter Palace, yet another reckoning."

Holmes surprised me by responding, "But if Miss Fatima, also known as Mary Jane Owens, alias Ghislaine Marie Zelle or possibly Margareta Gertrude Grumet, was in fact being financed by the Turks, she may be in possession of 'discretionary' assets. In addition to which, we've no way of knowing at this juncture what they might have uncovered in the Valley of the Kings."

"Did they even go there after Luxor?"

"I think it likely. The place is a mere twenty or so miles more and they'd come all this way. Suppose His Grace's horse by the name of Tuthmose the Fifth has actually come in."

From his drowsy tone and the expansive yawn which followed it, I inferred his eyes remained closed as well.

"Surely such a discovery would have made the newspapers by now. Whatever her real name, it all comes down to why our Miss Fatima was with him in the first place. Did it start as some kind of assignment and turn into something—?"

"Genuine?" my companion finished for me. "Or was it the other way around?" he mused. "An ardent infatuation discovered by the Turks leads to gainful employment? In any event, when they left Luxor, did the duke and the dancer remain together or split up?"

"Assuming they had no falling-out, I should think a couple certainly less conspicuous than a single woman travelling alone—especially in these parts," I remarked. "Then again, we may be reasonably certain she has well-placed friends."

"She may indeed," the detective conceded. I knew we were both wondering yet again about the busy and mysterious Turkish major Haki.

The train began to slow, causing us to open our eyes and peer about at our surroundings.

"Do you know what troubles me most, my dear doctor?"

"Why the man Mustafa was dispatched with an ancient Egyptian knife?"

"That is certainly a suggestive detail," the detective admitted. "Was an antique weapon employed for some theatrical effect? At present, it is hard to conceive of another purpose, but it is foolhardy to theorise in the absence of more data. Presently we are underserved in that department. But in fact I am puzzled by something infinitely more mundane. I simply cannot believe, wherever she ultimately travels, whoever she really is, and whatever her true motives, that Miss Fatima has not returned for her pearls."

There was silence as we both shied away from a troubling explanation.

The dig at Saqqara-Memphis was no great distance from the station, a structure itself hardly worthy of the appellation. Hundreds of fellaheen in soiled, sweat-stained white galabeyas and turbans made a clinking anvil chorus as they tilled and chipped at the rocky soil with mattocks, shovels, rakes, pick-axes, and trowels under the supervision of Howard Carter, whose centre of operations lay under a series of low-slung Bedouin-style marquees.* Around him were former egg crates, wicker baskets, and boxes snatched from other lines of work, now filled with catalogued and annotated samples from the dig, which seemed devoted to exposing a large structure.

Beneath the tents, on several aligned planks drooping between two sawhorses, we had no difficulty recognising Carter's precious charts. Note cards and additional papers with his drawings were held in place against the light breeze employing local stones as paperweights.

But dominating the entire landscape and driving for the moment all thoughts of our visit and the reasons behind it was a pyramid of the kind I—and I daresay few others—had never seen before.

---

* In modern times, Saqqara has proved the most rewarding of all Egyptian archeological digs.

"Interesting, is it not?" Howard Carter had been advised of our presence and now appeared behind us, his head covered by a battered topi. "A very early attempt to build such a thing as a pyramid. As you may gather, the original angle was too steep to be sustained and so the incline was softened part-way up with the crooked result you witness, the only example of its kind in the world. May I ask what brings you here?" he went on briskly. Carter was not a man for small talk.

"I was sorry to learn of your resignation," the detective began.

"No great misfortune. It was long overdue." His feelings on the subject were delivered in a studiously indifferent tone of voice, but I was of the opinion his exit from the important post that had so long been his was and would likely remain a sore point.

His Bedouin-style headquarters, I now realised, reeked of goat, whose distinctive, musky aroma in an instant took me back to my days on the northwest frontier where the odor was omnipresent. It is peculiar that smell has such a powerful effect on memory. In an instant I was transported back thirty years. Holmes, with no such associations, was querying the archeologist.

"And you've resumed work on this building—"

"The temple of Amun, king of the gods. Until he was replaced for a time by the Aten. I'm a busy man, Colonel. Would you mind coming to the point?"

Holmes glanced at me briefly.

"The point," he said softly, "is VK 61."

Carter, who had been occupied with his notes, now jerked up his head and glared at the detective, who returned his look with a steadfast regard of his own.

"Who are you?" the Egyptologist demanded.

"My name is Sherlock Holmes."

There was another pause, and then a faint smile. Had Holmes told him he was Tuthmose, he could not have astonished him more.

"I thought there was something."

"And this is Dr.—"

"Yes, yes," the other interposed, turning to me and easing his bulk into a canvas chair, evidently relishing this turn of events. "I follow your accounts of the great Holmes in *The Strand Magazine*. My cousin forwards back issues to me." His smile broadened. "'The Bruce Partington Plans'! 'The Speckled Band'! 'The Adventure of the Devil's Foot'! 'Silver Blaze'! He rattled them off like the lyrics to a patter song. "My favorite diversions. Well, well, Sherlock Holmes in Egypt! What brings you and your— Wait, don't tell me," he interrupted himself as he pieced the thing together. "It cannot be Tuthmose. Ah, yes." He removed his topi, wiping his sunburnt forehead with his sleeve as he surveyed us. "It's 'The Case of the Missing Nobleman.' Still no sign?"

He unscrewed a canteen as he spoke and held it out to each of us in turn.

"No sign," Holmes acknowledged, dropping his Windsor drawl and accepting the drink. "But he *was* on the trail of Tuthmose and recently went down to Luxor."

"Up," corrected the archeologist.

"I beg your pardon?"

"Luxor is *up*river. In Egypt compass headings like north and south only confuse geography. What most people think of as Lower Egypt is in fact Upper Egypt. And vice versa, wouldn't you know."

"I stand corrected. What is the precise total thus far of discovered tombs in the Valley of the Kings?"

"Sixty, to date. In time, doubtless there will be more."

Holmes glanced at me meaningfully, as much to say, "You see, Watson, your deduction is confirmed," before speaking aloud to the expert. "Uxbridge believes he has found the location of a sixty-first."

The archeologist continued to regard us thoughtfully. "And what makes you conclude such a thing? I ask because there is no such designation as 'VK.'"

The detective and I exchanged looks. Seeing our consternation, Carter smiled. "Now if you had said 'V*R*,' that would have been a very different matter."

"What?" we exclaimed simultaneously.

Carter smiled again. "As the French discovered the valley, their maps unsurprisingly originated and have been continued in that language. The designation 'VR' stands for 'Vallée des Rois,' French for 'Valley of the Kings.'"

"Dear God," I murmured.

"I beg your pardon?"

Out of the corner of my eye I could see the detective rearranging his thoughts as if they were pieces of a jigsaw puzzle wrongly jammed together. At length he looked up, shaking his head at the wonder of it.

"Ah, Watson," he addressed me. "You will recall that on other occasions I have observed that a chain of perfect logic can nonetheless lead one to an entirely erroneous conclusion. As it turns out, Mustafa wrote correctly from the first," he now realised. "It was merest chance that led us to what he was trying to tell us, and thence to you, Chief Inspector."

"I led us down a false trail," I found myself conceding bitterly. "He wasn't trying and failing to scrawl a *K*."

"Not at all, my dear fellow. Without your stroke of inspiration there would have been no trail at all."

It was now Carter's turn to appear flummoxed. "Who is Mustafa? I haven't the least idea what either of you is talking about."

"I know," the detective returned, "and I fear I have neither the time nor my client's permission to divulge any of it. I can only tell you it was a grotesque piece of good guesswork—yes, guesswork—by Dr. Watson here that accidentally succeeded in unravelling the duke's destination, which we otherwise might never have learned. 'VR' and 'VK' are not dissimilar, after all. Watson's brilliant serendipity managed to be wrong and right at the same time. Another time perhaps we will laugh about it, but time is not ours to waste at present." He stood. "May we examine your maps?"

"By all means." Intrigued to find himself in the detective's company, and his interest additionally piqued by the prospect of an investigation, Carter rose, put on his glasses, and rearranged the charts on his ad hoc work table. "But I'm not sure they will prove useful. Each tomb is numbered as it is found, but there is no sequence that suggests where the next discovery will lie."

We pored over the huge map with its indications and numerals set forth in the archeologist's meticulous hand. *VR* was omnipresent, albeit in tiny cursive.

"Where was the first Tuthmose's tomb discovered?" Holmes enquired.

"Far up the valley. Here." Carter indicated the place with a tapping forefinger. "You see it is labelled '1.' Subsequent generations have kept distributing their remains downwards towards the mouth or entrance of the valley. The numbers go up as the land itself descends, as you see."

"According to Professor Tewfik, Uxbridge spoke about a part 'down' in the valley that had not been explored."

Carter shook his head. "That's next to impossible, gentlemen. Even as we speak, fellaheen are crawling over every inch of the place, a veritable termite colony of activity, some of them my own people, digging on Lord Carnarvon's behalf, under my direction, to be sure."

Holmes stared at the map, pondering this answer. "Did he really mean 'down'?" the detective wondered.

"Who?"

"The duke."

Carter retrieved his canteen and secured the lid. "I don't follow."

"You said a moment ago that the compass confuses geography. As a relative beginner, isn't it possible that what Uxbridge referred to as 'down' might more correctly be termed 'up,' that is, towards the valley mouth, rather than its recesses? Especially if, as you say, the more recent ossuaries keep edging in that direction."

Wordlessly both men returned to their scrutiny of the map.

"I see nothing that answers your description," Carter commented at length, his brow beginning to crease with an impatient frown. There was only so much time the man felt could be spared from his labours.

"Is there any part of the valley mouth that is, for any reason, inaccessible? Geographically or perhaps legally off-limits?" the detective persisted, not raising his eyes from the map.

"Only the walkway trestles built near the site of Ramses the Seventh's tomb. The site is very popular with tourists and therefore it cannot be interfered with," the other answered matter-of-factly.

Then, hearing his own words, the archeologist froze, his small fists plunged down upon the chart beneath his gaze.

"Oh God."

"When you eliminate the impossible," Holmes offered

quietly, "whatever remains, however improbable, must be the truth."

"'*Trestles*'!" I now remembered.

"What?" They looked at me.

"Mustafa's cry that I couldn't make out as he ran towards me. I knew it began with a *T*! And I knew it couldn't be 'Tourette's.' It was 'Trestles.'"

Holmes pressed my arm with a greater force I am sure than he intended. "Are you sure?"

I nodded. "Quite sure now. He was trying to tell us and show us at the same time, delivering value for money as he—"

"No wonder the scoundrel wanted a free hand to dig where he pleased!" Carter exclaimed, referring, I knew, to Uxbridge. With an oath, he abruptly thrust aside the canvas flap and left the tent, shouting instructions in animated Arabic. Holmes and I waited where we stood, listening to an exchange neither of us could understand.

"Well done, my dear fellow. Well done," the detective murmured.

Several minutes passed before the gibberish outside ceased and the tent flap was again thrust aside.

"I've called off my boys," Carter explained, a trifle breathless, now rummaging among his papers. With an exclamation, he found a schedule and, putting on his glasses, ran his finger down the columns. This was succeeded by another shout. "If I bustle, I can be in Cairo tonight in time to make the seven-forty Star of Egypt to Luxor. The accommodations are designed for tourists, so the fittings are altogether excellent and single berths usually available on short notice. It's a fifteen-hour journey, so I recommend the Star, as travel at night helps pass the time."

"I shall also return to Cairo," the detective said, "but I

have additional considerations and arrangements which make it unlikely I will be able to join you until the following day."

The archeologist frowned. "Such as? I am still responsible for much in the Valley of the Kings."

Holmes threw out his arms in an all-encompassing gesture. "In addition to requiring more than what I'm standing in, I must inform my client of these developments."

"Your client?" Carter had missed Holmes's previous reference to his principal.

"Her Grace, the Duchess of Uxbridge. It was she who engaged me to find her missing husband. She and her brother-in-law are in Cairo and will likely wish to accompany me."

"I see." The Egyptologist carefully removed his glasses and folded them into a dented case, which displayed his faded initials. "In which case, perhaps we had best notify Professor Tewfik, as well."

"Most certainly, if you think it proper."

It took me but a moment's reflection to understand Carter's reasoning, namely that by alerting the director of the museum as to our intentions, the former Chief Inspector of the Egyptian Antiquities Service was hoping to repair some of the damage occasioned by his resignation from that body. A good word on his behalf from the professor should their expedition bear fruit might well serve to ingratiate Carter once more with the Egyptian authorities.

"Thank you, Mr. Holmes."

It was the detective's turn to frown. "As Sherlock Holmes is not officially in Egypt, might I ask you to continue addressing Colonel Arbuthnot?"

The idea of participating, however tangentially, in a case involving Sherlock Holmes appeared to please Carter enormously. "To be sure, Colonel Arbuthnot," he responded, proffering a mock salute, before turning to me. "And you, Doctor? You are still under your own auspices, I take it? You will join Colonel Arbuthnot on tomorrow evening's train, of course."

I stood between them, having said nothing to this point, but glanced at the detective, who by his expression I knew recognised my dilemma.

"There can be no question of my going to Luxor," I said.

"Why on earth not?" the expert demanded, making no attempt to conceal his surprise. "Have you no wish to see this affair to its conclusion? You are always the chronicler of such doings."

I thought I could sense on his part a vague hope that he might be included by name in such a chronicle.

"He has every wish in the world," Holmes answered for me. "Watson here is as much responsible as anyone in this business for the progress we have made thus far. But it cannot be."

"Thank you, but Holmes," I protested feebly, "you yourself said earlier, we don't know for a certainty that Uxbridge and Miss Fatima even reached the Valley of the Kings, only that they stayed three nights in Luxor. We cannot know if they found the unopened tomb of Tuthmose."

"'Fatima'?" Carter interjected, clearly puzzled. "*The*— What can that . . . 'performer'" was the word he settled on, "have to do with all this?"

Holmes ignored the question and looked at me, his grey eyes shining.

"Oh, they found it, to be sure, my dear fellow. That is the tragedy."

Holmes and I said little on the short journey back to town. Each knew what the other was thinking and all that needed to be said had been communicated within Howard Carter's Saqqara tent. For my part, while I ached to see the thing to its finish with all the curiosity that a lifetime's experiences by the detective's side had accustomed me, I cannot say that I dwelt on the matter. I had no intention of leaving Juliet for an unforeseeable length of time.

At Ramses Station, Carter bid us a hasty farewell, promising to see Colonel Arbuthnot in Luxor twenty-four hours hence. "Doctor, you shall be missed." He pumped my hand in the same vigorous motion as when we first met at the Antiquities Service, before hurrying off to purchase a berth on the sleeper. As he had ample supplies for himself in Luxor and often made the journey, his requirements were simpler than the detective's.

Holmes and I were left to bid each other perfunctory goodbyes.

"Do let me know how you get on," said I, shaking his hand, something I seldom did.

"Depend upon it, I shall, my dear fellow," Holmes responded, returning my grasp with a firm pressure of his own, before stepping onto the platform, his tall, thin form towering for a time above the rest.

I returned to the Khedivial Club in time for a wash and change of clothing before joining Juliet for supper. There I regaled her with descriptions of Saqqara-Memphis and its unique crooked pyramid, and spoke with pardonable satisfaction of Howard Carter's enthusiasm for my published accounts of Holmes's cases.

Juliet listened and put the occasional question to me, but I could see she was distracted. The more I endeavoured to amuse her, the more distant I sensed her becoming. When I queried her on the subject, she informed me Lady Cunningham had suffered what was termed "a setback" by Dr. Singh. I cannot say this news astonished me, for it was my medical opinion that her situation was not a promising one.

"I am so sorry to learn this. Let us hope her relapse is a temporary state of affairs and that she will soon be herself again."

Juliet toyed with her food in a way that made me uneasy. Loss of appetite is not a good sign.

"Dearest," I said, "are you also under the weather? You have been making such progress."

She stared at me for what seemed an inordinate length of time. "John," said she finally, "I may be a convalescent, but do you take me for a child as well?"

"Juliet!"

"Because you are certainly treating me like one, with the result that I begin to act the part. It is a role for which I am unsuited."

"My dear—"

"Your notions of the helpless female, the damsel in distress, and so forth, are out of date, romantically speaking. I am not to be confused with some Dresden doll to be dusted like a fragile porcelain, set on a shelf, and patronised, if I'm spoken to at all!" Her vehemence astounded me, but she was far from finished. "There are many subjects you have chosen to brush aside during our married life—women's suffrage being a prime example—and over time I have fallen into the habit of subservience to your views and judgements. In doing so I have gradually subsumed my own character. That is my mistake. Isolated here I have had time to think."

"Juliet, what on earth has brought this on?"

"What has brought it on is the fact that I can tell when you are keeping things from me. And it places me in a suspicious relation to you that I do not care for at all."

"What can you possibly mean?" I was sensible of my heart thumping in my chest and wondered if it were not about to burst.

"I don't know what I mean," she responded. "That is for you to say."

I felt myself turning scarlet. The sympathies between us were by this time so acute there was no point in persisting to deny what she had already intuited. My fictions had been detected, if not specified, and I had only succeeded in alienating her by the use of them. She was now staring across the table at me with unblinking eyes.

I heaved a tremulous sigh. Rather than degrade myself in a further series of entangling, and possibly contradictory, stories, I decided to make a clean breast of it.

"You are right," I began. "I have been dishonest. I will tell you what has happened."

She heard me out in silence as I related everything. If I expected exclamations or interjections during certain portions of my narrative, I was disappointed. When I confessed crawling inside the Great Pyramid with Holmes, she said not a word. When I described the performance at the Cave of Ali Baba, she remained mute. As I related the murder of Mustafa and my arrest, her eyes widened, but still she did not speak. Not stopping there, I informed her of Professor Jourdan's cut throat, Phillips's fall to his death at Abu Simbel, and Bechstein's mysterious neglect of his compass. She listened attentively to my entire recital, at the end of which I found myself sagging from exhaustion, my back taut as if it had been I, not Holmes, who had strained it shoving aside Fatima's unwieldy bed.

"And that, my dear, is the truth, the whole truth, and nothing but the truth," I concluded heavily.

After some moments of evident contemplation, Juliet resumed her supper. This was not what I expected. Unsure of what I was meant to say or do following my confession, I watched in silence as she ate. Finally, I could bear it no longer.

"What are you thinking? Dearest, please tell me. As I told you at the outset, I believed this to be nothing more than a simple missing persons case. But once it proved otherwise, I found I was unable to disengage my participation. That is intended as an explanation, not an excuse. I am truly sorry for having deceived you, but I knew you would disapprove. By the time matters developed as they did, my involvement was involuntary but total. Old habits die hard."

"They don't appear to have died at all."

What could I say to that?

"I cannot abide a liar."

Or that?

Finally she set down her cutlery and faced me once more. "Isn't the truth better? Isn't it now a load off your chest?" she asked. "It certainly is off mine. When I know you are keeping secrets from me, my brain leaps to the worst possible imaginings."

"What could be worse than murder?" I could not help wondering aloud.

"A husband and wife who fail to understand one another," she answered without hesitation. "John, if you are not on the Star of Egypt tomorrow night, bound for Luxor, do not bother returning home."

9

ALLAH'S BREATH

"Watson!"

It was not often that I succeeded in surprising Sherlock Holmes (I had done so recently, to be sure), but my presence with a valise just in time to board the gleaming Star of Egypt the following night as it was leaving Ramses Station clearly caught the detective off guard, as it did the duchess and Professor Tewfik. Seated opposite Holmes in the lounge car, they had clearly been told not to expect me, but as Howard Carter predicted, single berths were in fact to be had at the last minute if one did not object to sharing compartments with strangers. At the window the clerk asked if mine was to be a return ticket, as many sightseers typically preferred to journey back via *dahabeah*, a picturesque and stately steamer trip down the Nile, ending, if one chose, as far north as Alexandria. This choice I declined and I joined the others after depositing my bag onto the rack above the berth in my compartment, which, as it chanced, boasted no other occupant.

"We are advised to lock our windows whenever the train stops," the detective cautioned me, "as local thieves using fishing rods are seemingly adept at extracting one's valuables within less than a minute's time."

"Many thanks." I looked about. "Where is—?"

"Lord Darlington is indisposed," the duchess explained, "and will join us in a day or so. Assuming," she added pointedly, "that this excursion will last that long."

It occurred to me that fifteen hours in Her Grace's frosty presence might well seem like thirty and that it was a good thing part of the time we should all be asleep.

Professor Tewfik, as well, seemed out of sorts. He was determined to accompany us, and doubtless the last-minute nature of the trip had upset his own demanding schedule. He appeared flustered, searching furiously among documents and books as if fearing in his hasty departure he had omitted something of importance.

"Sorry. So sorry," he kept repeating. His eyes bulged with each repetition of the word.

The duchess did not acknowledge this or any of us, but stared fixedly out the window, ignoring the setting sun, as the train crept through the outskirts of the city, crossing the Imbaba Bridge to follow the Nile south along its western bank. We were just in time to see the pyramids of Giza and the Sphinx silhouetted in the gold penumbra of the Aten's dying glory. If the duchess was affected by this heart-stopping spectacle she gave no sign, and darkness shortly descended like a dropped curtain. Now only occasional pinpricks of light dotted the night's black velvet and soon even those intermittent glimmers lay behind us and the Star of Egypt, like a sinuous, lone glowworm, was wending its way across the Sahara.

Silence appeared to have descended with the sun as well. I was about to light a cigarette, but a sudden look in the window's reflection from Her Grace caused me to think better of it. Excusing myself from the charged atmosphere, I went onto the platform for a smoke, where Holmes shortly joined me.

"My dear fellow, I had no expectation you would find yourself able to accompany us. What happened?"

"It was a simple matter of putting my foot down," I explained. "I told Juliet she cannot expect to be treated like some Dresden doll, dusted like a fragile porcelain, set on a shelf, and patronised, if spoken to at all! I suggested her notions of romantic love were perhaps out of date and it was time for a new candor between us."

"Indeed." In the darkness the detective's eyes shone. I did not care to pursue the origin of that gleam.

"What have I missed?"

Holmes lit his own cigarette and blew smoke. "More of Her Grace's airs and graces. She wants to know why she is being asked to visit Luxor, a question I cannot answer to her satisfaction."

"What did you say?"

"I told her it was my belief that her husband did in fact locate the tomb of Tuthmose the Fifth—as he would have been—but that in order to understand what became of the duke afterwards, it was necessary to confirm the discovery itself."

"And the mysterious Darlington?"

He shrugged. "Continues mysterious. 'Indisposed' is such a convenient catch-all. It is always possible," the detective conceded, turning over the question in his mind as he spoke, "that Darlington is precisely what he seems, a shy schoolmaster from Staines with scholarly ambitions, who nurses understandably ambivalent feelings towards his elder brother and his squandered inheritance." But his tone belied his words.

"Have you had word from Mr. Carter? A telegram from Luxor?"

"No, but to my way of thinking that is not significant. If Carter has confirmed the find, I think he would believe it unwise to trust such information to the telegraph. On reflection, it might be argued the fact that he has not communicated augurs better than if he had."

"Ah, yes. The site would soon be as crowded as Piccadilly Circus with gawkers, the press, and thieves. Stop a bit," I added, holding him by the coat as he made to leave the platform. "Assuming you are correct and that Uxbridge dug in a forbidden section of the valley, how did he pay for the labour? I doubt fellaheen, experienced after centuries in these matters, would dig for promises."

"You forget, Doctor, the duke had a silent partner with resources of her own."

"Turkish resources?"

"Why not? If the duke unearthed the gold of Tuthmose, the Khedive would certainly claim the lion's share, which would unquestionably offset their expenses and more than justify their outlay. But there is another possibility," he added, as the idea struck him.

"And what might that be?"

"That Miss Fatima has invested Turkish dinars on her own behalf."

"Double-dealing?"

"Based on her passport collection it seems the only kind of dealing she knows."

"A dangerous game, surely."

"But one she has played before."

At this moment the train abruptly lurched to a stop, throwing us against the bulkheads.

"So sorry, gentlemen," a cheerful Levantine conductor announced as he passed us. "A camel caravan. We'll soon be on our way again."

"Is this a frequent occurrence?" the detective asked.

"Yes, but not so much at night. Good evening, gentlemen." With a crisp salute, he left us to contemplate this prospect.

"No wonder the journey takes fifteen hours," I commented.

"Shall we go back and face Her Grace's music?" Holmes asked. "Staying out here might be misinterpreted."

"Or it might not," I felt bound to point out.

The duchess was where we left her, gazing with unseeing eyes at her own immobile reflection in the window. The woman was as unknowable as when we were first introduced. I found myself remembering a comment Freud made to me during one of our Vienna walks, "What does a woman want?" he asked, though I'm not certain his question was addressed to me.

Professor Tewfik, preoccupied entering memoranda in the ledger propped unsteadily on his lap, looked up briefly, mumbling, "Sorry, sorry," yet again, before bending over his mysterious notations.

I now had the leisure to inspect my surroundings and must confess I was pleased. While the Star of Egypt was perhaps not on a par with such rolling masterpieces as the Orient Express, it was nonetheless a first-class affair, obviously—as Carter indicated—built to accommodate wealthy sightseers in this part of the world. The voices we overheard were invariably excited English or American. The fourteen carriages themselves were painted beige, an attempt, I imagined, to suggest or blend in with desert sands. The gilded lettering on each wagon-lit was named for an Egyptian deity. Inside, marquetry had been replaced by mirrors and the upholstery was leather instead of cloth, but otherwise the Pullmans were strikingly similar to their European counterparts, not surprising when one of the stewards (a Maltese, who, like the rest of the staff, spoke Arabic, English, or French with ease) informed me the coaches had been built in France. Our compartments were clean and ingeniously designed, the linens immaculate, and the furnishings never less than tasteful.

Uncertain in every sense of what was yet to come, I sat back and considered our silent company, for it occurred to me we none of us had much to say to one another, or rather, we had much to say, but I sensed each considered it prudent to keep his own counsel. The duchess, who might or might not be involved with her "indisposed" brother-in-law, could not hope to settle her husband's estate, much less inherit his title and device, until and unless Michael, eleventh duke of Uxbridge, was confirmed dead. Holmes was playing what he would term a long shot, believing that all such questions would be answered when we reached the Valley of the Kings. Tewfik, desperate for artifacts to include in his museum's insufficient collection, was likewise counting on the outcome. Would he startle the world by obtaining even the partial contents of the first unopened pharaonic tomb? And Howard Carter, not present, but doubtless anticipating our arrival in Luxor, was certainly counting on a major discovery, hoping such a find would aid his own rehabilitation.

And I? Was I here because, as the faithful water-carrier for the detective, I was bound to see where things led and ultimately write about them? Or was I present because of the ultimatum presented me by wife? It was apparent that from this point forward relations between us must be altered. I could only hope that henceforward they would be altered for the better. It is hard for the leopard to rearrange his spots (and still qualify as a leopard), but I had been given to understand in no uncertain terms that unless I made some fundamental change in my modus operandi, things would go hard with us. By this time I had absorbed enough of my wife's lexicon that what I regarded as "change" Juliet (always assuming she defeated her ailment) I knew would characterise as "growth."

At eight-thirty the dinner gong was mercifully sounded, breaking in upon my thoughts, and our little party, morose as ever, proceeded to the dining car. Each damasked table had an Egyptian rose centrepiece and the menu (which I managed to save but have since misplaced) offered an enticing variety, consisting of a choice of Pawpaw Cocktail, the ever-popular Nile perch in a remoulade sauce, or Crumbled Steak and asparagus with something called "Cream Sauce Princess." There was also, if memory serves, roast turkey with Liver Stuffing St. James, assorted vegetables, and Diplomat Pudding or Pêche Melba.

Had any of us known what lay in store, I wonder if we would have ordered differently.

"What a shame Lord Darlington was feeling unwell," I remarked in an effort to thaw the communal ice.

"Darlington will join us as soon as he can," was all the duchess offered, covering her wine glass before the steward was able to pour the chilled rosé. It certainly struck me we had no need of anything more chilled than things already were.

"Professor Tewfik," Holmes asked, spooning his pudding after a further uncomfortable silence during which we concluded our meal, "you've doubtless visited the Valley of the Kings?"

"To be sure, Colonel. On many occasions. I may say by this point I know it quite well."

The professor sounded relieved that someone had found a conversational gambit.

"It is easily accessible from Luxor, I take it?"

"Only about twenty miles distant. In cooler weather, such as this time of year, the trip is quite manageable. Luxor, as you know, is on the eastern bank of the river, while much of Thebes, the old capital, and the valley itself lie on the west, but the trip via felucca is mere minutes and the road thereafter to the ossuaries has been smoothed for tourists and is well maintained."

"So the fact now confirmed that the duke and his"— Holmes did not lift his eyes from his pudding—"associate were three nights in Luxor suggests they had ample time to cross the river and see what was there?"

"In theory more than ample." Tewfik also tried not to look at the duchess, who remained silent, concentrating on her Pêche Melba.

Our attempts at conversation appeared to have been exhausted following this exchange. It had occurred to me to mention Juliet and her experiences at the Al Wadi, but on further thought I rejected the idea. Matters here revolved around the duchess and her missing husband; my private concerns were none of hers. Or Holmes's, for that matter.

Shortly thereafter, the awkward meal came to an end and the unhappy group dispersed, heading for our wagon-lit. Holmes and Professor Tewfik had jointly reserved their compartment and naturally the duchess had her own deluxe suite at the end of the car.

Readying myself for bed, I briefly opened the transom to air the small room and was startled by the rush of wind and a slight spray of sand. In my drowsy state I attributed this to the great rate of speed at which I supposed we were travelling. After my recent conversation with Juliet and the ill-feeling aboard the train, the prospect of sleep was by no means unwelcome. As a rule I enjoyed trains and had no difficulty letting them sway me into the arms of Morpheus.

Mindful of Holmes's injunction regarding thieves amid the possibility of additional night-time camel caravans, I closed and locked my window before climbing onto my narrow bed. There, lulled by the gentle rocking of the train, I drifted off, looking forward with anticipation to whatever we would find in the Valley of the Kings and drowsily contemplating a triumphant homecoming that would reunite me with my wife.

It was some hours later and I was entirely unconscious when I became dimly aware of a soft but persistent knocking, which I finally realised was at my own door. As I was obliged to fumble for the blue night-light in unfamiliar darkness, it was some moments before I unfastened the bolt and opened the door to behold the Duchess of Uxbridge, dressed in night clothes underneath a belted robe of pink quilt.

"Your Grace!"

"May I come in?" She did so without waiting for an answer, shutting the door behind her. It was about this time that I realised the train had stopped; also, that it had begun to rain. In my dull state it did not occur to me that in Egypt this was impossible.

"More camels?"

"I don't think so. It wasn't a sudden stop. Something. I don't know. You are a doctor." I wasn't sure how this last fact figured into her computations, but the woman was clearly frightened and possibly with reason, for we could now make out shouting up and down our carriage.

"Wait here." Throwing on my own robe and slippers, I stepped into the corridor and seized a conductor who was rushing past.

"What has happened?" I demanded, holding him fast.

He favored me with a wild look. "Khamsin!" he cried. "Pull down all the shades and secure them!" before shaking himself free and rushing on, repeating his instructions.

I had no idea what "khamsin" meant or referred to (a horde of desert bandits out of The Arabian Nights was all I could manage; had they somehow blocked the train?), but I stepped back into my compartment, where the duchess, ashen-faced, sat where I had left her on the edge of the lower berth.

"What is it?"

"I'm not sure, but we're to pull down the shades," and leaning past her, I did, tying off the cord on the lower edge of the dark leathern curtain to the cleat on the sill. I now realised that the rain was improbably not striking the carriage roof, but pelting solely at the windows.

"It isn't rain," the duchess remarked, as though hearing my thoughts. "It's sand."

So it was—sand being buffeted by increasing wind. The sound was hypnotic, the aural equivalent of watching crashing waves or staring at flames in the grate.

"Talk to me. Please."

"What about?"

"Anything. Only keep talking." She looked about the small dimly lit place in search of a topic. "Are you married?"

"Yes."

"Happily?"

Before I could frame an answer there was another knock on my door, followed by the entrance of Holmes.

"Have you seen the duchess? Oh, I beg your pardon!" he added, spying her and directing a quizzical glance at myself.

The woman regarded the detective briefly but said nothing.

"Holmes, what is 'khamsin,' do you know?"

"I do now," replied the detective, who was already dressed. Professor Tewfik, also dressed, joined him in the doorway. "Khamsin is what one would call a mistral in the South of France," he explained. "Is that correct, Professor?"

"Yes, meaning 'Great Wind.'" The museum director nodded. In the gloom, his eyes were starting from their sockets and he was breathing in the wrong places. "Khamsin is our name for a sirocco, or kamikaze, as they term it in Japan. Here it denotes a typhoon of sand, the winds capable of whipping up the Sahara at speeds of over a hundred miles an hour. The natives call it 'Allah's Breath.' It is rare for this time of year," he assured us hastily, "but one closes tight the shades to prevent injury from flying glass in case the windows should break."

The duchess had not moved from where she sat but pressed a fist to her mouth.

"How long does this last?"

As we looked at him, Tewfik hesitated, then shrugged unhappily. "'Khamsin' literally means 'fifty.'"

"Fifty?" The duchess moaned.

"Fifty what?" I demanded. "Hours? Days?"

The man shook his head. "There's no telling, but there's no going forward until it slackens, that much is certain."

Far from slackening, however, the wind only appeared to be gathering force. The sand no longer resembled rain but rather hail and, shortly thereafter, pebbles that clattered everywhere like a regiment of cavalry cantering down a stretch of macadam. The ensuing racket made speech impossible.

Holding on to various bulkheads, we stared at one another. The howling redoubled in fury, and now the entire wagon-lit began to tremble. How long could such a horror last? It couldn't, we told ourselves. But it did, and grew still worse. *Fifty*. Fifty hours of this was inconceivable; fifty days unsurvivable.

"What's happening?" the duchess yelled, as though she'd not heard the professor's explanation.

Before anyone could answer, there was an explosion and my window was smashed inwards, the shade snapping up as the cord was severed and a tidal wave of sand blowing in with shards of glass, prompting a muffled shriek from the duchess, who doubled over in an instinctive contortion. Whether this posture was adopted for protection or from terror it was impossible to say; possibly both considerations were at work.

The carriage itself now threatened to tilt entirely. The detective and I exchanged looks.

"We must decouple this car," Holmes decreed. "For if it rolls over, it will take its neighbours with it, or they do the same to us, which would greatly complicate any attempts at rescue."

His logic was clear enough.

"If Your Grace will excuse me," I shouted in her ear, "I must dress!"

She gave a spasmodic jerk of her head but did not speak. I nodded to Holmes, who tugged a blanket from the upper berth and wrapped it around the duchess, then pointed his finger beyond the door, indicating he and the professor would wait for me there.

As the wagon-lit continued to be buffeted by shrieking wind and pelting sand granules, I managed to slip on my clothes and boots, one hand pressed against a bulkhead to preserve my balance. I made feeble attempts at decorum, but speed was of the essence and space was limited. How much of these arrangements were noticed by the duchess it is impossible to say, but when I made a move to the door she seized my arm with a convulsive strength and a wild look.

"Where are you going?" she demanded.

"To help."

"No!"

"I'll return," I promised. "Stay right here. Will you do that?"

She made no answer as I pried her clenched fingers one by one from my sleeve and squeezed them around the blanket. Thinking quickly, as one does in such circumstances, I seized an extra shirt and tied it about my head, endeavouring to cover my nose and mouth, knotting the sleeve ends tightly at the base of my neck.

Seeing my appearance thus in the middle of the night amid such a tempest prompted her to jam a fist again into her mouth as if she would swallow it.

"Stay right here, Your Grace!" I knew I spoke but could not hear my voice muffled through the cloth that covered my mouth. "I'll reconnoiter."

And with that, I was out the door and into the corridor. No windows on this side of the train were broken, as the khamsin was barrelling in from the west, but the car itself was rocking to and fro as though being tossed about amid an earthquake. Sand had contrived to coat everyone and everything within. My teeth instantly gritted with it.

Towards the front, I could see Holmes, Tewfik, and some others gathering, and I made for them, the flooring quivering beneath me as my feet struggled for purchase. Hats and face coverings were being improvised and distributed.

"Remember," Holmes was saying as I reached him, "this operation must be performed twice, once at each end of the car. Is that understood?"

There were muffled nods and five travellers whom I had not met squeezed past, heading for the rear of the car. "This way, pardner!" cried one. "Right behind you, pal!" yelled another. Spying me, the detective offered a grim smile before pulling up his own face covering.

That said, we pulled open the platform door, to be greeted by a blast of sand that sent us reeling backward into each other, our eyes stinging from grit.

"Push us!" the detective ordered Tewfik, and, with our heads lowered, we were thrust onto the platform where the storm had already smashed in the door that faced the wind. The skin on my face and arms, even the part that was nominally protected, felt it was being stung by a thousand nettles, or stabbed by the very glass shards whose forced entry my window shade had dismally failed to prevent. My forehead was instantly cut open, but my hands were the worst. Had I thought more clearly while dressing in my compartment at that confusing time, I would have devised some protection for them. I would pay dearly for that neglect; now, however, there was nothing for it but to follow the detective.

As he crawled out and dropped underneath the couplings, I did likewise, more or less falling in his wake. There matters only worsened. Where we crouched it was a veritable wind tunnel, and above us our wagon-lit and the one attached before it rocked alarmingly in opposite directions, producing high-pitched squeals that rivaled the volume of the tempest.

Professor Tewfik, who had followed us, almost suffered a more dire fate. The wind made a snatch at him as he descended and threatened to whirl him into a dark oblivion had Holmes not seized him by his collar, which promptly came off in his hand. Fortunately, his other fist snagged the man's coat and, dragging him back, forced him up and into the car. The professor gave the detective a heavy nod of gratitude and left us to our work. Everything was so dark I could not tell whether it was day or night.

And to crown our difficulties, what we could see only further confused matters. The coaches, cunningly painted to blend with ochre desert hues, now acted as malevolent camouflage, disguising where they began and the storm left off.

Amid our struggles to undo the coupling, it was all one could manage not to think of one or both cars overhead rolling over in the midst of our efforts and crushing us both. It did cross my mind that if such a thing occurred it would prove a ridiculous end to our two lives, but I told myself, as the sands assaulted me like pummelling Furies, perhaps all endings are ridiculous and this would prove no worse than many others.

Thanks to the steward who earlier had informed me the carriages were built in France, it was no great matter for Holmes and myself to know what was required to decouple them. The difficulty lay in withstanding the onslaught of sand and accomplishing the task before one or more sections of the train were toppled by the ferocious khamsin. It was useless to speak, but by dint of gestures I indicated to Holmes that I would stand with my back to the wind, thus shielding him as he worked the coupling. I had not thought to bring any sort of winter garb, but with my robe thrown over a singlet, a shirt, and my Norfolk, the layers I had improvised proved sufficient for me to shelter the detective from wind and sand as he strained to unwind the giant screw-tension turn-buckle and throw off the two heavy link safety chains. The only flaw in my choreography was that I was compelled to expose the backs of my hands as I grasped pieces of both carriage handles to brace myself in place while he worked. Blood was shortly running in rivulets under my sleeves, sliding towards my elbows. The absurd thought flashed through my mind that regardless of whether I lived or perished, my Harris Tweed was irretrievably ruined.

I don't suppose the entire procedure lasted more than two minutes, but the backs of my hands were a red-soaked, slippery mess as we clambered back aboard the train, as if I had donned a pair of crimson gloves. Blood from the cut in my forehead trickled into my right eye, prompting a repeated involuntary wink and a half-blind search for a towel in the lavatory. In the mirror above the pewter sink I was a sight to behold. As a battlefield surgeon I had certainly experienced gouts of hemoglobin during my time of service, but not since Maiwand, when Murray, my orderly, saved my life by throwing me over a packhorse after I'd been struck by a Jezail bullet, had that blood been my own. The sight made me momentarily dizzy and I clutched the basin to steady myself. As the carriage rocked in the skirling wind, I briefly saw myself as Lady Macbeth with chapped and flaking lips and tottered out of the washroom, wondering if the others thought so, too.

"Watson, dear man, are you alright? Let me see." The detective, who generally eschewed displays of emotion, now let slip his mask of imperturbability if only for a moment, suggesting how problematic our situation must be.

"'Tis not so wide as a church door nor so deep as a well," I managed, surprised and pleased by his concern.

We were shortly rejoined by the Americans who had successfully worked the coupling at the rear of the car. Their lips, I noted, were as cracked as my own.

Someone suggested we might be safer lying flat out of doors on the sand, but the prospect of being struck by flying debris discouraged any such recourse. I thought of Juliet and hoped I would live to see and smile with her again.

Eager hands now rushed to create ad hoc bandages using water and towels from the washrooms and items from other compartments to cleanse my wounds. Others had suffered injuries as well. As the khamsin continued to bellow and shove at the coaches, we endured as best we could in silence, for there was nothing that words could accomplish even had they been heard. Occasionally the distant crash of more window glass breaking sounded through the wind's cacophony, punctuated as well by distant cries elsewhere on the train. As those who uttered them were beyond our reach, I for one tried to ignore them.

It was hard to judge the passage of time in all of this. I had not brought my watch, which would certainly have been destroyed, and as it was totally dark outside, it was impossible to say whether or not the sun had risen. The swirling sand obscured everything that might have been light.

And then we heard a distant crash unlike any other. This was accompanied by faint shrieks. Holmes understood at once.

"One of the cars behind us has rolled over."

"Holy cow," one of the Americans responded in his own tongue.

I stood unsteadily with the evident intention of heading towards the source of the noise.

"Not you, old man," the detective stopped me. I was so feeble it didn't take much effort to restrain me. "We'll go and see what we can do. Might I trouble you to look in on my client?"

I nodded, too exhausted to argue.

"Say, maybe I should check on my old lady!" yelled another, but the rest, including Professor Tewfik, who, I realised, was in fact a vigorous, not to say athletic, figure, chose to follow the detective towards the rear of the train. The other cars must literally stand or fall on their own. For the rest, we would simply have to wait.

The roar of the sandstorm sounded not unlike a freight train rumbling through one's drawing room, mingled with echoes of children sobbing in a distant chimney.

For a time I perched on one of the trembling leather armrests and let my mind wander. It flitted uncertainly, bouncing from one aspect of this mysterious business to another. There had been the missing suite 718 at Shepheard's; there was Akhenaten, his repulsive features distorted by Marfan Syndrome, married to his elder brother's attractive widow, what was her name? Nefer-something. Thence my idle associations drifted to the striking Duchess of Uxbridge and Lord Darlington, her improbable brother-in-law, who, like Akhenaten, was also heir to a kingdom, a dukedom at any rate, should his own brother predecease him. What had Tewfik said about "older than Hamlet"? And what of the murder weapon used on our hapless waiter, a dagger of ancient vintage? Surely the peculiar choice of weapon was what Holmes would term "suggestive." But suggestive of what? And what of Bechstein, Phillips, and Jourdan, all of whom—professional or amateur plunderers—seemed to have met their fates on a quest for gold? Finally I settled on the enigmatic Fatima. Which thread in this tangled skein was hers? Was she indeed playing a double game—and if so, with whom? The duke? One-handed Major Haki and the Turks? Mycroft and his "clubmen" of the Diogenes? Or possibly herself? I longed to put a great many questions to her should we meet, but finally blinked away my speculations, rose, and clumsily made my way back to my berth. My compartment door remained unlocked and the duchess sitting where I had left her. And then, for the second time in my life, I fainted.*

Having lost all sense of time, I have no idea how much had passed before I came to myself. I found the duchess leaning over and sponging the cut above my eye with a cambric handkerchief soaked in cool *patchouli*. I remember being surprised to recognise it as the same scent Juliet wore. How had I not noticed this earlier?

"Is that better?" She now gently applied salve to my parched lips.

"Yes." I struggled to sit up and she helped me.

"What time is it?"

"Where is your watch?"

I thought about this. "Under my pillow?"

---

* Writing around 1911, Watson was still adhering to the text of "The Adventure of the Empty House," in which he described fainting when seeing Holmes alive years after supposing him dead. It was not until 1939 that he acknowledged the entire case had been a fabrication, designed to conceal Holmes's time in therapy with Sigmund Freud. If *The Seven-Per-Cent Solution* is to be believed, aboard the Star of Egypt was arguably the *first* time Watson ever fainted.

I held the timepiece to my ear, relieved to find it still running. The fact that I could hear it suggested something else, namely a change in the velocity of the wind. Squeezing shut my eyes to distinguish more clearly, I thought it might be abating, or was that merely wishful thinking? I decided not to mention it, as I did not wish to raise false hopes.

"Can you wind this for me, please? I'm afraid my hands are—"

She took the watch from me and wound it.

Having sat up on the floor, we regarded each other in the faint glow of the blue night-light.

"Thank you for last night. I expect I lost my head."

"Small wonder."

"When I was ten years of age, my grandfather, assuming it would interest me, brought me down with him—the better part of a mile it must have been—into a shaft of one of his copper mines. Attempting his idea of a joke, he abandoned me in that dark, underground place for perhaps less than a minute, though to me it seemed an eternity. Regardless, the damage was done. Ever since that day I have nightmares of close confinement."

She fastened my watch about my wrist.

I remained for the time being on the floor while she, tightening her robe, resumed her place on the edge of the lower berth. She was doing something with her hands, opening and closing them as if to flex the fingers.

"Why did you ask about my marriage?" The question popped unbidden out of my mouth before I knew what prompted me to ask it. It was curious how our situation had unleashed a different aspect of her personality, and, for all I knew, of mine, as well. The formerly icy and unknowable Lizabetta del Maurepas had been thawed by an onslaught of sand, going so far as to share childhood reminiscences with a comparative stranger.

"Did I?" She confessed dully, "I expect I was making comparisons."

"With your own?"

"Mr. Holmes—is he alright?" she asked instead of replying. I had overstepped.

I considered her question, tentatively touching my scalp. "He was when I left him."

"Try not to do that."

I obeyed. The coach continued to quiver. Sucking air in jerky inhalations, she reached for one of the upper-berth supports.

"Where is he?"

"Holmes? One of the cars—perhaps more than one—has rolled over towards the rear. He has gone to help."

She nodded, convulsively clenching and unclenching her fingers again. "I have done him an injustice."

"He may have done you one as well. In any case, he is not one to carry a grudge."

"What do you think he knows?"

"Knows?" I slowly got to my feet and in the gloom inspected the shambles of the compartment, crunching window glass shards under my boots.

"About my husband."

"He has not communicated his thoughts along those lines to me," I began, but held up a bandaged hand, forestalling her next question, "but even had he done so, it would not be my place to say."

She accepted this answer with a philosophical shrug as much as to say she expected nothing different from me. It was at that moment that we both realised the wind was well and truly slackening. Indeed, as I looked again, patches of blue were appearing outside the broken window.

She followed my look, then directed her gaze at me, her features resuming their accustomed expression.

"It is over."

10

LUXOR

In the end, eleven died, including three women. Thirty-four all told were wounded (fourteen seriously), out of a total of ninety-seven passengers and crew. The last three coaches of the Star of Egypt, including the lounge car, were overturned and damaged beyond repair. Not having been disconnected, they toppled together, each dragging the next, thereby increasing the number of injured. With the rear of the train thus disabled, in theory we could go forward; in fact, we could not possibly go back.

By my watch, it was almost noon under a windless azure sky when, singly or in small clusters, passengers and staff descended or tumbled uncertainly from the train to take stock of the situation and themselves. The air was now so still and the temperature so mild, it was as if "Allah's Breath" had never happened. We had been lucky. The big wind had not lasted fifty hours, let alone fifty days.

In the event there were six doctors aboard the train; seven, if one includes an Alienist from New York. Most, like myself, had not thought to bring medical bags or instruments on the journey. Fortunately, the Star of Egypt did boast a rudimentary stock of emergency supplies in the larder next to the galley and these, accessed with some difficulty, proved largely intact. There was nothing like enough bandages but plenty of compartment bedsheets, made, as luck would have it, of that same Egyptian linen in which their mummified kings were shrouded. These, to coin a phrase, were pressed into service on behalf of the injured—and the dead.

The wood-burning galley stoves were still in working order and these were used to sterilise what instruments could be conjured into being, most of them adjusted cutlery or Sheffield dining car utensils. If, as must inevitably be the case, the galley's supply of wood gave out, engine coal being unusable for lack of ventilation, destroyed items of the train's burnished wood trimmings could feed the oven fires and water from the locomotive's boiler siphoned off and re-boiled in the galley for purposes other than locomotion. Needles and thread would prove essential. Women, who (like my wife) typically never travel without sewing kits, were asked to donate these to the medical rescue effort and willingly did so.

Because of injuries suffered by my hands, I was scarcely able to assist in caring for other wounded, but I did attempt to function in an adjunct advisory capacity as best my own condition would allow.

Holmes's situation I judged tolerable. He was exhausted, to be sure, his face and forearms black with grease from the couplings and pockmarked all over with sand grains, as was Professor Tewfik, who marched beside him as they strode the length of the Star of Egypt ascertaining our state of affairs.

Behind me, the creaking of a platform door torn off one of its hinges and hanging by the other drew my attention. I turned in time to see the duchess, haphazardly dressed, but with a certain undeniable rag-tag flair, descending our car with assistance from one of the porters. She now stood irresolutely below our behemoth wagon-lit with its shattered windows. Though several of the gilded letters above her head were missing, I now recalled our carriage had been called Hatshepsut, who I'd read somewhere was an Egyptian queen, an irony I judged inappropriate but inescapable. Lizabetta del Maurepas, like everyone else, I knew, was attempting to understand what might or must happen next.

For the moment, our happenstance community remained immobile, stranded amid motionless waves of piled-up sand, with no means of communication at our disposal. My earlier assumption about moving forward I now realised had been ill informed. The metals immediately before us were obliterated for who knows how many miles. Any thought of progress in that direction was out of the question.

There was, to be sure, some food in the pantry, though it would not suffice were our circumstances to remain prolonged.

"That will not be the case," Basil, our Maltese steward, assured us. He had suffered a broken arm which I directed others to set and bind as we spoke. "When the khamsin struck and we failed to arrive, our plight would quickly be understood in Luxor." Basil winced but did not cry out as I felt clumsily to inspect the splint. "They will dispatch help from along the river, as it is close by our route. But they also have a sixteen-wheel engine with a snowplow for use in just such cases. She is probably already on her way."

"And from Cairo?" I enquired, thinking suddenly of Juliet for the first time in hours. "Surely, as we failed to arrive, Luxor will have telegraphed word."

He shrugged. "If the wires were not severed by the storm, *effendi.*"

The stoker, with whom I exchanged a few words, calculated we were somewhere in the vicinity of Girga and thus assured me not far from the Nile itself, as our route consistently parallelled the river.

His estimates, overheard, raised some spirits, if not mine, and indeed some half-dozen stalwarts made preparations to leave the train and trudge across the Sahara for the Nile, where they anticipated river traffic would pick them up and carry them either up- or downriver to safety. This struck me as a problematic, not to say foolhardy enterprise, as no one could say how far we were from the river or what conditions might be like between the train and the water.

Holmes had returned in time to hear the stoker's assessment and I knew it was in his mind to undertake the exploit, but felt bound to caution him on behalf of the duchess. It was one thing for the detective and the professor to try the expedient, but she was hardly in a position to do so. As my own weakened condition would preclude such a stratagem, it was obvious I could and should remain with Her Grace. Realising all of this in less time than it takes to describe it, the detective ultimately discarded the entire proposition. Detectives are not physicians, but Holmes regarded his client as the equivalent of a patient and now understood we must stay with her and the train to await rescue. He attempted to pace, kicking furiously at the sand that surrounded his ankles. As a rule he was patience itself when pondering a problem or, like a hunter, when he stalked or waited motionless for his prey to break cover, but passivity in the face of difficulty or danger was anathema to his temperament.

"But there's nothing stopping you from joining the river party," he informed Professor Tewfik, who was not only unscathed by our experience but whose wiry frame remained trim and energetic.

"Nonsense," the latter replied. "In due course we shall reach Luxor safe and sound, join Howard Carter, and learn what has become of the Duke of Uxbridge."

"There's a good fellow," the detective proclaimed.

Holmes was not infallible.

As we stood deliberating these courses of action and their possible outcomes, we were approached by a small deputation that included the conductor and some of the train's crew, as well as a score of passengers. All appeared in tattered garments and filthy bandage wrappings, mirror images of ourselves.

"I am begging your pardon, *effendi*." The Levantine touched two fingers to his cap, addressing Holmes. For having taken the initiative in decoupling most of the cars, the detective had, by default, seemingly assumed a mantle of leadership, if not authority. "What do you propose regarding the burial detail?"

In our eagerness to deal with the wounded and survivors, we had not confronted the grisly reality of eleven bloating corpses.

Holmes, finally at the limit of his endurance, dragged a blackened hand across his blackened forehead.

"Is there no way they can be stowed abroad the train until we reach Luxor?"

"*Impossible, effendi, je regrette infiniment.* They would never make the journey in their condition and no one would ever board this train again if they did."

"But your brochure says you carry ice to cool the coaches," the detective recollected. "Could it not be diverted on this occasion to a more humane use?"

"We only carry such ice in summertime, *effendi*."

Holmes and I once more exchanged beleaguered looks. "Some of these passengers may refuse to leave their loved ones behind," I speculated quietly.

There were murmurs of agreement from several hovering nearby.

"I won't leave Harry in the middle of nowhere," a woman declared.

"We can bury them temporarily," Holmes suggested. "Leave markers and return with coffins to recover their remains as soon as we can."

"In a mass grave?" a German wondered.

"Unmarried men alongside women?" objected an American.

"Beg pardon, *effendi,* but one of the deceased is a Muslim female."

This intelligence elicited further murmuring.

"Wogs, too?" now scornfully chimed in an English voice.

"How many shovels have we?" the detective enquired of the stoker, as questions and objections continued to rain down.

"Just the two from the tender," the man, an Australian, answered.

"Unless you count soup ladles," the chef added. I couldn't tell if he was attempting to be humorous.

"We've not sufficient tools for more than a single pit," Holmes endeavoured to explain. "One temporary grave it must be."

"That won't happen!" threatened another.

At which point Sherlock Holmes, at the end of his resources, lost his temper, a thing I rarely recall seeing him do before.

"Very well," he returned, raising his voice as if the khamsin were still screeching. "Sit here. Do nothing. Or construct pyramids, if you please. Perhaps the rescue engine will arrive with room for the dead before they explode. Perhaps not. In the interim you can inhale the stink of your relatives and hope for the best."

With which malediction, he stalked off, his back to us.

His blunt ultimatum shocked all to silence. I could not in that moment decide whether it was my friend's crass behavior or his brutal truth that distressed me most.

The others stewed for a time, some glaring furiously at his retreating form, others at the ground, and some at the bodies laid side by side in the shade of the overturned cars.

In the end, however, the detective's argument proved irresistible. Grumbling among themselves, they took the shovels, retreated to the rear of the train, and there angrily took turns heaving sand over their shoulders.

I watched their labour in silence. More bed linens were now brought forth from the train and used for the same purpose they had been put to three thousand years earlier, as winding sheets for the dead. One of the passengers—I was standing too far off to make out which it was—appeared to be delivering some sort of prayer or collective eulogy for which the others, doffing hats and bandanas, stood respectfully still, but I could not make out his words. His talk was accompanied by a number of emphatic hand gestures, after which the digging resumed.

After a time I trudged to the front of the train, where I found Holmes standing beside the belching locomotive, his face still turned away, but from long familiarity between us he soon sensed my presence.

"Watson, what on earth have I said?"

"It's not what you've said but what you've done," said the duchess, who had followed me, laying a hand on the detective's shoulder. "You've saved most of this train and those on it. You made the only logical suggestion."

He turned slowly—reluctantly, I judged—and regarded her with a hangdog expression, somewhere between gratitude and bewilderment.

"You have nothing with which to reproach yourself, *senhor*."

Without replying, the detective now cast about him as if searching for another topic of conversation.

"I wonder if there's enough water in our carriage for me to have a wash."

It was after three when, preceded by puffs of black steam, the oversized snowplow engine from Luxor finally crept cautiously into view, pushing aside mounds of sand and clearing the metals as she approached. As Holmes feared, the heavy locomotive brought no carriages or freight cars in tow. With only sand—sand again!—to support the metals and ties, Egyptian engines and rolling stock could never exceed a certain weight for fear of dislodging the alignment of the tracks on the unstable rail bed. Nonetheless, faint cheers greeted its arrival and in another hour or so, with steam up and our train reboarded, the Star of Egypt slowly followed the retreating snowplow, leaving behind three overturned coaches and eleven fatalities in shallow graves. We passed Karnak, stared at by workers on the station platform as we made our way south, and I thought briefly of Professor Jourdan, who had met his death here from decidedly unnatural causes.

It was nearly six before we pulled into Luxor. Immediately the seriously injured were taken off to the town's small hospital in a variety of improvised conveyances. The most serious cases were placed in such motorcars as were to be had. Others rode in wagons and still others in the local version of rickshaws.

It was understood that in due course the train's abandoned coaches would be righted or destroyed and the dead exhumed and packed in ice-filled coffins for interment elsewhere. The ancient Egyptian art of embalming, even if its secrets were known today, would have been too late to preserve the remains of those unfortunate souls. In all probability it would be difficult, if not impossible, to inter them in their countries of origin. The Coptic cemetery in Cairo would become the final resting place for most.* Needless to say, the arrival of the overdue Star of Egypt after her harrowing encounter with the khamsin occasioned much excitement in the Luxor station and its environs. The khamsin had spared the city, but news of the storm had been received from Karnak before the telegraph went down in midtransmission. As it happened, many folk, both the relatives of tourists or guides or hotel greeters, had arrived hours earlier to meet the expected train, only to learn what had befallen. In an agony of suspense, not daring to leave, they had been obliged to wait here long hours, trying now and then to nap on uncomfortable wood benches or pacing for news of the lost express.

Vociferous cheers heralded our entry into the shed behind the plow engine, but the scene shortly disintegrated into a miasma of confusion and emotion. On learning the details of our experience and, in some cases, the fates of friends or family, lamentations grew clamorous.

A relieved Howard Carter, forcing his way through the distraught mass, was on hand to greet Holmes, the duchess, Professor Tewfik, and myself.

---

* In fact, the remains of two Frenchmen and four Americans were shipped home.

"Are you alright, Colonel?" he asked, signalling his bearers to collect our bags.

"We seem to be," was the detective's terse comment.

"Good lord, what has happened to your hands?" the expert exclaimed on beholding my bandages.

"Dr. Watson was injured saving the train," Professor Tew-fik informed him.

"I need to send a telegram," I said.

"You'll find a shorter queue at the hotel," the Egyptologist assured me, pointing to the line outside the telegraph kiosk, "and perhaps by then the lines will have been repaired. Presently, Luxor is cut off."

"Can we go now?" asked the duchess.

"Of course. This way, Your Grace. What a perfectly dreadful business," Carter did his awkward best to soothe the exhausted woman. "I expect you'll want to rest and clean up after your ordeal," said he. "As the Winter Palace is chockablock, I've managed to book rooms for you at Amenhotep House."

"I want to sleep," was her curt rejoinder.

"We must thank the crew," Holmes said, looking about him as if waking from a dream.

Carter was solicitous, to be sure, parting the undulating throng with his boys to usher us from the place, but also, I could not help noticing, impatient. He was clearly on fire to communicate something but aware that given what had occurred and the condition of the detective and myself, this was hardly the moment.

But Holmes, as it proved, was equally impatient to learn his news. "Did he find it?" he brusquely demanded as we finally began to wedge our way into the mass of jostling bodies.

Carter's eyes widened at this and he looked briefly over his shoulder.

"He did," was all he said, laying a finger on his lips.

As I was struggling amid the press, it was difficult to detect the effect this news had on our party. As Holmes was walking before me, I was unable to see his reaction. Tewfik's eyes did their usual trick, but it was the duchess, by my side, whose response most intrigued me. Her husband's horse had apparently come in, albeit the bet he placed on it was likely made with another woman's money. From the duchess's frozen features it was impossible to say what she was feeling. I knew from previous experience (was it only at dinner the night before?) this was an expression she could sustain for hours on end.

Squeezed into the Lancia Epsilon sent by Amenhotep House, with the boys running behind, our bags balanced on their heads, Holmes thought better of his question.

"This matter will have to wait 'til morning," he realised, looking at the duchess, whose eyes were already closed. "We will need clear heads but presently are at the ends of our tether. Certainly I am," he conceded with a remorseful glance in my direction. "A hot soak and a deep sleep is the first order of business."

Carter, who was intelligent enough to perceive both necessities, nonetheless greeted the reality with exasperation. "That will entail a twenty-four-hour wait," he muttered.

"Why so long?" I demanded. "Surely we can set out in the morning."

The expert shook his head. "When your train was scheduled to arrive this morning, I allowed the day to rest, for we can only visit the place by night. You're arrival now in your present condition rather alters things."

"Why can we only go at night?"

He looked at me as one might regard a simpleton. "For the

simple reason that the dig in question was illegal. As I direct another dig not far off for Lord Carnarvon, I have the paperwork that will allow us to enter the valley after hours and grant us access to the site. But whatever VR 61 proves to be, for the present only we may see. Therefore it must be at night or not at all," the archeologist repeated firmly. "When word gets out, and it will, the wrangling will begin between Egyptians, British, and Turks over digging rights and it will be the End of Days before any of us ever get to view, let alone catalogue, what's inside."

"Then you've not opened it?" Holmes asked.

Carter shook his head. "That seemed inappropriate. We have found the flight of steps where the duke anticipated. They lead down to an ancient door where the original seal remains unbroken, so there I stopped and posted guards with signs warning of 'hazardous ground.'"

"*Quis custodiet ipsos custodes?*" Holmes repeated.

"Yes, they are all susceptible to *baksheesh*," he conceded, "but there was no other way. The duke's instinct proved correct, but illegal or not, with His Grace not present, clearly the duchess, his wife" indicating the sleeping woman with a tilt of his head—"has the right to be present when we first go in."

"That is the proper way to do such things," Tewfik, turning back from his seat beside the driver, agreed.

I said nothing but privately wondered whether a woman with a terror of closed-in spaces would be prepared to undertake anything of the kind. Had she not endured enough by this point?

Luxor, compared with Cairo, was a provincial town, whose revenue largely depended on only two related sources beside the always beneficent river: Egyptology and tourism, the former obviously fomenting the latter. In either capacity, Luxor did most of its business during the cooler, winter months and hotel space was consequently at a premium.

Unlike Shepheard's or Luxor's newly opened Winter Palace, each with almost three hundred rooms, Amenhotep House boasted a mere tenth that number, and these were booked. We were then surprised when Howard Carter informed us there were in fact beds for us all, if the colonel and I doubled up.

"How can this be?" the professor wondered. "At the height of the season."

Carter appeared embarrassed, awkwardly explaining the rooms had been held in the names of two families who did not survive the storm. These were certainly sobering tidings, but under the circumstances there was little choice but to make use of the fortuitous vacancies.

Before ascending to our rooms, I went to the desk with the intention of asking the concierge to send my telegram the moment service was restored, only to find Holmes in the queue before me, evidently with a telegram of his own.

"Holmes, please let me go first. Juliet must be frantic."

"My message is terribly important, Watson."

"More important than my wife's peace of mind?" I demanded tetchily.

He looked at me, hesitated a moment, then stood aside.

It was a concession that almost cost both of us our lives.

I wrote to Juliet, thus:

DARLING DON'T WORRY. IN LUXOR WITH HOLMES. ALL WELL HOME IN A FEW DAYS. MISSING YOU TERRIBLY J.

When the man had finished writing, I thrust some Egyptian pounds at him according to the local custom. "Very important," I emphasised. He nodded and swept the money from the counter, whether into a drawer or his pocket I could not see.

I did not remain for Holmes's telegram and in truth now felt rather ashamed of my impatience, but told myself that Holmes, a perennial solitary, had no one (possibly Mycroft or Mrs. Hudson?) waiting on news of his well-being.

The rooms at Amenhotep House more resembled my accommodations at the Khedivial than the lavish appointments offered at Shepheard's. The small place was simply decorated in what I suppose was the Egyptian equivalent of French provincial; the rooms and amenities were spare and small, such wood as was in evidence, sere and unvarnished.

Filling the tin basin with water from a terra-cotta pitcher designed to evoke ancient Egyptian antecedents, I gingerly unwound my bandages and tenderly bathed my hands. Once the blood had washed away in soap suds, I was surprised to note the damage far less severe than the pain I had endured at the time it was inflicted.

My Harris Tweed Norfolk was less lucky. As I'd feared, those stains would never come out. Holmes and I unpacked in silence, both dead on our feet.

"I say, Holmes."

"Yes, my dear fellow."

"I am sorry to have jumped your place in the queue. It was entirely unnecessary. I didn't wish to give Juliet an extra moment's anxiety."

"Don't give it a thought, old man."

The detective had begun to pace. I knew all too well that once he began, it was difficult to stop.

"Sit down, Sherlock.* I have a tweezers."

After the briefest hesitation, the detective obeyed and sat backward in a chair, remaining stoically motionless as we faced each other. Employing expertise from campaigns of yore, I extracted grain after grain of sand from his face as if it were so much shrapnel.

It was about nine in the evening when, our ablutions completed, we piled into that bed and were both soon fast asleep. Or at least I was. It was some time later when I woke to realise the detective was lying next to me, wide awake.

"You can't sleep?"

"Apparently not."

"You should, you know. Tomorrow night promises to be . . ." I searched for the right word. "Demanding."

"Yes," said he. "I expect it will be."

With that he rolled away from me and was soon snoring.

We were both more spent than either of us imagined and did not wake until after ten the following morning, only just in time to breakfast before the little dining room closed 'til luncheon.

It was a an odd, disorienting day as Holmes, Carter (who had his own lodgings in town), the duchess and myself sought ways to pass the time until four in the afternoon, when Carter judged it time to leave. It was some twenty-five miles to the Valley of the Kings, including the river crossing, and Carter wished to time our arrival by dark. I took a short walk in the vicinity of the inn, for in reality it was little more than that,

---

* One of the only times I think Watson has addressed the detective by his Christian name.

then sat in our room and arranged these notes. It was while I was performing this chore I heard a knock on the door and the boy presented me with a telegram.

DEAREST BRING BACK AU 79 LOVE J

I stared at the message in some confusion. "What the devil?" I exclaimed.

"What is it?" Holmes asked from across the room, where he was studying hieroglyphs.

I handed him the telegram. "I don't know what she means."

Holmes read the telegram and offered a faint smile. "You've forgotten your chemistry." Using the smallest finger of his right hand, he pointed to the message. "The fact that teletype is all capitals doesn't help. *A* lowercase *u*, which is how it should correctly be written, is the proper element designation for gold. And seventy-nine is the element's atomic number. 'Bring back gold,' your missus urges you. Your wife has a wit worthy of a Shakespearean heroine."

"You don't say." I had to laugh. "What a clever girl she is." I was so relieved to hear from my wife in good spirits that it was a moment before I looked back at the detective, who had returned to his study of the ancient symbols. "No answer to your own telegram, I take it?"

"Unfortunately." He did not look up.

Later we met the duchess and Professor Tewfik for tea. We were all in better spirits for having had a good night's sleep, but Holmes felt it important to be candid.

"Your Grace, it is my recollection from our conversation at the Great Pyramid that you have a fear of closed-in spaces."

"My condition is technically termed 'claustrophobia.'"

"Professor Tewfik can correct me if I am wrong, but I believe there is every possibility that where we are going this evening may prove to be just such a space."

"That is so," echoed Tewfik, his blue eyes protruding briefly once more.

"This being the case"—Holmes smiled—"are you sure you wish to accompany us?"

She smiled in turn, quite unlike the woman I had first met.

"Colonel Arbuthnot, yesterday you and Dr. Watson showed me what bravery is. I don't know what my nerves can withstand, but I haven't come all this way to back out now."

Holmes did not often regard women with more than skeptical or professional interest, but I could see her remarks impressed him. But then she went on in quite another vein:

"Besides, my husband spent a large part of my fortune these last years in pursuit of his own. If he has in fact found something of value I am at least entitled to share in it. I intend to have something to show for this madness."

Holmes said nothing to this but looked at the floor.

Shortly afterwards, Howard Carter, dressed for the evening's events and with a dark jumper draped over his shoulders, joined us.

"The desert will be chilly at night," he warned. "Dress accordingly."

11

IN THE VALLEY OF THE KINGS

The setting sun, seen from the deck of the felucca that carried us across the Nile from Luxor into its dying rays, was a sight to behold and remember. Compared to all we had endured, the tranquility of our passage served as a balm to our recent hardships and peril. The river at this juncture could not have been a mile in width, but appearances on water are deceptive and our journey took longer than I anticipated. Were it not for the sense of urgency felt among us all, I could have relished the time it took for our transit. Even the duchess appeared soothed by the experience. We were silent, lost in our thoughts or some, like myself, perhaps, in simple contemplation of the scene, the only sounds being occasional muttered instructions from the boatman to his one-man crew and the slapping of water against our bow. Next to me, Holmes, shielding the flame with his hand, lit his briar. "If only it could always be thus," he murmured. I was sometimes surprised by my friend's poetic streak. If he was in any way apprehensive about what was to come this night, he gave no sign.

There was a fair amount of river traffic, some vessels jour-neying up- or downstream and still others crossing in the opposite direction to ours, fellaheen and tourists alike heading back to hotels and homes on the Nile's eastern shore. But for all, the serenity of the time and place seemed to inspire silence.

Waiting for us at the western landing stage was one of the largest automobiles I have ever seen. I had just time to make it out, but not to discern its colour, before the sun disappeared and darkness replaced daylight in an instant. Almost immediately, the temperature dropped as well.

"It's a Knox 7," Howard Carter informed me, following my look. "From America. His Lordship is a great automobile fancier and owns several varieties. He chose this one specifically for this work as, by its name, you will understand, it carries a great many. Also, it is equipped with the new radiator springs, which makes travel on such roads as these less onerous than might otherwise be the case."

As he spoke, the Lascars were lowering sail and tying off the felucca. Ashore, I saw the acetylene gas headlamps of the Knox 7 being fired up by a driver whose face I could not make out.

"That's Ahmed," the Egyptologist explained. "Been with me for years. He's very good."

The duchess was first ashore, helped across the gap by Professor Tewfik, followed by Holmes, myself, and finally Carter, who exchanged some Arabic with the boatman. Handing over *baksheesh*, he explained, "He will wait here for us all night if need be."

Now we climbed into the commodious vehicle with its three rows of seats, and again Carter issued instructions, this time to Ahmed, standing by the bonnet, who immediately worked the crank, bringing the engine to life, its roar echoing across the night-time river. I imagined they could hear us in Luxor.

Ahmed moved to the boot and with Carter's help erected

the canvas top, securing the grommets, before climbing behind the wheel. Not for the first time, it occurred to me that I should like to add driving to my meagre list of accomplishments.*

As we'd been warned, the road was primitive, comprised of local limestone pounded into gravel chips, but well maintained, as a steady stream of vehicular traffic in daylight carried workers and sightseers to and from our destination. By this hour, as Carter had foreseen, it was empty. It was some fifteen miles more to our destination, hence we had a longish drive before us. There wasn't anything to be seen except the road immediately ahead, lit only by our faint headlamps. Occasionally we would pass Bedouin campfires and by their yellow flames behold turbaned faces of diggers, curiously inspecting us as we passed.

As I grew accustomed to what would typify the next two hours, I became aware that I was nestled among supplies and equipment packed snugly at my feet, leaving them little room. These, on examination, proved to include two large canteens (their contents sloshing within as we jounced), sandwiches in waxed paper, three electric torches, a kerosene lamp, a Graflex camera, and a tripod. There was, in addition, a coil of stout rope and a tool belt laden with differing instruments whose specific uses I could not make out in the darkness, save for a smallish ball-peen hammer. When I asked the expert, seated beside the chauffeur, the purpose of the rope, his only comment was, "You never can tell."

His words caused me to think wistfully of the duke's carbine from Purdey's, left behind by His Grace—and us—at Shepheard's. Sitting to my right, the detective read my mind.

---

* Watson soon became a good driver. See *His Last Bow*.

"I suspect artillery won't do us much good where we're going," was his dry declaration.

After a time, Carter spoke again. "The Colossi of Memnon are nearby to our right," he informed us, pointing. "But too dark to see."

The road itself gradually inclined, and in the inky gloom on either side I sensed hills encroaching on what had earlier felt like openness. Notwithstanding the innovative "radiator springs," the ride was anything but smooth.

"It's chilly," the duchess allowed. She was—as always—dressed for the occasion, wearing boots, jodhpurs, and a heavy woolen blue turtleneck I suspect belonged to either her husband or Lord Darlington (I wondered which), but even with the canvas top, the car was open, boasting no windows other than the windscreen. It was the breeze created by our forward movement that contributed to the cold.

Huddled in my bloodstained Norfolk, I must have fallen asleep, only to be roused by a large bump and Ahmed jerking us to a stop.

Before us a barrier, modelled more or less on those of provincial railway crossings to be found everywhere, was illumined by our headlamps. Within their beams two fella-heen with rifles slung over their shoulders stood with palms upraised in our direction, the clearest possible signal that we were forbidden to proceed farther.

"Wait here," Carter instructed. "This shouldn't take long."

He climbed out of the car and withdrew what I presumed were his certificates of authorisation.

"Let's hope they're not fussy enough to scrutinise the date," I mumbled, aware that Carter was no longer an employee, much less Chief Inspector, of the Department of Antiquities.

"Let's hope," agreed the detective.

"I daresay they can't read," struck in Tewfik. "But in the end, they always succumb to *baksheesh*."

The reverberating noise of our engine turned the exchange before us into a kind of pantomime, not that we could have understood more had it been audible. There was some back-and-forth in the light as we watched, some pointing and nodding, before the expert walked back to us, pocketing his documents as the two guards set about raising the barrier.

Carter climbed into the vehicle and spoke to Ahmed, who nodded.

"That's alright then. It's only a quarter of a mile more."

By now we were hemmed in by walls of stone, rising in ominous blackness above us on either side.

"Welcome to the Valley of the Kings."

I am not normally given to what is generally known as "the creeps," but this phrase, uttered in this dark and desolate place, home of the dead for thousands of years, I confess sent a shiver down my spine.

We rode in silence until we saw, spanning the road above us, a lacy network of human construction.

"There are your trestles, Doctor. Scaffolding designed to help sightseers get from one burial site to the next without risk to life and limb." He said something to Ahmed and the car stopped a second time. Carter took a breath, like a horse collecting itself before a jump. "We're here," he announced. "Bring the torches and gear, if you please."

Stiff from the confinement of the journey and perhaps from accumulated tension as well, we eased ourselves out of the car. Carter strapped on his tool belt and handed off the canteens. Taking one of the electric torches and switching it on before passing it to him, I briefly observed the Knox 7 to be a dull red in colour, unsurprisingly now covered with dust.

Carter again spoke to Ahmed, who extinguished the headlamps, plunging us into utter pitch, save for the torch beams. With the engine additionally switched off, we were now surrounded by oppressive silence as well as towering stone.

"Follow me and stay close. The way is slippery, but it's not far."

We did as instructed, and before we had travelled a hundred yards Carter's torch illumined a second barrier, more clearly improvised than the first, with crude exclamation points and signs in English and French, warning visitors this area was dangerous and off-limits. Above barbed-wire fencing, the dark hills stretched up and out of sight. Directly behind the ad hoc barrier was a flight of descending stairs, hewn from the omnipresent limestone.

"Behold VR 61," the expert said.

Shoving aside the barbed wire barrier, Carter led us to the cavity.

Alongside the top step was a heavy stone flag with a ring of some sort embedded at its centre. Roughly the size of the aperture itself, the stone had clearly been cut and placed over it to conceal the opening, a sort of Egyptian manhole cover.

"This was what he found first." Carter gestured with the torch beam to the ring.

Tewfik at once knelt to examine the ring, running his fingers over the metal. "Iron, no less," he declared. "Preserved by the aridity from rust."

On either side of the man-made crevice, shovels and wheelbarrows lay alongside massive piles of sand and pounded limestone chips of the same sort that comprised the road on which we'd driven. These had self-evidently been dug up and cleared from the steps by the duke and his workmen.

"When they'd buried their courtiers and kings," Tewfik explained, "they filled in all traces with what they'd carved out"—he indicated the piles of sand and stone—"and in the end, no trace could easily be detected."

"Unless one knew where to look," the detective murmured. The hush of night made us talk in whispers. No birds or crickets or sounds of any life except our own disturbed the stillness.

I stared down the flight of steps leading into the earth and tried not to think of hell.

"Ready?"

Without waiting for any affirmation, Carter extended his hand to the duchess, who took it, and slowly they led the way down. Cramming one of the sandwiches into his pocket, Holmes followed, shouldering the rope, the tripod, and carrying one of the canteens. Tewfik and I followed, holding the second canteen and juggling the camera and other two torches between us, as we brought up the rear. The torch batteries were exceptionally heavy and I hoped we had not far to carry them.

I counted twenty-seven steps in all. At the last we congregated before a pair of desiccated doors that looked to have once been cedar. Across the handles was wound an intricate knot of petrified rope or twine, and over that Gordian contrivance dripped a coating of what I took to be hardened tallow.

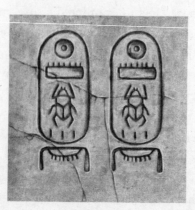

Carter knelt and lit the kerosene lamp, greatly improving our ability to see, and inspected the seal. The two door panels themselves bore the remains of hieroglyphs, eagerly perused by the Egyptologist.

"Professor?"

Tewfik squeezed past us and squinted at the doors and their markings.

"Amazing," he breathed.

"Tuthmose, Eighteenth Dynasty. You concur?"

"And unbroken, with the *cartouche* of Tuthmose," Tewfik responded, reverently touching the ancient rope and tallow with the tips of his fingers.

"This is the perennial dilemma of the archeologist," Carter sighed, tremulously stroking the seal. "How to unearth the past without destroying it?" He shook his head as if to say he had no ready answer. "Very well, I shall now—"

"Just a minute," the professor interrupted, standing up and looking about the way we'd come.

"What is it?"

The urbane museum director seemed perplexed and suddenly uncertain. "I don't trust that lot at the barrier. Carter, you'd best go back and read them the riot act."

"What?"

"You'll probably end up offering *baksheesh*, but as an Egyptian I tell you I know these beggars. They're capable of anything. Take one of the torches. We'll wait."

"Nonsense. I'm not leaving at a moment like this and I've no intention of waiting. This thing must be over and done with before dawn."

The professor shook his head like one unconvinced. "Very well, give me one torch and I'll go myself. Better safe than sorry." He stretched forth an impatient hand.

"Are you sure?" Carter asked doubtfully.

"Quite sure. Start without me and I'll catch you up."

"Would you like me to accompany you?" Holmes asked, handing him one of the torches, which he switched on.

Tewfik scratched his head. "Perhaps that would be best," he began, then apparently thought better of it. "Very kind of you, Colonel, but I think I can manage. We've got Ahmed up there and I doubt they'll try anything with the two of us, but I want to make sure they're not planning any sort of mischief."

Carrying the light, he warily mounted the steps and disappeared over the lid. We waited in some bemusement, broken by Howard Carter's handing me the kerosene lamp, fishing into his tool belt for the implements he knew by touch, and slipping off his rucksack.

I held the lamp aloft and watched as the Egyptologist, with a surgeon's expertise, pricked and pried at the rigid rope and its wax-like seal.

"There's no way to break this seal without ultimately breaking it," he acknowledged, "but one wants to preserve as many of the pieces as possible for future examination."

This he proceeded to do. There was another pause as we watched his delicate manipulations and listened to the trickle of debris dislodged by his efforts. With mounting impatience we stood over him while he used one of his camelhair brushes to sweep the bits he had created into a rectangular canvas envelope, before replacing the whole into the rucksack.

"Can't this wait 'til our return?" the duchess enquired, but Carter, absorbed in the work, either didn't hear or chose to ignore her question.

When he finally completed the task to his own satisfaction, the Egyptologist sat back on his haunches, running the back of his sleeve across his mouth, and looked up at us.

"That's done it," he said, employing a deliberately casual tone.

All that was now left, we knew, was to open those long-closed doors.

"Go on," the duchess commanded in a faint voice.

"Very well."

As we watched, Carter tugged gently at the handles, as if fearing they might crumble, but finding they did not, gradually applied more force. After some initial resistance and with a deal of crackling, the doors finally opened outwards towards us on hinges that hadn't functioned in three thousand years and gave way as they did. Again we exchanged looks. The duchess briefly put a hand to her brow. I stole a look at Holmes, who followed the proceedings, attentive as a pointer.

"Follow me," Howard Carter commanded, taking back the lamp, and we did, leaving behind the cool night air, and entering what proved a long inclined corridor, eerily lit by the kerosene flame, whose yellow light meandered as we walked downwards.

In contrast to the crude and confined robbers' entrance I'd traversed within the Great Pyramid of Cheops, this thirty-foot hallway was engineered to plumb line perfection. I judged it perhaps eight feet high and almost as wide. Both walls and the ceiling were covered with innumerable hieroglyphs and extraordinary paintings in vibrant reds, shimmering blues, greens, and gleaming gold, denoting lives lived millennia before ours, but as fresh as if the colours in which they'd been daubed had not yet dried. The lamp showed them piecemeal as we inched our way forward and down. Scenes of gods and animals, sometimes both the same, of farmers threshing wheat, of priests praying, or folk bathing in the river. Carter wanted to study each and every one, to sketch and possibly photograph them, using flash powder, but the duchess would have none of it and kept urging him forward, her excitement—or should I call it by its proper name, greed?—overcoming her fear.

Even I by this time could now recognise the ubiquitous *cartouche* of Tuthmose.

The air within was somehow different from any I could recall inhaling before. It wasn't precisely musty; neither was it entirely clear, being faintly infused with an odor I could not at the time identify.

"I don't see any images of the Aten," Holmes observed, his voice echoing slightly.

"Nor will you," Carter responded. "The gods depicted here were the old gods, not the Aten later favored by Akhenaten. Tuthmose died and was interred before his brother's religious epiphany."

We continued.

"West by one and by one," the detective murmured after a time.

"What?" demanded Her Grace, more loudly I suspect than she'd intended.

"'And so under,'" I finished, smiling in the dark. The last time Holmes and I had uttered these enigmatic phrases we had also been searching for buried treasure.

"Ah, yes, 'The Adventure of the Musgrave Ritual,'" Howard Carter, ever the Holmes enthusiast informed the duchess, holding the lamp as high as he could. "But if I'm right, there will be far more of value here than a rusty old English crown."

"Are you alright, Your Grace?" I enquired.

She nodded in dumb fascination, never taking her eyes from the pageantry on the walls and ceiling as the corridor inclined downwards into the mountain.

Presently we came to a second set of doors, but here we were confronted by a disagreeable and inexplicable shock, for the rope and tallow seal that formerly bound the panels had been brutally sundered, with crumbs of rope and waxen fragments scattered all over the floor before them, the handiwork of predecessors.

"The devil!" exclaimed Carter. "He was already here."

"The duke?"

"Who else? I'll wager the treasure is gone. Curse the man."

"One moment." The detective laid a hand on his arm. "If the outer seal was intact just now"—he jerked his head back in the direction we had come—"how is it possible that this one is broken?"

We stared at one another lit by the glow of the lamp.

"There can be only one explanation," said I.

"Correct, Watson. The outer seal was a fake of the sort Professor Tewfik warned us about in Cairo. He said they were prevalent and convincing."

"If the outer seal is fake, what was the object? To keep us out?"

"Or lure us in?" the detective mused.

"Where *is* Professor Tewfik?" Carter suddenly wondered. "Ought we to stop here and have our sandwiches while we wait for him to join us, or go back and see what has become of him?"

"No!" declared the duchess, her voice bouncing off the painted walls. "I don't want any more splintering off in different places."

That logic made sense as far as it went, but again she was not finished. I noticed a sheen of perspiration on her forehead. Her nostrils flared now, twitching as she imagined the scent of gold. "I must know what is on the other side of this door and I am not waiting or going anywhere else but forward until I do."

I daresay she spoke for all of us. We were now all in the grip of that spectral, heady aroma. Speaking for myself, I had by now forgotten what we had originally come for. *Bring back Au 79,* Juliet had wired me. I will forever retain the smell of gold in my nostrils, a dizzying perfume as difficult to describe as it is to forget. The prospect of uncounted riches on the far side of these open panels literally affected my ability to see, let alone think. It pains me even now to acknowledge that like the rest of mankind, I was not immune to gold.

We stared for some moments at those opened doors, but now, like someone having the first intimations of a sore throat, I began to feel a nameless, inexplicable dread at what lay beyond them.

But acceding to her wishes, Carter, with abrupt decision, pulled apart the panels, which fell to pieces at his feet from their second use in three millennia. This time the duchess, in a fever of impatience, did not wait for him to scoop them up but proceeded to cross the threshold.

How to write about what followed? Even now, secure and safe as I am, the palm of my hand as I hold my pen becomes damp with terror as I remember.

The smallish, low-ceilinged room we were facing contained but two objects but was otherwise entirely bare. All the golden contents, the iridescent treasures and possessions Crown Prince Tuthmose intended for his next life had been taken by the duke, leaving only the walls covered with still more paintings and messages in hieroglyphic writings that included his name.

"He has made off with all of it, the wretch!" exclaimed his wife, stamping her foot, quivering and white with rage in the lamplight. "He and that creature!"

The tomb indeed had been stripped clean, like all yet discovered.

But I saw at a glance the two objects remaining that made this room different from all others.

The first was a giant stone sarcophagus, topped by its monumental convex lid.

The second, the figure on the floor, shrouded head to toe in torn linen and gazing at us through bandaged eyes, while reclining in seemingly tranquil repose, propped against the coffin's base.

In addition, I became again aware of the unusual odor, more noticeable here than before. If this was the smell of gold, I could do without it.

We should have fled at that moment and I wish we had. Had we done so, we might have avoided what was to come, but riveted by the horror we froze where we were and stared, at which moment the duchess gave a muffled cry at the sight of the mummy and Holmes caught her as her legs gave way. He lowered her gently, propping her back against the wall beside the doorway.

"Don't move!" the detective commanded, seeing that Carter and I had started forward. We stopped, obedient to his authority. "What do you see?" he enquired of the expert and myself.

"What looks to be a mummy," the Egyptologist responded, again making to go towards it.

"Stay where you are! I insist!" Holmes's tone brooked no contradiction. "Look at the floor, gentlemen. *What do you see?*"

In our astonishment at beholding the sarcophagus and the shrouded corpse before it, we had not observed a cluster of footprints in the thin layer of dust on the floor. Taking out his magnifier and aiming his electric torch, Holmes proceeded to examine them, muttering a string of exclamations, whistles, and a sort of running commentary as he moved cautiously among the imprints.

"Most are flat sandals, scuffing about, doubtless removing the treasure— Hullo, but see here, a pair of bespoke hiking boots alongside a much smaller pair—a woman's beyond question. Observe the dainty heel. They both make directly for the foot of the sarcophagus. And, hullo, what's this?" He paused, bending closer. "A third pair of boots, these with square toes, but *only* the toes! The heels are not present. Why?" He looked at us, a teacher examining his pupils.

"Possibly the third man was running to catch up," I hazarded. "That might account for no heel prints."

"No, Watson, the length of his stride is too short for someone running, and why trouble in this small space? No, this third man was walking on tip-toe. He was creeping up behind the other two."

The detective stood, stretching his back, which evidently still troubled him, before returning to his scrutiny of the floor. At length, satisfied he had extracted all there was to learn from the confusion of footsteps in the dust, the detective fairly rubbed his hands. "We may now proceed to examine him who has been so patiently awaiting us." He motioned us forward.

I followed Holmes to where he squatted beside Carter next to the body. As he raised the kerosene lamp above it, we now could see the linen that swathed the corpse had blackened and shredded with time. The mouth contained few teeth.

"Yes, it is a mummy," Carter proclaimed. "But whose? And why does it still reek?"

"It doesn't," Holmes responded grimly. With the tenderness of a lover, he gently unwound the tattered bandages surrounding the head. Spellbound, Carter raised no objection.

"That is Tuthmose the Fifth," said I, peering closely at what was revealed.

The Egyptologist looked at me in bewilderment. "How can you know?" he demanded, perplexed by my show of expertise.

"Because, like his younger brother, Akhenaten, he has Marfan Syndrome," the detective answered for me. "The bandages cannot conceal the distorted elongation of the face and fingers, peculiar to the disease, which, according to the good doctor here, runs in families."

I hadn't realised Holmes was paying such close attention the night we spent in gaol.

Carter blinked in astonishment and again regarded the mummy. "So this is truly Tuthmose . . ."

"Which leaves three questions unanswered." Holmes was minutely examining the head, his slender fingers roaming with dispassionate dexterity over the skull.

I cast a look at the duchess, who was sitting motionless with dead eyes. It was impossible to determine if she was watching the proceedings or not.

"What three questions?" Carter demanded.

"*Primo,* who murdered him? Oh, make no mistake, three thousand years ago this man was killed." Delicately parting more wrappings atop the corpse's head, the detective might have been leading an anatomy class. "Observe this crushing blow to the parietal bone, splitting the skull. There can be no question. Tuthmose the Fifth was murdered and must have died instantly. The first question is thus, murdered by whom?"

"Wouldn't that be obvious?" I asked. "As in any murder investigation, the first question is: Who profits?"

"Very good, Watson. Murdered by Akhenaten or those in his employ. The proper term for such a crime is 'regicide.'"

"And the second question?" pursued the Egyptologist, regarding the detective with something like awe.

"*Secondo,* why is Tuthmose outside his sarcophagus and not within it?"

"Possibly to make room for something else," I responded before I'd had time to consider the implications of what I was saying.

The detective looked up at me. "Which might explain this dreadful smell, for it does not emanate from His Majesty."

"Not after three millennia," agreed the Egyptologist.

"Which brings us to the third question." Holmes's grey eyes gleamed in the lamplight.

At this the duchess gave another moan. She had now curled into a fetal ball on the polished floor.

"Holmes, perhaps we should move her away from here."

"I think Her Grace's logic still holds, Watson. It may be difficult, but let us stay together for now. Whatever happens, we don't want to be disbelieved later by Her Grace. At the end of the day, of course, the choice is hers," he added as an afterthought.

It was a brutal calculus, but entirely logical. Logic, as always, was the detective's Polaris.

"Your Grace? If you care to leave, all you need do is say so. The way back is clear. You can bring one of the electric torches and you've only to retrace our steps to be in the open air where you can wait for us with professor Tewfik."

Staring with wide eyes from her prone position, Lizabetta del Maurepas did not answer. I unscrewed the lid of my canteen and held it up to her, lifting her head so she could drink. She swallowed some of the water, nodding gratefully and sitting up, brought back, for the moment, to herself.

For the rest of my life I will reproach myself for leaving her then as she was, but in the moment, caught up in the same frenzy of the chase, I abandoned her and returned to the sarcophagus, which drew us like so many iron filings towards a magnet.

"It will take all three of us to move that lid," Carter noted.

"Which means more than one person lifted poor Tuthmose from his coffin and sat him here. All those sandal marks."

We regarded the dead man in silent pity. The fact that he had been killed so very long ago did not, as might be expected, lessen our feelings on his account.

"Yes, more than one man," the expert agreed, "because many would have been needed to unearth those steps outside and cart off the gold."

"Shall we?" Holmes stood. We set the lantern on the floor at the head of the sarcophagus and I turned on both electric torches. "We must lower it on the farther side," the detective reasoned, "or we risk dropping it on His Majesty."

The duchess, now also unable to resist the magnet's attraction, drifted closer, wrinkling her nose as she neared the sarcophagus.

The convex lid having been previously removed, its replacement was subsequently misaligned, allowing fingers' purchase at the head and feet, where Carter and Holmes placed themselves. I stood ready at the midsection and with a nod the detective and the Egyptologist inched the lid towards me until my fingers could lodge their own grip beneath the edge of the stone.

"On three," Holmes commanded. "One. Two. *Three!*"

With a mighty collective effort we managed to slide the thing off its base and attempted to lower it to the floor where Holmes indicated it must go, but got only part-way before the weight tore it from our hands and it landed with a crash, splintering in two amid a cluster of discarded digging tools and the stumps of a dozen or more candles we had not seen from the front.

The thieves had left behind much of their gear; doubtless they had no further need of it. The treasure was more important to them.

At the thud, the duchess moaned again and thrust her fist into her mouth, an action I had seen her perform before when frightened.

"Holmes, we really should—"

I was interrupted by a wave of horrific putrefaction and another cry from the duchess, who swayed, but whose feet nonetheless remained rooted to the spot as if nailed there.

"What in God's name is that awful stench?" Carter demanded, instinctively shielding his nose and mouth. The only bodies the expert had ever examined were thousands of years old and had been embalmed by masters of the art. But Holmes and I knew at once what we were smelling, though a lifetime's familiarity had never inured us to its revolting effects.

Inside the sarcophagus was a beautifully painted wood coffin, red, blue, and black with gold trim delineating, among other things, the serene features of the late prince. The lid was not heavy and the detective and I easily and gently removed it.

The nauseating smell grew stronger yet, now filling the small chamber.

There was another coffin yet within the last, this one painted in still more detail. As Carter had first made the comparison, I was reminded of those wooden Russian dolls, one nestled inside the contours of the next.

Glancing at each other over its top, Holmes and I were now impelled to tie handkerchiefs over our noses, breathing through our mouths only as we prepared ourselves for the inevitable.

Then, with a nod, in rapid unison, we raised and set aside the final lid.

On top was a torn map with faded markings, drawn on

what looked like papyrus. It was doubtless Ohlsson's Egyptian purchase, initiator of the entire tragedy, for tragedy it was, as Holmes had foretold.

Under the map, folded at the knees and mashed together almost beyond recognition with decomposition, were the hideous, liquified, and partly congealed remains of the eleventh Duke of Uxbridge and his mistress.

Breathing through his mouth, the detective peered more closely.

"I believe that is a hairbrush," he murmured.

"Eighteenth Dynasty?" enquired the archeologist, gagging through his fingers.

"Yardley's," returned the detective.

The duke's widow began to scream.

Even knowing by this point what we should find, for us this had to be the last straw.

Scooping up the woman, the lamp, the torches, the canteens, the camera, and our gear, we now beat a hasty retreat through the second door, tripping in our haste over its fragmented remains as we stumbled up the corridor towards the first set of doors, longing for the open air.

When we first entered, we had left those cedarwood doors open.

Now they were shut. Puzzled and not thinking entirely clearly, we merely pushed at them.

They refused to open.

The duchess's howls tore her throat to shreds.

All our nightmares had come true.

12

AÏDA

"They won't budge!"

"You don't want them to! Don't touch them, for God's sake! Look!" Carter pointed with the torch and we followed its beam to the base of the splintering doors where we discerned a telltale anthill of sand.

"They've filled it in, the scoundrels! Poor Tewfik was right! They must have planned this from the first. The stuff up top was only waiting to be pushed in. There's no telling what they've done to him or how much they've piled outside by now."

"Or how many are piling it," Holmes added as he lowered the duchess to the stone floor. "I've read of unfortunate farmers in America crushed to death when their grain silos overhead give way. Physically we now find ourselves in a situation with much the same potential."

Out of the frying pan and now into the fire. "Those rotting doors won't hold forever," I felt bound to point out. I couldn't seem to tear my eyes from them.

"They won't," Carter agreed, his voice registering a slight tremor. "And when they burst we will be overwhelmed by an avalanche of sand and stone, with gravity carrying the stuff downwards until it fills this corridor." He gestured to the incline. "We'd suffocate before we dig through it and up those blocked steps."

At this Lizabetta del Maurepas moaned and her eyes rolled upwards in their sockets, leaving only ghastly whites in the lamplight as she tilted over like a wrongly positioned doll before I could prevent her. I endeavoured to prop her upright, but the detective restrained me.

"For the moment she may be better off where she is, poor woman. It's a very pretty problem," he added, staring at the swollen doors and the obstacle behind them that spelt our doom.

This struck me as an unnecessary understatement. "But why have they done this?" I demanded. "Once they obtained the gold—"

"This is the first unopened tomb discovered in modern times," Carter theorised, "and word must have got out. Once I thought it proper to wait until Her Grace got here, they had ample time to plan. Burying us and concealing the site entirely, they ensure their own escape. The false outer seal, as I worried, was simply an enticement to lure us in."

"Someone gave a lot of thought to this," I remarked dully.

"I wonder how long we can last," the detective mused aloud. "How much air, food, and water have we? And how much light?"

These were sobering considerations. We had indeed made free use of the kerosene lamp and the electric torches. We sat in silence, for the moment numbed by our predicament. Presently it was the detective who spoke again.

"I for one do not intend to sit idly and await my extermination. I don't think it would be in character," he added for my benefit, smiling slightly. "I don't think your readers would accept it. I therefore propose the following. Let us first abandon this corridor and make our stand in the crypt."

"But the stench!" I protested.

"Nonetheless, if Mr. Carter here is correct, it may prove safer. We can replace the inner coffin lids and then light all those candle stumps left by the thieves, which ought to help. If we stay here, we risk being obliterated by a limestone avalanche."

We did as the detective suggested, retracing our steps with our confounded load of gear, and carried the duchess back to the odiferous crypt where Tuthmose patiently awaited our return. There, retying handkerchiefs across our noses and breathing again through our mouths, we replaced the inner coffin lids over the rancid corpses and planted the dozen candle stumps around the edge of the sarcophagus. Intent on saving our supply of matches, I lit only one candle and used it to light the rest.

"It's an improvement," Carter allowed after several minutes.

"Not a great improvement."

On the floor, the duchess remained inert, still curled tightly in upon herself, almost as if, like a snake trying to swallow its own tail, she hoped to make herself disappear.

"I don't think she wants to wake," Carter intuited. "I can't say I blame her."

"We had best turn out the kerosene and the torches to conserve them," Holmes advised.

"And sit here in the dark?"

"We can think by candlelight."

"How romantic."

After a moment's hesitation, Carter turned out the kerosene flame and I switched off my torch.

In the gloom we became more conscious of the smell. We sat in silence, each preoccupied with his own thoughts.

In the blackness, the duchess began to weep. At any rate, I mistook it for weeping. But in the gloom my hearing became more acute and I soon realised we were listening to a kind of sniggering. Somehow the sound of that dark amusement I found more disquieting than anything that had come before. We listened without comment to the low giggles, which gradually tapered off into muffled silence once more.

"Should we eat?" I asked after a time. "We have the sandwiches."

"In this?"

"We'd do well to keep up our strength."

"The doctor, as usual, has a point. But we must ration both food and water."

With a rustling of waxed paper we extracted our sandwiches and, gagging, forced ourselves to eat small portions amid the vile perfume of mortality, before rewrapping the remainder and washing down the bread with sparing sips of stale canteen water. I tried without success to get the duchess to swallow, but her jaws were now clamped rigidly shut and the precious water when I poured it merely dribbled down her chin. I wasn't sure what, if any, remedy for her condition lay to hand.

"We're in rather a Venus flytrap," the detective noted between mouthfuls.

"What's that?" Carter asked.

"A plant whose fragrant blossom tempts its prey within and then abruptly closes its petals upon them before they can escape."

I gestured to the sarcophagus, the rim now bizarrely framed by a ring of candlelight. "It seems the trap has already claimed two victims."

"I suspected as much when they disappeared so completely," Holmes responded. "And I'm not sure but that it hasn't claimed more."

"You refer to Bechstein and the others?"

"As an element, gold appears to manifest some singular effects. I was unaware of its magnetic properties 'til now. Though perhaps I should have been," he added with a trace of bitterness he made no attempt to conceal.

"Look at him, sitting there grinning at us." Carter pointed to Tuthmose. "Having the last laugh."

"Who knows?" I felt impelled to suggest, commencing to feel giddy myself. "Perhaps he's having the first laugh."

Holmes regarded Tuthmose with an inscrutable expression.

"*For God's sake let us sit upon the ground and tell sad stories of the death of kings,*" he whispered. "*All murdered. For there the antic sits, grinning at his state, scoffing at his pomp, allowing him a little scene to monarchise, be feared, kill with looks, filling him with self and vain conceit and at the end with a little pin bores through his castle wall and farewell king.* I'm sure I've garbled it, but that's the gist," he conceded.

"What I wouldn't give for some Uxbridge Elixir," I remarked.

Carter glared at us with something like fury, but fortified by his snack, Holmes slapped his palms on his thighs with sudden resolve and, switching on one of the electric torches, began to inspect the small room, examining every inch as I had first seen him do decades earlier when he first exhibited his astonishing skills at Lauriston Gardens.*

---

* Watson first witnessed his new roommate in such action during their first case together, *A Study in Scarlet*, over twenty years earlier.

Watching his efforts now and thinking of Juliet, I heaved an involuntary sigh. The thought of never seeing her again pained me from her perspective as well as my own. Would she ever learn what had become of Holmes and myself or would all trace of us be forever buried under the sands of Egypt?

"Ahmed would have put up a fight," Carter maintained, speaking more or less to himself. "He would never have joined with them in such a scheme."

"By 'them,'" the detective asked, now crawling on his hands and knees, running his fingers along the seams between wall and floor, "are you intimating that a cabal of nameless fellaheen murdered the duke and his"—eyeing the duchess, who couldn't hear him in any case—"mistress on their own initiative, a sort of slave revolt?"

"Even slaves have their leaders," Carter remembered. "Spartacus. Toussaint . . . Whatever his name was. In any event, these men aren't slaves. They are paid wages."

"Slave wages," Holmes persisted. "Did they also murder Professor Jourdan and that man Phillips who fell from the statue of Ramses at Abu Simbel? I find that notion hard to swallow. I suspect Mr. Square-toed Boots could tell us a great deal more."

Carter made no answer, but the detective's skepticism echoed silently in the darkness.

Strange thoughts percolate at such times, as I was now in a position to appreciate. The senses of time, of day or night, almost of up or down, were all in question. Some of these thoughts I am ashamed to relate. I spent some time sullenly blaming Sherlock Holmes for my fate. Hadn't I always hastened to his summons, blinded by curiosity and a certain canine fidelity? Was it not in fact the detective, sitting and paraphrasing Shakespeare, who had led me to this sorry pass? Years ago I should have broken free of him and his Siren-like claims on my time, my health, my obedience, and now, indeed (and not for the first time but assuredly for the last!), my very life.

I wandered up and down this fruitless path for some time, staring into the Stygian dark, hoping the detective would feel my evil eye trained in his general direction. But Holmes, understandably preoccupied with more urgent matters, left me to my profitless ruminations. In time, I grew unsatisfied with these and forced to acknowledge that my fate was the result of own folly, of decisions no one had forced me to make, my mood lifted slightly, and I turned down a different path, one that made perhaps no more sense but which pleased me to contemplate.

"Holmes, has it occurred to you that we are participating in a sort of reenactment?"

"How do you mean?"

"Perhaps 'sequel' might be a better word. Three thousand years ago, our friend"—I gestured to Tuthmose—"was murdered by his younger brother, to gain the throne and his beautiful sister-in-law."

"What are you getting at, my dear fellow?"

"Why did Lord Darlington not accompany us?" I asked. "'Indisposed,' we were told, but what does that really mean? Does he not in fact have the same motive as Akhenaten? With the duke out of the way, he stands to inherit the title and estates, in short everything that goes with it, including, quite possibly, his rich widow. Men have been killed for less. Or more," I conceded, gesturing again to the dead man sitting quietly among us.

"Aren't you forgetting something?" the detective asked. "The desirable sister-in-law in question is here, trapped with us."

"But perhaps she is no longer essential to his plan." I cast a look at the duchess, prone and glassy-eyed. "Without her or any children to interfere, Darlington's claim to the dukedom and title is much less likely to be contested in a court of law. With husband and wife out of the way, I would hazard his schoolmastering days are over."

"The same crime three thousand years apart," Holmes considered the possibility. "Hamlet redux. Nothing very much seems to change, does it? But your theory, gratifyingly *Grand Guignol* though it may be, fails to account for Bechstein, Phillips, and Jourdan. These deaths are evidently related, yet they could not possibly be connected to a schoolmaster from Staines."

He was right, of course. One does have strange thoughts at such times.

Holmes's inspection of the room had yielded nothing, and in the end the detective was forced to sit with the rest of us, blocked at every turn. Now even Howard Carter, with years of experience in sites such as these, began to lose his composure.

"You're the great detective. Do something!"

"I'm a detective," my friend replied calmly, "not a magician."

As if to reinforce this fact, we now heard a sharp *crack* from the far end of the corridor whence we'd entered, and presently the room began to vibrate.

"What's happening?" I shouted.

"The doors have given way!" the expert answered, his voice rising an octave to match my own.

Indeed, as the initial crack gave way to a rumble the very walls and ceiling began to vibrate, threatening at any moment to collapse upon us. There was not a thing any of us could do but remain frozen where we were, our palms reflexively pressing against the shuddering walls as if to hold them upright.

The duchess's only reaction was to curl still tighter into herself, her eyes squeezed shut as the sound and trembling grew. The rumble now became a perfect roar as a tidal wave of stone and sand slid into and filled the corridor leading to the crypt of Tuthmose, where we cowered, each, I suspect, trying our best on short notice to make peace with our maker. It is curious the things one notices at such times. I was briefly entranced by the jittering candle flames dancing merrily around the lip of the sarcophagus.

The whole inundation could not have lasted less than a minute, but a minute can seem like an hour in such circumstances as these.

Eventually the roar subsided and the tide of sand stopped, grains and limestone chips lapping just over the entry to the chamber of Tuthmose. The silence that followed seemed somehow as deafening as the din which had preceded it, silence so complete that the sounds of our shallow breathing almost pained the ears.

No one moved. Time was passing . . .

Who in the aftermath of this final blow would be first to speak? It proved to be me. I unbent my stiff leg, which I had instinctively drawn towards myself moments before.

"Holmes."

"Yes, my dear fellow." His voice was as calm as if we were sitting together in Baker Street.

"Did you ever think it would come to this?"

The detective offered a dry chuckle. "Doctor, you of all people should know: it always comes to this."

But I was now wallowing aboard my morbid train of thought, unable to shake off my despair. "How does *Aïda* finish, Holmes? I can't think."

The detective looked over at me from the far corner of the room, his hawk-like features illumined from beneath by the fading torch.

"Radamès and Aïda are buried alive but go happily to their deaths because each is with the one they love. There are perhaps worse ways to go," he added under his breath.

It wasn't until much later that I grasped the full import of his words.

At this point, as if she had overheard us, the duchess began to talk, but chose to address us in a foreign tongue.

"I take it no one here speaks Portuguese," I said.

"That's not Portuguese, Watson. That's not even Swahili. She's gone. I could be mistaken, but I very much doubt she'll be back."

Indeed we now realised another victim had been claimed, this one alive but off her head. As I remembered our experience together during the khamsin and her care for me, my heart ached. She had, it is true, been overcome in the moment by avarice, but which of us had not?

"With the corridor now filled, how much air do you imagine we have left?" Carter enquired in the gloom. Holmes grunted with a kind of satisfaction, as much to suggest that here at least was a problem he was capable of solving.

"It shouldn't be too difficult to calculate," he began. "There are four of us and how many cubic feet do you think this small chamber con—"

"Holmes, I beg you."

The detective fell silent.

In time—how much time?—the electric torches both gave out, the kerosene lamp was finished, the sandwiches eaten, and only the stumps of candles remained.

Holmes, Carter, and I were now alone in the remaining

light with only Tuthmose and Duke Michael's mad Brazilian widow for company. Not visible but far too close for comfort, were the duke himself and the famous Egyptian dancer. Whatever air remained was, in any case, horrible to inhale.

Perhaps, indeed, we were using up our supply for I felt myself sliding into oblivion and was grateful for this mercy when I was startled to hear the detective's voice once more.

"Why are the flames wavering?"

It was some moments before I blinked, shaking off the stupor whose pull I had been embracing only moments before.

"What?" Carter likewise awakened now demanded.

"Look at them!" the detective exclaimed. "They shook before with the room, but now they should be static. Yet they are wavering. Something from somewhere is blowing at them or they would remain upright."

"The avalanche must have loosened something," Carter said, sitting up.

We had seen but had not observed.

With renewed energy we converged on the flickering lights, licking our fingers and holding them up like sailors searching for the wind.

"It's from there!" Carter shouted, moving to the wall behind the stone sarcophagus.

Holmes eagerly ran his hands along the smooth surface, stopping abruptly, one palm pressed tightly against a painting of Ra's face.

"Yes, here! Faint but sufficient to stir the flames. Let's have the pickaxe."

Not waiting, he seized that item left behind by the diggers in their flight, and without ceremony struck at the wall, which crumbled with the first blow.

In response, the duchess did not move but mumbled excitedly in her nonexistent tongue.

Carter instinctively groaned at the destruction of the mural.

"It's just mud!" the detective yelled. "Hardened mud—like adobe. Let's have the flash powder!"

Carter didn't have to be told twice. With unsteady hands, he poured all the powder intended for use with the camera into the fissure created by the pickaxe.

"It may light up briefly for a photograph, but do you think it will have any other effect?" I wondered aloud, twisting tight Ohlsson's wretched papyrus map for use as a fuse.

"It will if we use all of it," the archeologist predicted. "Always assuming it doesn't bring the rest of this place down about our ears."

I looked at the detective. "We have little to lose," was his rejoinder.

I struck a match and we crouched back.

"Cover your ears!"

Rather than cover his own, Holmes clapped his hands on either side of the duchess's head. The explosion that followed seemed bigger in the small space. It pummelled our eardrums, but it also dislodged more wall as the crypt shook with a single tremor.

The duchess, writhing free of the detective's hands, now mumbled more loudly.

"Watson!"

Using every discarded tool at our disposal, we attacked that false wall like madmen, astonished to find it concealed an adjacent niche or rather a small cave where the current of air, emanating from above, was decidedly stronger. The ceiling was in fact much higher than that of the crypt. Rather than trouble to fill all the space, the original builders had chosen the simpler expedient of walling it up.

We now took turns whacking at the ceiling with the pick-axe and poking upwards at it with shovels, causing a drizzle of dirt to fall on our heads. It was difficult work as the angle was unfortunate and out of reach. Eventually nothing would do but Holmes—being the lightest and tallest—taking turns sitting on my shoulders or Carter's, and striking upwards as chopped clumps of earth flew down upon us. But in fact we were making good progress, so much so that after what I guessed was an hour we stopped to rest, panting and dripping with sweat and excitement. The only question was how much overhead lay between us and freedom, or would we ultimately encounter solid limestone?

The fact that air had penetrated so deep gave us hope, and after a mere five minutes' respite we resumed, too exhilarated—and desperate—to stop. Holmes climbed back on my shoulders and shortly after that a cluster of rock and sand tumbled onto his head, revealing dark sky speckled with stars above us. There was never such a welcome sight in my life, but it was still out of reach.

"Where's the rope?" Holmes asked from his perch on my shoulders.

Carter ran and fetched it.

"Watson, rather than sit, I must stand. Can you still support my weight or should Carter try?"

"Happy to be of service," the expert enthusiastically volunteered.

"Don't worry about me." I staggered slightly as the detective rose, one hand pressing on my scalp, and carefully placed one foot and then the other on my shoulders, gingerly reaching down to take the rope proffered by the Egyptologist.

As I tottered to and fro like a circus acrobat, continually modifying my stance under his altered position, Holmes reached his arms through the hole and with a mighty leap that sent my game leg buckling managed to claw his way to freedom as I collapsed.

I sat gasping and looking up with Carter. For the longest time, there was no sign of my friend. The expert was on the point of regarding me dubiously when several feet of rope abruptly tumbled down through the hole between us. This was followed by the sight of Sherlock Holmes, his features hardly discernable, squinting down from above.

"Be very quiet," he whispered. "They're still at work down there. Once the doors burst, it was very like pulling the plug in a bathtub. The steps must have been exposed again, so they're at work refilling them. It will take two of us to haul Her Grace. One must climb the rope to help me pull her from here, the other bring her into the cave and secure the other end under her arms, then help lift her when we're ready."

"I'll bring her," Carter offered. "You get out of here, Doctor. You've done enough."

It had been aeons since I had done climbing of any kind (it was an apple tree in our neighbour's orchard and I recollect I was about twelve), but the adrenaline now coursing through my pores enabled me to scramble up that rope as if I had been a gymnast.

Outside, amid a rocky outcropping, the air was cold and my sweat instantly turned clammy. I had shed my Harris Tweed but nothing on earth could have induced me to go back for it. Holmes had lassoed his portion of the rope around a substantial boulder. He pointed and I followed his look.

Below us and almost out of sight, two dozen fellaheen were still industriously pushing sand and stone over the top of the almost entirely invisible steps. In less than an hour there would remain no trace of the cavity or its trapdoor entrance. All would be smoothed over with local stone. I was hypnotised watching their efforts.

"Watson!" Holmes impatiently waved me to crouch and together we crept back to the hole. Peering down, we could make out little, but presently heard Carter's whisper.

"She's still muttering. What if she screams?"

Holmes yanked off my regimental green tie and tossed it down.

"Gag her."

"Right." There was a pause, then— "She's not heavy. I'll lift her from this end and you'll pull?"

Holmes leaned down. "Give us a minute."

So saying, he made a loop in the slack and coiled it around his waist, one end secured by the boulder. Cautiously the detective paid out the line into the hole where the archeologist tugged gently to signify he had possession. We both grabbed hold of the remaining slack and waited until we felt another gentle tug, informing us Carter had secured the duchess.

"On three," the detective whispered, cupping his hands. "One. Two. *Three*."

We both pulled hand over hand, Holmes planting his back against the boulder as Carter hoisted the woman as high as he could manage. As the hole was not large, it was necessary to tug carefully so as to avoid any collision which might injure the poor creature or cause her to cry out.

The duchess continued to babble through the gag, but neither that restraint nor being hoisted by a rope beneath her arms seemed to especially alarm her. She had entered a mind palace of her own and looked to be taking up residence there.

After Holmes and I lowered the rope a third time, Carter

soon joined us, his chest heaving from his unfamiliar exertions.

For several minutes, we sat shivering on the cold stones, endeavouring to marshal our faculties and in some fashion digest our ordeal. By any measure it had been a narrow escape.

"Now what?" I asked quietly.

"An excellent question," a cultivated voice close by agreed. "But one I can answer."

In the early light of dawn, Professor Hassan Tewfik and a half-dozen fellaheen had climbed up behind us. The latter had rifles slung over their shoulders, now aimed in our direction. At this range, there was no chance of missing their targets.

To say I was surprised is to understate the case, but the duchess, her gag now removed, failed to react to the man, his men, or his words. Lost in the catacombs of her own circumscribed realm, she continued her mumbled soliloquy.

Holmes likewise appeared unfazed. "I surmised it must be you," he said, gesturing to Tewfik's square-toed boots. "That night at Shepheard's after you saw Mustafa and divined his intention when I asked the location of the Great Mosque and the time of Isha, the weapon you chose to lay your hands on at short notice was a knife from your own museum. You had just time to dash there and back to the Great Mosque, to literally cut the man off in the alley before he reached us. Why not simply employ a steak knife from our dinner table?"

Holmes, I understood, wished to keep the man talking. And, his vanity invoked, Tewfik obliged.

"I would not have dreamed of stealing cutlery from Shepheard's," he declared with cool disdain. "The knife I did use was another Egyptian fake. Fitting, don't you think? Certainly I would never have squandered the real thing."

"All this for gold?" I asked. I too wished him to keep

talking, if only to prolong the moment before he ordered his men to fire upon us.

"It's nothing to do with gold," the professor replied, his voice rising only slightly. "It's about the bodies."

"Bodies? What bodies?" Carter wondered, staring at the museum director as if the man he'd known forever turned out to have come from the moon. In this he spoke for all of us, as it was impossible to tell what the professor was talking about.

"Our bodies! Ours!" Tewfik gestured furiously to himself and those standing on either side, pounding his chest with a fist. "Egyptian bodies! Our ancestors shipped off to New York or Paris to be gaped at by giggling schoolchildren! I saw it with my own eyes at the British Museum. Don't try to tell me I didn't. Grave robbers. Desecrators of the dead! The ongoing humiliation. When does a man's right to lie in peace expire? Would you care to be exhibited for the amusement of the mob? Dug up from your resting places and displayed under glass? Or is it because we are only, after all, 'boys' or 'wogs' that the concept doesn't apply? Good enough to hold your stirrups, serve at mealtimes, and do your laundry? In fact, some of us were kings. It wasn't for the gold. It was for Egypt!"

As he spoke, his shoulders squared, but his eyes reverted to their protruding tic.

Holmes regarded him with interest. "So on the night of January second you telegraphed the duke in Cairo saying his map was correct and you had located the crypt of Tuthmose."

Recovering his poise, the other nodded complacently. "I took a leaf from Mr. Carter's rule book and said I would wait for His Grace to arrive before entering and that I had booked rooms for him at The Winter Palace Hotel."

"He and his mistress left Shepheard's in such a hurry the next morning he forgot one of his hairbrushes."

Tewfik shrugged. "He would have no further need of it. And you will do without yours."

"Colonel Arbuthnot saved your life during the khamsin," I reminded him, pointing to the detective. But for the rifles aimed in our direction I would have cheerfully throttled the man.

"So he did," the professor acknowledged, "but not before I'd saved his when I vouched for him at the Consulate and extracted him from gaol. I'd say we're quits. I mastered all your ways," he now felt obliged to point out. "But you've learned none of ours. You weren't even curious. It was only about the gold."

"What do you plan to do with us?" Carter asked.

"Oh, I don't think that's in question. Poetic justice and Western efficiency. We shall deposit you down the hole from which you so cleverly emerged, making sure, this time, that you will not succeed again. There you can join that other grave robber and his Turkish whore."

"Are you so certain she was Turkish?" a new voice enquired.

Major Haki and his men now appeared behind those of Tewfik and quickly disarmed the astonished fellaheen, even as a skirmish broke out below us between the remainder of the gang and military police surrounding the place where the stairs formerly began. There was brief, sporadic gunfire, bullets whining, ricocheting and reverberating off the rocky hillsides. The short-lived fusillade was followed by silence as resistance ended and the surrender took place.

Tewfik accepted this sudden turn of events with a phlegmatic air, almost as if he anticipated something of the sort.

"When you didn't answer my telegram, Major," Holmes replied, endeavouring to sound calm, "I assumed you hadn't received it."

"Certainly I received it, Englishman, but very late. Realising there was no time to be lost, I dashed here before taking the time to answer. I commissioned a special and they'd only just cleared the wrecked coaches of the Star of Egypt off the tracks when we came barrelling through." Using his covered club hand, he stroked his beard beneath his chin in that self-satisfied manner I recalled from our previous meeting the night of our arrest.

"A good thing, as you barely made it," Carter said. "If matters had gone according to his plan"—he indicated Tewfik—"we would have been dead by now and no trace of our existence ever found."

With a start I suddenly recalled forcing Holmes to send his telegram at Amenhotep House after I'd sent mine to Juliet. The detective had acquiesced, though he knew full well what the stakes might ultimately be. Truly I would never fully understand Sherlock Holmes.

Two military policemen now began roping up the sullen accomplices, tying them to one another. They offered no resistance. Briefly, like their leader, they had been men; now they were once more "boys."

Carter approached his old comrade, who stood with stoic calm as Haki clamped manacles on his wrists. The museum director, having recovered his poise, smiled amiably.

"Don't imagine for a minute that with my arrest you have squelched the aspirations of the Egyptian people," he told the Turk without the least trace of rancor in his manicured English. "Today we are only hundreds, but in time there will be thousands of us, and one day Egypt and, yes, even the canal will be ours."

"Not in my lifetime," retorted the major.

"Where is the gold of Tuthmose?" Howard Carter demanded.

Tewfik smiled once more, his only sign of agitation being his pulsating eyes.

"Safe in Egypt. Where it will remain. Where neither you, Lord Elgin, Lord Carnarvon, nor the British Museum will ever lay hands on it."

They led him off as the sun rose over the tops of the hills.

As the Turkish police prepared to dig up the remains, Holmes and I gratefully sniffed the bracing morning air. It was chilly at this hour but the heat would soon become insupportable.

"Remember Nietzsche's dictum," the detective remarked, lighting his pipe. *"Nothing not written in blood is worth reading."*

"Or writing, in this case," I rejoined.

He smiled in agreement. "Definitely one for the books. One of *your* books," he added.

The train back to Cairo found me sleeping for hours. When I woke, I splashed some water on my unshaven face and stumbled to the dining car, where I found Holmes with Carter, drinking tea and profligately buttering a scone.

"Did you sleep well?" the detective enquired, smiling.

"I should say I did."

"I took the liberty of wiring your wife we were safely on our way back."

"Goodness, Juliet! Thank heaven you thought of that. Bless you, my dear fellow."

As we trundled north, he filled me in on several points. "Obviously the remains of the duke and Miss Fatima must be accorded some sort of rites."

I tried not to think of the grisly task which would involve separating the bodies from each other and from their effects, which Tewfik had tossed into the sarcophagus with them.

"He," meaning Tewfik, "didn't mind Tuthmose being left there?"

"On the contrary. By his lights, that is where the prince belonged, though I daresay he will now wind up in some museum or other, to be gaped at by lisping school brats as Tewfik and his cohorts feared. Make no mistake," he added, "those ubiquitous, faceless fellaheen we see but do not observe are men with feelings even as we are." The detective sat back in a meditative frame of mind. "They may have a point, you know."

"There we disagree," Howard Carter responded. "I'm of the opinion that knowledge trumps faith. In any case, one can hardly argue today's Egyptians are the true descendants of the pharaohs."*

"Putting that issue to one side, is it a question of knowledge versus faith?" Holmes wondered. "Or is it, rather, what is the statute of limitations on death? Does its expiration differ for these 'lesser breeds without the law,' in Mr. Kipling's loathsome phrase? Do their remains become fair game because they *are* 'lesser breeds'? As professor Tewfik wondered, would we wish our own bodies unearthed for whatever purpose, rather than left in peace? Should we now display the Duke of Uxbridge?"

"Certainly not. How absurd," Carter protested.

---

* In 1922 Howard Carter, still working for Lord Carnarvon, unearthed the only unopened tomb in modern Egyptian history, that of Akhenaten's young son, Tutankhamun. (Tut's tomb was in fact right around the corner from that of his murdered uncle, Tuthmose.) The fabulous treasure, which periodically goes on tour, can also be viewed online.

"Because he is white? Because his death is recent?" The detective lit his pipe. "I could not see what linked the murders of Jourdan, Phillips, and Bechstein other than gold. As an Englishman, I could not conceive another motive."

From the Egyptologist's silence and blank expression, it was impossible to divine his thoughts. Did he have arguments or did he feel it wiser to withhold them?

Sitting across from them, I could see both sides of the argument.

"And the duchess?"

The detective sighed, relieved, I suspect, to forgo metaphysics. "She's under sedation two cars ahead in her drawing room suite. Darlington will meet the train and I expect take her back to England, where, if there's no improvement, she'll go to some sort of facility where she can be properly looked after."

"Were they lovers?"

"How can we ever know? And I expect it's an open question who will finally inherit the dukedom. If past is prologue we're doubtless looking at Jarndyce versus Jarndyce ad infinitum."*

"And Major Haki?"

"Ah, Mycroft's gift, timely as always."

"A double agent?"

"At least! As my brother observed, Egypt is deuced complicated."

"One thing is sure." Howard Carter sat back with something like a smile. "That is the first and last time I will ever wish to be a participant in a case of yours, Mr. Holmes. I prefer my corpses long dead and without the reek of mortal-

---

* Holmes refers to the interminable lawsuit in Dickens's novel *Bleak House*.

ity I doubt my memory will ever expunge. In the future, I will much prefer my old habit of reading your exploits from the safety of an armchair before a good fire of a winter's evening."

I had the rest of the long train ride to ruminate on this and everything else. Who was Fatima, really, and for whom was she working, if anyone besides herself? I suppose I'll never learn.*

And what of Holmes, sitting across from me, lighting his pipe and gazing tranquilly out the window as he smoked? Would I ever fully understand this man who advertised himself as a thinking machine, but who, when he thought death was imminent, unfolded his feelings to me in such a subtle but elegant fashion? Perhaps, after all, I do have all I need to know.

It was night when we finally drew into Ramses Station, where Lord Darlington was indeed awaiting our arrival. With him were two men in white coats. They had presciently fetched a wheelchair. Holmes and I were there to help the duchess—still conversing with herself in a guttural undertone amid occasional cackling—and to attempt goodbyes. Wrapped in one of the blankets from the train, she looked past us with unseeing eyes and heard us with unhearing ears.

"I am so very sorry," the detective addressed the schoolmaster. Holmes was, I knew, understating his contrition. I have noted previously my friend's proprietary feelings for his clients and his keen sense of obligation where their interests and safety were concerned. In the present instance, he had

---

* Was it really Fatima in that sarcophagus? A Dutch woman with a name similar to one of her aliases was shot by a French firing squad in 1917. She was then calling herself Mata Hari.

solved the mystery the Duchess of Uxbridge had engaged him to unravel, but in the process had failed to prevent her own collapse.

"I will take her back to England as soon as possible," Darlington informed us in his peculiar neutral fashion. "Perhaps once more among her own surroundings and familiar possessions, she will recover her wits."

"We can only hope so," I replied, as Holmes found it difficult to speak. We watched as the future twelfth Duke of Uxbridge, putative progenitor of the cadet branch of his line, wheeled away his sister-in-law in the company of the two orderlies. He insisted on pushing the chair himself. I don't believe either of us had ever encountered anyone quite like him.

"It's almost as if the man casts no shadow," Holmes said, reading my thoughts.

It was only when I turned again to face the detective that I confronted a surprise of my own. My wife stood on the platform, having evidently witnessed the entire exchange.

"Juliet!" I rushed to her side.

She threw her arms wide. "John, dearest, did you find gold?"

"I have just done so," I answered, taking her in my arms.

"Watson, you'll excuse me," said the detective, bowing slightly in the direction of my wife, who inclined her head in return. "I've no wish to intrude on your reunion and I suspect Major Haki has more questions for me." Almost as if in flight, he started down the platform towards the building.

"Holmes, when will I see you again?" I called after him.

"Soon enough, surely, my dear fellow. London is not so large a place, after all."

And he was gone, his tall, somehow melancholy form swallowed up among hundreds.

I turned and faced my wife.

"John, I have the most wonderful news. Dr. Singh says we will be home in time for the coronation! My cough is entirely gone!"

My news could wait—but I would tell her everything.

10 November, 1911. Today I received not one but two parcels in the morning post. The first was from Holmes, a slight envelope with a note addressed to me in his familiar hand:

> *My dear Watson, I trust this finds you well. The enclosed was sent me from Cairo by Major Haki. I thought you might want it as a souvenir of our Egyptian adventure. H. PS: Don't worry, it has been cleaned.*

Provoked by this singular postscript, I opened the small packet to find a German passport made out to one Hildegarde Von Stroheim, 24, born in Hamburg, but there was no mistaking the face in the photograph. Holmes had been correct: Fatima had been carrying an additional passport when she met her fate.

The second, larger parcel contained a slender volume published by the Oxford University Press: *Thoughts on Napoleon's Egyptian Campaign of 1798 with Special Emphasis on the Conduct of Admiral Lord Nelson at Aboukir* by Lord Darlington, Duke of Uxbridge, along with a card, *Compliments of the Author.*

16 March, 1912. A newspaper clipping stating that *at St. George's, Hanover Square, Lionel, 12th Duke of Uxbridge, married the widow of his brother, the 11th duke, in a private ceremony.*

Wherever he now lies, Akhenaten must be smiling.

HERE ENDS THIS PORTION OF WATSON'S JOURNAL.

ACKNOWLEDGMENTS

There are worse ways, it turns out, to endure the COVID-19 lockdown than to spend it in the company of Sherlock Holmes. The great detective and his biographer are, as we all know, the brainchildren of Sir Arthur Conan Doyle, who must as a consequence be always first in line when thanks and credit are being handed out. I know I am not alone in running low on superlatives and explanations for his two indestructible creations, so let us leave it at that.

This particular book was the result of a suggestion made by my longtime agent, manager, and dear friend, Alan Gasmer. It is hard to overstate Alan's contribution to my work and to my life. This book is an attempt to express my gratitude.

I would also like to thank Charlotte Sheedy, my indefatigable literary agent, and Keith Kahla, my attentive and subtle editor, who both supported this endeavor with expertise, enthusiasm, and patience.

A host of indulgent friends have previewed the novel, which has benefited from their observations, objections, and many suggestions. Among these contributors must be numbered—Leslie Fram, Les Klinger, Richard Rayner, James Spottiswoode, Michael Philips, Dylan Meyer, Frank Spotnitz, Robert Wallace, David Robb, Roger Spottiswoode, Barbara Fisher, Madeline Meyer, Gary Lucchesi, Robert Hollander, Nelson and Maydee Lande, Dan Colanduno, Madeline Meyer, Laurent Bouzereau, Thomas Barad, Ken Reinhard, Michael Elias, and Jonathan Tiemann.

I must acknowledge a special debt of gratitude to Professor Willeke Wendrich, director of the Cotsen Institute of Archaeology and professor of Egyptian archaeology at UCLA. It is hard to overstate what I owe to her close reading of the manuscript and her painstaking attention to Egyptian details therein. I admit I have, on occasion (tomb numbering, Egyptian-born museum curators, and the year Howard Carter was dismissed from the Antiquities Service) allowed the demands of fiction to override historical precision as provided by the professor, but I hope she and any colleagues who read the book will forgive these liberties. I made up the story I wished to tell. (I may have even made up a pharaoh, but I tell myself Homer would never pass the smell test, either.)

Finally, a good deal of additional research went into this novel. In addition to tuberculosis, Edwardian England, Edwardian English, and the usual Holmes arcana, I was obliged to learn something about nineteenth- and early-twentieth-century Egypt and its politics, geography, topography, and railroads. That was a lot of ground [sic] to cover before I, magpie-like, could pick and choose, mix and match, what I thought I needed. Any howlers were either intentional or accidental, my fault or possibly Watson's; none can be laid at the door of my impeccable sources, partially listed below, for those curious to read the nonfiction version:

Akhenaten: Egypt's False Prophet, by Nicholas Reeves

The Murder of Tutankhamen: A True Story, by Bob Brier, Ph.D.

The Riddle of the Labyrinth: The Quest to Crack an Ancient Code, by Margalit Fox

Loot: The Battle over the Stolen Treasures of the Ancient World, by Sharon Waxman

The Search for the Gold of Tutankhamen, by Arnold C. Brackman

Egypt: The Treasures of the Great Pharaohs, by T. G. H. James

City of the Sun: A Novel, by Juliana Maio

Valley of the Kings: A Novel of Tutankhamun, by Elizabeth Eliot Carter

The Riddle of the Pyramids, by Kurt Mendelssohn

Luxury Trains: From the Orient Express to the TGV, by George Behrend

Venice Simplon Orient-Express: The Return of the World's Most Celebrated Train, by Shirley Sherwood

Not to mention the internet and a whole raft of Hollywood spear-and-sandal movies, including *Land of the Pharaohs, Valley of the Kings, The Egyptian, Cleopatra, Alexander the Great,* et cetera. For additional pleasure, if it's still available online, visit: https://my.matterport.com/show/?ref=fb&m=NeiMEZa9d93.

You won't be sorry.

JOHN HAMISH WATSON was born in England in 1847. After obtaining his medical degree from the University of London Medical School in 1878, he enrolled in the course at Netley for army surgeons, after which he was attached to the 5th Northumberland Fusiliers and sent to India. He was wounded at the Battle of Maiwand during the Second Afghan War in 1880, after which he returned to England with nine months' veteran's pension. In January the following year, he met Sherlock Holmes, who was looking for someone to share his lodgings. Watson found his niche, chronicling sixty cases of his detective friend. He resumed his practice of medicine, was married twice, and died in England in 1940.

NICHOLAS MEYER is the "editor" of four previous Sherlock Holmes novels, including *The Seven-Per-Cent Solution*, which was on the *New York Times* bestseller list for a year. He's a screenwriter and film director, responsible for *The Day After* and *Time After Time*, as well as *Star Trek II: The Wrath of Khan*, *Star Trek IV: The Voyage Home*, and *Star Trek VI: The Undiscovered Country*, among many others. A native of New York City, he lives in Santa Monica, California.